BACKSHOOTERS!

Harlan felt a prickling sensation on the back of his neck and across his shoulder blades. He had felt that same thing once before, outside a bank in northern Arkansas.

Now Harlan wanted away from Walking Bear's place just as far and fast as he could do it. Instead of walking the gray across the open yard he vaulted into the saddle and whipped the horse into a run for the woods that surrounded Walking Bear's shack. The brown balked and tried to fight the halter but had no choice except to run also. That or be dragged off its feet. Both horses bolted into a run and seconds later Harlan heard whooping and hollering behind him.

A flurry of shots pounded the air around him. Two, three, as many as a dozen. Harlan heard the bee-swarm buzz of at least four bullets that passed close by his head . . .

Harlan

Frank Roderus

WITHDRAWN

LEISURE BOOKS NEW YORK CITY

A LEISURE BOOK®

November 2009

Dorchester Publishing Co., Inc.
200 Madison Avenue
New York, NY 10016

ISBN 10: 0-8439-6220-8
ISBN 13: 978-0-8439-6220-8
E-ISBN: 978-1-4285-0762-3

The name "Leisure Books" and the stylized "L" with design are
trademarks of Dorchester Publishing Co., Inc.

Printed in the United States of America.

10 9 8 7 6 5 4 3 2 1

Visit us online at www.dorchesterpub.com.

HARLAN

HARLAN

Frank Roderus

WITHDRAWN

LEISURE BOOKS NEW YORK CITY

A LEISURE BOOK®

November 2009

Dorchester Publishing Co., Inc.
200 Madison Avenue
New York, NY 10016

ISBN 10: 0-8439-6220-8
ISBN 13: 978-0-8439-6220-8
E-ISBN: 978-1-4285-0762-3

The name "Leisure Books" and the stylized "L" with design are trademarks of Dorchester Publishing Co., Inc.

Printed in the United States of America.

10 9 8 7 6 5 4 3 2 1

Vernon Kinder grabbed the dipper and tried for the third time to rinse the sharp, acid taste of vomit from his mouth, but water was not what he needed here. Whiskey might work but he hadn't brought a bottle with him, dammit. He wondered if maybe Kenny had. Or . . . Vernon shook his head. It didn't matter if Will Howard had any inside his soddy. Vernon wouldn't set foot back inside that house even if he would get a lifetime supply of bonded whiskey for doing it. The sight of what was in there . . . Vernon gagged again just from thinking about it. He spun around and bent over with the dry heaves. Christ, he'd already lost everything he'd eaten for the past three days. A thin stream of mucus was all he could get out. Jesus! He straightened up and reached for the water dipper.

"D'you think they did the kid too, Vern?" Kenny asked, ignoring Vernon's puking.

Vernon spat, rinsed and spat again. "I don't know and I ain't gonna look. I ain't going back in there. Not for love nor money."

"Somebody has to. They've got to be buried, you know."

"Fine, but I ain't gonna do it. Let the marshal come out and do that shit."

"The marshal doesn't have jurisdiction out here, Vern. That'd be the sheriff."

Vernon scowled. "Then don't hold your breath. That sonuvabitch ain't been to this end of the county since just before the last election. And we'uns voted for Delton then so I don't expect we'll see our sheriff anytime soon."

"Somebody has to do something though, Vern. Jesus God! Will is laying dead in there and both them kids and . . . and Margaret buck naked and . . . and . . . what all was done to Margaret wasn't human, Vern. Wasn't even human. It must've been Indians that killed them all. Must've been. Couldn't be no white man cut . . . did all that shit to them. Couldn't of been."

"Maybe," Vernon said cautiously, looking around as if he expected to see a screaming horde of wild savages spring at them from Will Howard's hog pen or possibly the hen house. "Maybe it was Injuns at that. I guess, hell, it must've been."

"What are we going to do about the bodies, Vern?"

"Shit, I dunno. But I'm telling you straight out, Kenny. I ain't going back inside that house. No, sir, not never."

"We have to tell somebody. Do something," Kenny said.

"I told you what I think. We'll ride back t' town. Tell the marshal there. The justice o' the damn peace too. An' the doc. Prob'ly make him puke too when he sees what's in there. That fancy college Doc went to, the war, I bet he didn't see the like of this in none of that shit." Vernon shook his head. "Jesus God, Kenny. Jesus God!"

"I guess we ought to, I don't know, shut the door at least. Keep the coyotes out and all them."

"If you know a way to keep the stinking flies out, it'd be a blessing, you know that? Some of them flies crawled on me when we was in there, Kenny. Makes me feel like they was rubbing some of that shit on me. You know what I mean?" The thought made Vernon's gorge rise again and he once more doubled over in an attempt to empty an already vacant stomach.

His friend Kenny quietly walked around to the front of the sod house and pushed the door closed. The latch was broken—there must have been a struggle—so he used Margaret's churn to prop the door closed. It was the best he could do at the moment. And like Vernon, Kenny had no intention of going inside that place again. In his mind's eye he could still see the ugliness within. For the rest of his life he would still see that, he suspected.

Kenny fetched their horses from the rickety corral that Will Howard had built and tried to lead them over to Vernon, but neither horse was willing to go near. Most likely they could smell the blood. Horses generally will shy from the scent of blood.

"Come on, Vern. Quit your puking and mount up. We got to go tell somebody about this."

Chapter One

Laura Hannigan felt a flutter of excitement. There was a man, a stranger, talking with Jim. They stood beside the barn, shielded from the ever-present wind. It was nigh onto suppertime and Laura considered whether she had time enough to freshen up and change into a nicer dress. Something with the color in the material not quite so washed out and . . . oh, good heavens, this old thing had a patch on the pocket. She could not allow the gentleman—and from the way he was dressed, this man was a very fine gentleman—she could not possibly allow him to see her like this.

But if she ducked into the bedroom now her biscuits might burn. If she took them out of the oven now, they would be half raw on the inside.

Laura stood at the window, peering out and dithering, staring at the visitor as if she were a little girl with neither sense nor manners. She had to change. But if she went in now . . .

Abby saved her. Laura and Jim's only daughter came rushing inside, all a-bubble with excitement. "Mama, Mama, did you see, there's a man out there talking to Papa, oh he's a fine-looking man, dressed like out of a picture book or something. Did you see him, Mama, can we invite him in to dinner, well, can we, Mama, can we?"

"Settle down, sweetie. Your papa knows enough to invite the gentleman to stay, and I have already seen him, thank you very much." Laura hurriedly reached around to her back and untied the strings of her apron, then yanked it over her head. "I have something I need you to do, dear. I want you to watch those biscuits. Mind what you are doing now. They shouldn't be brown on top, just a nice light gold color. You remember what I taught you."

"Yes, mama, but . . ."

"No buts, if you please. I have to go change. I won't be a minute." She left Abigail alone in the kitchen while she herself darted into the tiny, nearly dark cubicle she shared with Jim. Abby slept in the loft overhead.

The gentleman. Wherever should they put the gentleman? Abby was too old to take into her parents' bed nowadays, and Jim worked hard. He deserved a sound sleep in his own bed with his wife at his side. But the gentleman. She was not sure how she should treat him. An ordinary drifter or cowhand she could ask to go up the ladder to Abby's loft, and they could lay a pallet on the floor down here for Abigail. But . . . a gentleman? Oh my. Whatever was she to do?

She was not immobilized by her indecision though. While she gave thought to the problem of where to sleep everyone she was a whirlwind of activity. Grabbing her Sunday dress off the peg. Fingers flying to unbutton her patched and faded old housedress. Throwing the garment off and hurriedly yanking her best dress over her head. Oh dear.

She stepped to the mirror and squinted in an effort to see in the poor light. She reached up to snatch some of the pins from her hair, then quickly brushed and tucked and pinned the curls in place again. She was sure she had done a dreadful job of it but it was the best she could do. And if she waited too long . . .

"Oh!" She hadn't heard the oven door clatter. Whatever was Abigail doing out there? The biscuits were sure to be ruined. She grabbed her apron off the bed and ran back into the kitchen. Abby was at the window, staring out at her papa and the visitor, the oven forgotten.

"Abigail Jane!"

Abby jumped. She knew it was serious when her mama called her by both her proper names. "They're all right, Mama, really." Laura knew the reassurance was meant at least as much for Abby herself as it was for her mother. Her daughter bent down to the oven and cracked open the door just enough that she could peep inside. Laura knew without looking that no harm had been done when she saw a wave of relief spread over Abby's dear and freckled face. The child was eleven years old and the apple of Jim's eye. Of her mother's too, if the truth be known.

"They're all right, Mama. See? I told you."

"Are they ready to come out?"

"Yes'm."

"Then you can put them on the table, if you please."

The biscuits were suspiciously dark on top when seen outside the oven but not badly so. They would do. They had to do. Laura lifted the heavy coffeepot off the stove, placed four enameled bowls and four plates onto the table, used her apron as a potholder so she could get both hands on the big pot of bacon and Mexican pinto beans—thank the good Lord for pinto beans—and mentally declared herself ready . . . well, almost . . . for their guest.

"Abby, you can go out and tell your father that supper is on the table. Mind now, don't just ring the iron to call him. We have a guest. Go out . . . slow and ladylike, mind . . . and tell him."

Abby gave a little giggle, then gathered up her skirts and went larruping out the door like a wild Indian and not at the serene pace her mother would have preferred.

The truth, however, was that it was all Laura could do to keep from dashing out there with her.

They had not had a stranger come visit in . . . goodness, not since last Christmas, she thought.

She patted her chest and tried to slow her breathing and her racing heartbeat.

A stranger. A *gentleman* stranger at that. Oh my.

And so, *so* handsome. Abby was right. He did look like something out of a drawing in one of the finer catalogs or an elegant magazine. Before he entered he very carefully wiped his feet on the rag rug at the door and removed his hat. He was tall. Had to stoop a little to make sure he did not bump his head on the lintel. And his clothes. Goodness.

Laura could have swooned when he smiled at her. Without thinking about it she dropped into a little curtsy and the gentleman responded by bowing. She hadn't been treated like this in . . . in ever so long a time.

"Mrs. Hannigan." He smiled that smile again. It deepened the cleft in his chin and made his eyes—they were the brightest blue she thought she ever saw—made his eyes bright and merry. "I want you to know how much I appreciate Mr. Hannigan's offer to take this stranger into your home for the evening. I hope I'll not inconvenience you. And of course I shall be willing to pay for my lodging."

"You'll do no such thing, sir. We are always happy to have guests. You can catch us up with the latest news if you would. Have you met our daughter Abigail, sir?"

"I've had that pleasure, yes, ma'am." He bowed to Abby too as if meeting her again. "My name by the way is Jarrett. Harlan Jarrett. I am a land speculator. I

buy when I find a property and a price that I like and
sell at a modest profit after. It is a particularly pleasant
occupation because it allows me to meet so many fine
folk such as yourselves."

"Oh, dear. Please excuse my manners, Mr. Jarrett.
Here I'm keeping you standing by the door when you
and Mr. Hannigan should be at the table enjoying your
dinner. Please. Take that chair there, Mr. Jarrett."

"Thank you. May I have the honor of saying grace
over the bounty Mr. Hannigan provided and you have
prepared?"

"We are the ones who would be honored, Mr. Jarrett.
Abby, fetch the ladle and put it in the beans, then we
can all sit and . . . and Mr. Jarrett will offer the blessing."

Later—Laura found the beans too salty and the biscuits overcooked but even so the meal seemed to have
gone well enough—Jim leaned back in his chair and
signified his pleasure by unfastening the top button
on his trousers to make more room. Not that he really
needed it. Jim was a lean man. A good man too and she
was lucky to have him. He did not smoke or chew and
rarely drank. He never beat or so much as smacked
Laura and was patient with Abby. If her life was not
perfect, it was nonetheless quite good and she was
thankful for what she had.

"Tell me," Jim said, "what is the news? We don't take
a newspaper and have mighty few visitors."

"Not even neighbors?" Harlan Jarrett asked.

"None close enough to count. We get into town every
month or two. That's about it."

"Then you haven't heard about the raiders?"

"Raiders?"

Laura's attention was piqued too but she was a little
concerned that Abby was there. "Excuse me, gentle-

men. Abigail. It is time for you to go upstairs and to bed."

"But I haven't . . ."

"I shall finish the dishes myself and we will do your lessons in the morning after you feed the chickens. Go on now." Her tone of voice made it clear that she would brook no disagreement, while Abby's expression made it just as clear how very much she thought the order unjust. "I said go."

"Yes, Mama." Abby dropped the cutlery into the wash pail and turned away. She climbed her ladder slowly instead of scampering up at her usual furious pace.

When Abby had disappeared into the loft Laura turned to Jim and Mr. Jarrett. "I apologize for the interruption. Please go on with what you were saying."

"Actually, Mrs. Hannigan, I am pleased that you sent the child out of the room. She shouldn't have to hear any of this."

"Raiders, you said?" Jim prompted.

"Yes. A small gang apparently. There is disagreement whether they are red Indians or renegades of some other stripe, coloreds perhaps or Mexicans, even whites. No one knows. The reason no one knows what they are or how many is that they have never left any survivors behind to tell tales. They do . . . excuse me, but I do not wish to elaborate. They do terrible things. Simply terrible.

"They rob and kill and worse. Hit isolated places like this one." Jarrett leaned close to Jim and said, "Never leave these handsome women of yours alone, Hannigan." He sat back. "Not that it is my place to tell you your business, sir. But my advice is that you should be vigilant. And never leave your lovely ladies by themselves."

The warning was shocking. Yet Laura could not help feeling a thrill of pleasure. Handsome women, Mr. Jarrett had said. Lovely ladies. Gracious! To think he would say such a thing about her, married a dozen years now.

"Might be I should take the birdshot out of my old scattergun and put in a charge of buck instead," Jim said, nodding toward the door where the shotgun rested on pegs above the opening.

"That would be a good idea, Hannigan. Keep that and whatever other guns you have close to hand. Close to hand, sir. With savages on the loose a man cannot be too careful."

"Thank you for the warning, Jarrett, and for the advice. Thank you very much."

"It is the least I can do, Hannigan, and small recompense for such a fine meal and excellent company to take it in. I am in your debt, sir." Jarrett smiled. "If you wouldn't mind talking about something less troublesome, tell me what crops you intend putting in. I've heard a little about prices on the speculative markets, you see, and I might be able to give you a little advance knowledge of what will be selling well on the Chicago and Kansas City markets this fall."

"Oh, we don't sell that far away. No way to transport our produce, you see."

"Perhaps not, but the prices there will affect what your local buyers pay."

"Yes, I suppose that is true. Well, I have three fields prepared. I expect to put the east field in barley, mostly for our own use, you see, for feed. And then in the north field . . ."

Laura took that as her cue to quietly remove herself to the stove, where she drew hot water from the reservoir to wash the supper dishes. The men's voices receded into a half-heard drone while her hands went though the routine of scrubbing and rinsing and wiping. But her mind heard over and over again Mr. Jarrett's opinion that she and Abby were handsome and lovely. Oh, she would not soon forget something like that. It was the nicest thing she could remember happening to her in ever so long. Ever so long indeed.

Chapter Two

Harlan Breen felt the bed shift very, very slightly and heard the muted creak of steel springs moving. He lay still, eyes closed and breathing regular, but his right hand slid out from under the covers and reached ever so gently for the smooth, hard grip of his Colt. The gun was hanging from the bedpost. Always. Harlan never allowed himself to become so drunk as to forget that small but important detail.

The .44 was where it ought to be, positioned exactly the way he liked it.

On the far side of the room he heard the slither and fall of cloth and a very faint jingle of metal upon metal. Harlan lifted the Colt from its holster and draped his thumb over the hammer, sliding his index finger inside the trigger guard.

A floorboard groaned as a foot stepped onto it. Then another. By the door, that one. He was sure of it.

The picture his senses painted was as clear in his mind as if he could see through his closed eyelids. His supposition was confirmed when he heard the light rasp of the lock bolt being drawn aside.

Harlan tensed. Then leaped off the bed with an ear-shattering roar.

The big Colt came steady. Hammer drawn back to full cock now. Harlan beside the bed in a crouch, naked as a jaybird but as lethal at that moment as any grizzly.

"Bitch!" he bellowed.

"Oh, God," the equally naked whore squeaked. "Oh, Jesus-Mary-and-Joseph." Harlan's trousers fell to the floor with a thump while the girl held her dress in front to cover herself. Damned if he could figure out why she would bother doing something like that though. Not considering the fact that she'd been naked in his bed for half the damn night, twisting and contorting into 'most every shape one small human person could get herself into. She hadn't minded him getting an eyeful then. Now she did?

"Drop the dress," he ordered, emphasizing the instruction with a gesture of his pistol barrel.

"I didn't—"

"*Drop* it. I ain't gonna tell you twice."

"God, honey, I never . . . I was gonna . . . you gotta believe me, baby."

"Drop the dress or I'll drop you with a bullet. Now do it."

She dropped the garment and it struck the floor with a suspiciously heavy thud. Harlan figured his belt and knife and buckle were enough to account for his pants being heavy. But whatever could be in her dress pocket now to make that heavy? It was only a wisp of cloth a little while ago when he took it off of her. Goodness gracious sakes alive, whatever could that be in her pocket now?

"Get in the corner over there. Face to the wall. Don't look around. Don't say a word. Not a peep. Not one."

"But—"

Harlan crossed the hotel room in two quick strides. His gun flashed in his hand. "Are you gonna shut up now?"

The girl squeezed her eyes tightly closed and screwed her face into a caricature of misery.

She turned and scurried into the corner, the only sound coming from her that of her bare feet padding across the floor. She left a puddle behind where she'd been standing and every time her left foot stuck the floor, it too left a wet patch behind.

Harlan picked up the dress, tucked the Colt under his arm so he would have both hands free, and examined the pockets. He was not exactly amazed to discover his own coin pouch there. He tossed the dress down and used the ball of his foot to wallow it around on the floor so as to wipe up the whore's urine, then kicked the dress toward the foot of the bed.

Harlan retrieved his trousers—thank goodness none of her piss had got on them—and returned the coin pouch to its proper place before he dropped the Colt onto the rumpled and sour-smelling sheets, then sat and pulled his pants on and stuck his feet into the boots sitting beside the bed. He stood and finished dressing, then went to the wardrobe in a corner of the room and got out his saddlebags, bedroll and carbine. He'd had about enough of this place.

It was . . . he didn't have any idea what time it was. Closer to morning than to midnight, he judged. And he didn't have any idea which rooms the other boys were in.

Didn't matter, he decided. He'd just go up and down the hall and pound on doors until he found them. If the other guests didn't like that they were welcome to say so. But Harlan figured he'd do the door pounding with the butt of his Colt. That very likely would cut down on the complaints from those who answered his knocking.

Get the other boys, have a bite to eat at the café down the street—he wasn't sure if the café was an all-night outfit usually but it would be tonight—and wake the hostler at the livery. He figured they would be miles down the road before daybreak.

Thought they'd go up to Kansas this time. The Nations was wearing a mite thin for him. It was about time they stepped outside the I.T. and pulled another robbery or two. Or three. Before they came back to the safety of the Indian Territory where state law couldn't touch them and where the marshals didn't much give a shit as long as there were no federal charges against a man. Convenient, that. Awful convenient.

Harlan touched the butt of his Colt and repositioned it a quarter inch or so. He liked for it to hang just right. He was fussy about that.

When he was satisfied that he had everything in order he tugged his hat brim down and draped the saddlebags over his shoulder, then shifted the bedroll and carbine to his left hand. He walked over behind the whore. She was standing in the corner where he'd put her. She was shaking so bad it was surprising she hadn't fallen down, but she'd been paying attention to what he said. She hadn't made a peep or turned her head since he put her there.

"You're lucky," he told her. "Lucky I paid for you downstairs or I'd make you give it back. Reckon I can't do that now. But I think I might just take me a souvenir to remember you by. I think I'm gonna scalp you."

He heard her snuffling and gasping and her shoulders shook as she bawled and cowered. But she didn't say anything. Not one word.

Harlan pulled his knife. Took hold of one of the little whore's pigtails—he didn't know who she thought she was fooling with that little-girl hairstyle, for she was thirty if she was a day—and sliced it off right up close to the side of her head. Now wasn't that going to make her look pretty for some months yet to come?

"I'm gonna be in the hotel for a while longer. Maybe the whole day. You'd be smart to stay inside this room until sundown because if I see you outside o' this room you'll be sorry. You understand me?"

He waited a moment and said again, "D'you understand me?"

The girl nodded. But she did not speak.

"Bitch," he grumbled.

Harlan Breen turned and left the room, still feeling grouchy but not quite as much so as he had a few minutes earlier.

Now to find the other boys so they could get themselves around and head up into Kansas. Hell, they were needing some money anyway. And money was easy enough to come by.

Harlan grinned to himself. A fella just needed to know how to ask for it, that was all. Like over the barrel of a .44-40 Colt, for instance.

All of a sudden he was eager to get on the road and get back to work.

Chapter Three

A body couldn't ask for a more perfect day. Bright and warm and sunny, with puffy white clouds drifting overhead and hawks circling high above the fields in search of mice or rabbits or whatever. Too nice a day by far to waste inside a stuffy old schoolroom full of stupid girls and giggly little kids. No sir, this was just about a perfect day to catch a fish.

Tommy agreed with him, which was not exactly a surprise. The two of them always walked to school together. They had been doing that pretty much as long as Willie could remember. Except this morning they walked along the road just far enough to get out of sight of the Eglestons' barn, where Willie's father was busy putting a harness on the mule, then cut across through the woodlot and down the path to the river.

They stopped long enough to unearth some fat worms from the loam in the shade of a droopy old oak, then retrieved their fishing poles from the patch of poison sumac where they had left them. Among the sumac seemed a likely hiding place because most folks believed it would cause rashes and itching just the same as poison ivy or poison oak, but that was just a tale that people told. The sumac never bothered Will or Tommy, and others' belief in its powers to harm acted as a protection for their things when they left stuff there.

Like the fishing poles now. Perfect.

They walked on down to the river to the log where

they liked to sit to do their fishing. They knew the spot well. They had been here before.

Most days they caught nothing, but that was all right. If they caught something they just had to throw the fish back anyway, otherwise the fish would get them caught. Neither one of them could take a fresh fish home in the evening without giving away the fact that they had been playing hooky.

Oh, that had really hurt the time Willie caught the big catfish. Why, that cat might have been the biggest old catfish ever. And they'd had to throw it back.

Then to make matters worse, when he tried to tell the kids at school about his monster catfish some of the older boys taunted him, saying he was just telling a fish story. He'd gotten in three different fights about that. Won one of them too. But then Henry Leinart was big but he was soft, so in a way he didn't hardly count.

This morning Willie would like to catch something, just not anything that awful big.

This morning too he had thought to filch some matches out of the box his mother kept close to her stove. This morning if he caught a big old catfish—or a little one, for that matter—they could build a fire and have it for their lunch, along with the butter bread and chunk of fried pork Willie's mother had put in his pail today.

Willie nearly always had the same boring stuff in his lunch pail. And Tommy's mom nearly always put cold biscuits and chicken in his pail. But then Willie's family raised hogs. Tommy's had chickens.

More days than not the two would swap lunches.

Today, though . . . today they would have a fat old catfish and sit down to a proper dinner.

Willie settled onto his accustomed end of the log, unwrapped the scrap of cloth full of dirt and worms that they laid between them and plucked a juicy worm out of the dirt.

"Now if I was a fish I'd sure want to eat a fine-looking worm like this'un here," he observed.

"If you want t' eat that worm you go right ahead," Tommy said, "but tell me first so's I can watch."

"I'll be sure an' let you know if I decide to slurp one down." Willie pursed his lips and held his breath and ever so carefully threaded the worm onto his hook. He checked to see that the twig he used as a bobber was set at a depth he liked, then flipped the baited hook into the powerful flow of the river. He hoped the weight he had on the line was enough to take the worm under. The river was flowing strong today, and he did not have any more buckshot to put on the line.

Perhaps he could devise some way to tie a stone onto the line as another weight. He was puzzling on that when Tommy said, "See if you can snag that doll baby."

"What are you talking about? Doll baby? What would a doll baby be doing in the river?"

"Some kid lost it, dummy. What other reason could there be? See if you can snag it. If the water hasn't ruined it I can take it home to my sister."

"And how will you tell her you come by it?"

"I'll think about that later. Now help me snag it, will you?"

Willie shrugged and looked upstream, toward Tommy's end of their log. He could see the doll now. It was barely floating, hanging low in the water. It had long hair and no clothes on . . . and it was awful big for a doll. What kind of baby doll was that big anyway? Now that it was floating closer he could see that it was near about as big as a real girl.

It was . . . oh Jesus!

"Don't touch it, Tommy, *Jesus!*"

Willie's fishing pole slipped out of his hand and dropped into the water. It floated downstream unheeded.

"Jesus Christ, Tommy, oh Jesus."

Donald Egleston shifted his chew into his other cheek and spat a stream of dark tobacco juice onto the rocks at his feet. A sense of nervous decency kept him from staring at the more private parts of the naked body that bobbed at the shallow edge of the broad river.

Not that there was anything appealing there to look at anyway. There might once have been, but the girl had died a terrible death and terrible things had been done to her before she died.

"Who d'you think she is?" Egleston's neighbor Matthew Schenk asked.

Egleston shook his head. "I never saw her before. I'm pretty sure of that."

"The way she's all battered and puffed up," Schenk said, "she could be anybody and we'd not know it. Not so much as recognize her."

"No, if she was from around here we would've heard something about a child being missing. She isn't very old. Looks like she wasn't, um, much developed." He forced himself to look, really look. If he thought of the body as a puzzle to be solved it was easier to bear. "She's been in the water quite a spell, I think. Can't say for how long, but a good while."

"She could've come from anyplace," Schenk said. "The Arkansas is one long old river. She could've come down from all the way over into the mountains, I suppose, and that's a mighty long way. There or anyplace in between."

"Do you think . . . I mean . . . do you suppose all

that, uh, that damage . . . it could've come from being pounded on the rocks? If she fell in, I mean? Maybe it wasn't anything human as did this to her. Maybe it was the rocks."

"Whatever did this *wasn't* human, that's my opinion."

Schenk sighed. "However she come to be here, whether she fell in or was thrown in, it's up to you and me to pull her out and see her proper into the ground."

Egleston shuddered. The thought of touching that bloated, mottled flesh made his skin crawl. It had to be done, of course, but he hated it nonetheless.

"Stay where you are, Don. I'll get down in the water with her and ease her up to where you can get a good hold on her. We'll lay her on the bank then . . . do you think you can get your wagon down here to her?"

Egleston nodded. "I think so."

"We'll take her over to the Corners and bury her behind the church. Get Rev. Simm to read over her."

"And the sheriff. We'll have to tell the sheriff. He may have heard something about a missing girl. If she has folks somewhere who are looking for her, they need to know. It's a blessing she'll be in the ground, though, and they won't have to see what's been done to her."

"The rocks, Don. Just believe it's the rocks that did all this. Now give me a hand so's I can ease down . . . Jeez, that water is cold."

Chapter Four

Roger Bailey paused at the end of the row. He wiped his face with a kerchief that was already sweat-soaked and soggy. The gesture probably did no more than re-arrange the spit-warm moisture but it made him feel a little better anyway.

"You look as tired as I am, old girl. What do you say we call it a day? Go in and clean up a mite. Have ourselves some supper. Does that sound good to you, girl?"

There was still a little daylight remaining, but the mare was heavy with foal and Roger did not like to push her too hard. The foal was important to him. To him and to Maria. If it turned out to be good enough, with the size and the muscle and the bone to pull, it would bring in some badly needed cash. Even if it proved to be ordinary he could put it to work on his own farm.

His own farm. What a wonderful thing it was to be able to say those words. His own farm.

Roger turned now and took a moment to look back over the field he was breaking. Natural grass that had never felt the plow, not until now.

It was beautiful, the soil warming with the spring, moist now after the winter snows. God, he hoped there was enough moisture in the ground to nourish the barley he intended to plant.

They had said he could expect little rain here. That did not make sense to him, not when he could see how rich the carpet of wild grasses was. If there was enough moisture to sustain grass, he reasoned, there should be enough to bring in a crop of barley.

And one crop, one decent crop this first year, and he would be able to pay off the balance he owed to the railroad corporation he had bought from.

His own farm.

Roger could not help grinning at the thought.

He pulled out his kerchief again, wiped his face again. "What do you think, girl? Are you ready to go in?"

Roger unhooked the traces and moved up to the big horse's head. He carefully sorted and coiled the driving lines, then draped them over the neat hames and led the mare a few paces distant. "Whoa now. Stand, girl."

He went back to the plow, sitting upright at the end of his newly turned row, and wrestled it around to face the other way, then straightened the chains ready to hook to at first light tomorrow.

Again he took a moment to look out over his field—*his* field, by gum—and to marvel at the beauty of the earth.

"Roger? Are you done for the day?"

He turned, smiling, to see Maria approaching from the direction of her chicken pen. Not that it was much of a pen. And not that it had much of anything to protect. She had had thirty birds when they got here last fall. Maria had had notions about pickling eggs to sell on the rail cars, when one of these days a railroad was built. Now there were two hens remaining and one of those was crippled. Hawks took them. Owls, weasels, foxes. Maria grieved over each bird that she lost.

They could get along without the chickens though, thank goodness, and when you thought about it, thirty birds was too many until or unless a railroad came to give Maria a market. Perhaps when this country was more settled and they had more money to build a proper hen house, she could try again.

In the meantime they had two sows, a cow with a heifer calf already at her side, the pregnant mare, and seed already bought and stored in rat-proof barrels in the shed. Lord, he was one lucky man.

Someday they would have a proper house. For now they had a perfectly comfortable soddy that they had built as soon as they got onto the land.

Well, almost perfectly comfortable. It was warm and secure and had protected them all through the cold and the winter winds. The sod roof dribbled dirt onto everything though, and oozed mud when snow melted on top of it. Roger suspected it would run mud even worse when the rains came. And surely, please God, the rains would come.

Just let him get his seed in the ground first.

Roger sighed. And smiled as Maria reached his side.

"Do you know," he said, "that you are the most beautiful girl in the whole world?"

Maria dropped her eyes. Her dear face flushed with pleasure.

"I mean that. The most beautiful girl there ever was."

"Hardly a girl," she said. "I'm an old married lady."

"A very beautiful married lady. And you are going to be the most beautiful mother too. Uh, do you still think . . . ?"

Maria bobbed her head. "Yes, I'm almost sure of it now."

He moved to wrap her in his arms, then hesitated.

"What's wrong?"

"I'm all dirty. I'm too sweaty to be holding you."

"I like for you to hold me. I hope you will want to hold me for all your life." She hugged him and laid her face against his damp and sticky shirt.

"God, I'm lucky," he whispered.

"Do you think so?"

"I know it."

"I'll help you with the harness and the feeding," Maria said. She giggled. "Then maybe we could go inside and I'll give you a bath." Roger had been shocked to discover that his innocent bride professed to actually like bathing him.

He had been even more shocked—but awfully pleased—to learn that those baths usually led to much more than simply getting clean.

"Do you think . . . I mean if you really are, um, with child . . . do you think we can still, uh . . ."

She laughed. "Of course we can. I'm not sick, you know. I'm just going to have a baby. That's all."

"That's all? That is more than all. That is everything. Are you sure it won't hurt you . . . or the child . . . if, um . . ."

"It won't. I promise."

He held her tight and buried his nose in her hair, breathing in the scent of her and marveling anew at the fact that she was his.

She was far and away the prettiest girl he ever knew. Seventeen years old now, sixteen when he married her. Gleaming black hair that fell below her waist when she let it down in the evenings. Dark, smiling eyes. Tiny dimples, one on either side of her soft and eminently kissable mouth. Long, curling eyelashes. Tiny waist and full bosom. Oh, she was a beauty. His beauty.

And now she carried his seed within her.

"Come on then. Let's put the mare up and see to the evening choring."

Maria laughed. "Why are you in such a hurry now?"

"I . . . oh, gosh darn."

"What's wrong?"

Roger nodded toward the lane that led over the rise from the direction of what passed for a public road. "Someone's coming."

A buggy or light wagon was coming into view at the brow of the rise.

"Who could that be?" Maria asked.

"I'm thinking it might be James Dewey. I asked him what he would charge to have his boar breed our two sows. He said he wouldn't charge anything, but I offered him his pick of whatever litters we get. He said that would be all right with him. I'm thinking he might have that in mind now."

Maria got an impish look to her and said, "Then can I watch? I've never seen hogs do it."

"Maria!"

She giggled. "Don't look so scandalized."

"You shouldn't . . . aw, you were just teasing me, weren't you?"

"Of course I was. But I really would like to watch. I'm already in the mood. That might put me to boiling over. And I know you'd like that, now wouldn't you."

"Shush, girl, I . . . oh, never mind. That isn't Dewey. That isn't his rig and the man driving it looks like a city fellow. He's wearing a suit."

"Damn," Maria blurted. "We'll have to invite him to supper. But don't let him come in right away. I have to change clothes and get out our good dishes and . . . oh, I have lots of things I need to do. So you keep him outside as long as you can."

Maria disengaged herself from Roger's arms and ran toward the soddy. Roger took hold of the mare's bit and began leading her back toward the shed where he kept her.

Chapter Five

"Remember now," Harlan Breen warned his men, "no trouble. None. We don't want to call attention to ourselves. You three can ride in first. Get yourselves something t' eat, then find a saloon. A nice quiet one, mind. Have some beer and pretzels or something like that. No heavy drinking though and don't be giving anybody any shit. If somebody walks up an' pokes you in the eye, you smile an' beg his pardon. You got me?"

"What are you gonna be doing while we're in there minding our manners?" Danny Hopwell asked. Danny was in his early thirties but he looked as if he could still be in school. He had a button nose and freckles, and the ladies always wanted to mother him. Not that mothering was what Danny generally had in mind.

"I'm gonna take a look inside that bank, o' course," Harlan told him. "I'll go in. Ask if they can change some currency for me. Which reminds me. Any o' you got a twenty-dollar bill? I'll swap you twenty in gold for a paper note."

"I think I got one," Carl Adamley said, digging into his britches and coming out with a fistful of currency. Adamley peeled the sweaty, crumpled bills apart, straightened them and thumbed through until he found a goldback. Handing it to Harlan, he said, "Here y' go, boss."

Harlan made a sour face. "When's your birthday, Carl?"

"November. Sometime in November, why?"

"'Cause I'm gonna buy you a snap purse or a wallet so's you can keep your money without it looking like chickens been nesting in it." But he took the twenty and stuck it in his pocket. He pulled out a handful of change, selected a shiny double eagle and handed that to Carl. "I hope they don't throw me outa the bank when they see what you done to this bill, man."

"If you'd told me ahead of time I woulda took better care of it maybe."

"I got one cleaner if you want it," Little Jim Toomey offered. Little Jim was tall and burly. He swore he lifted an ox off the ground once on a bet. Harlan had never seen the man perform that exact trick but Little Jim was without question the strongest man he had ever seen. He almost believed the yarn about picking up the ox. Of course Little Jim never specified just how big the ox was, or how high he got it off the ground.

"Thanks but this will do." Harlan grinned. "Likely we'll get Carl's nasty bill back when we take the bank anyhow."

"Unless they pass it along quick so it don't infest the rest of their bills," Danny said.

"If we do get it again it has t' go to Carl in his share," Harlan returned. "That seems only fair. Now let's get back to business. You boys mind what I told you. No trouble. And no excuses neither. Anything happens, it don't matter what, you boys smile an' apologize. If you see me in town, you don't know me, right? You don't even look in my direction. But keep your eyes open. You know what to look for. Leastways you ought to by now. We'll meet back here an' compare notes after sundown."

"Do you care what we do in town so long as we don't cause no trouble or call attention to ourselves?"

"You got something in mind?"

"I was thinking I might want to get laid." Danny grinned. "It'd be something to help pass the time."

"D'you ever think about anything else, Danny? Never mind. I know the answer to that. Anyway, shit I don't care. If you want t' get laid an' have the money, go on an' enjoy yourselves. Just meet me back here at this spot come sundown, *an' don't get in no damn trouble*. Now get outa here. I'll be along directly."

Harlan squatted beside what was left of the fire and watched the boys saddle their horses and ride off.

He was pleased with what he saw. They were a good bunch, far and away the best crew he'd ever put together. Everybody got along, one with another. More importantly, every man of them was steady. They didn't get excited or nervous. Didn't start throwing lead all over the landscape at the least excuse. And they didn't kill. That was the most important thing of all. Start killing people and the law would be all over you like stink on shit. They wouldn't let up until you were laid out ready for burying.

What was more, these boys didn't brag on themselves afterward. They spent their money and they had plenty of fun doing it. Whiskey, women and wagering. That was the ticket. But they didn't crow or so much as hint about what marvelous robbers they were. As far as anybody knew, they were just some drifters enjoying themselves between jobs. Cowhands or mule skinners or whatever. They never exactly said.

As a result of all that, there were no stories going around about the Breen gang like there had been about the Jameses or the Youngers or the Lincoln County Regulators. No songs or poems or exaggerated penny dreadfuls written about them.

And that was exactly the way Harlan Breen liked it. The less people knew about them, the better.

Harlan watched until the boys reached the public road that ran parallel to the watercourse where they were camped, and then he put them out of mind. He reached for the tin can that served as a coffeepot and poured, carefully so as to not disturb the grounds. The coffee was terrible. It tasted like a cow had pissed in it. And come to think of it, maybe one had, this creek winding past some dairy farmer's pasture.

On the other hand, it was better than having no coffee at all. He took another swallow, scowled, drank again.

He finished the coffee, then dumped the grounds and rinsed out the can, setting it back beside the dying ashes in the fire pit. The ring of stones had already been there when he and the boys arrived. This thicket was apparently popular with bummers and line riders and other ne'er-do-wells.

That was to the good. Locals passing by would not likely get excited about there being strangers around if they were already accustomed to seeing smoke here. The less notice folks took of them, the better. Even when they were busy robbing a place Harlan did not like to make it obvious just how many of them there were. Or how few. Quiet in and quiet out, that was the best.

Harlan washed out his enameled tin cup and set it on a flat rock beside the pot. No one was apt to bother it there—they damn sure better not anyway—and he needed the room in his saddlebags for the next few hours.

He pulled the makings out of his shirt pocket, peeled a leaf of rice paper off the packet, creased it and spilled some Cutty Pipe onto it. Good stuff, Cutty Pipe. You could roll a quirly, pack it into a pipe or chew it, and it would taste good any way you had it. Rolling it was the way he generally preferred. He licked one edge of the paper, rolled it into a cigarette and twisted the ends. Rather than waste a lucifer he stuck a twig into ashes in the fire pit, waited a moment until he got a flame, and used that to light his smoke.

He stood there for a moment, then unbuckled his gun belt and rolled it around his holster so that the .44 and cartridge belt made a compact package, which he stuffed into one pocket of his saddlebags. There was nothing wrong with wearing a gun into a bank but it was not necessary either, and why call attention to himself unnecessarily?

That done, Harlan saddled his bay and tied the saddlebags in place. The right side hung a little low because of the weight of the revolver, but that could not be helped.

He stepped onto the saddle and eased the bay's head around, setting off at a walk. He was in no hurry. The bank they intended to hit was but five miles away, and he wanted to give the boys plenty of time to get there ahead of him. That way no one seeing them would have any reason to connect them with the stranger who stopped to make change at the bank.

But if anything wildly improbable happened and Harlan found himself in a jam, they would be there to back him up.

He put that out of mind and sat easy, enjoying the scent of the air and the feel of the sun.

This was going to be a nice, clean job. He was sure of it.

He reached the road and reined west, keeping to a walk even on the rutted highway. He tugged the brim of his battered old Kossuth a little lower to keep the afternoon sun out of his eyes.

Half the men west of the Mississippi wore the same

style of black slouch hat. That was exactly why Harlan insisted that he and his boys wear them too, even though he liked a fashionable Stetson as much as anybody. The thing was, the Kossuths, cheaply available by the tens of thousands as army surplus, were not distinctive. One man wearing a linen duster, a Kossuth hat and a mask that hid most of his face looked exactly like any other fellow. Witnesses could not put you behind bars if they could not identify you.

Anonymity would get a fellow out of more scrapes than a revolver would, Harlan believed. The guns just sort of got a bank clerk's attention. Did a right fine job of it too, he reflected, a slight smile tugging at his lips.

Yes, sir, a fellow in his line of work wanted to grab a banker's attention. But quietly, with no fuss or bother.

Go in easy. Take what was available. Leave quickly. It was a process that made him and his boys a very good living.

It would annoy the hell out of him to have it interrupted. Especially by something as bothersome as a hanging.

No, he would leave fame and excitement to the other fellow. Fortune was enough for him, thank you.

Harlan's musings came to an end when he reached the outskirts of the drab, sun-baked Kansas plains town where farmers for miles around came to sell and to buy and to dream.

The town did not look particularly prosperous, but that too was the sort that Harlan preferred. More people and greater prosperity led to a police force that was serious about peacekeeping.

Harlan liked the boring little places that might have a fat old town marshal sleeping in the shade somewhere.

A bank in a town like that would for one thing have

no competition, so whatever money there was in the community would all be in one place. And while there might be less of it to take, the risks would be very small as well. No one ever expected trouble. Few men carried weapons. Often there were not even any saddle horses immediately available to mount a pursuit.

This place, Harlan thought, wrinkling his nose with wonder at the idea that anyone would actually choose to live here, was just about perfect.

He stopped in front of the larger of the two general stores on the very short main street, dismounted and tied the bay to a post there. There was not even a rail where saddle horses could be hitched; rather there were half a dozen stout posts with rings bolted to them planted in the ground so harnessed horses could be secured. But then this was farm country, not ranchland.

The storekeeper, a middle-aged man with a large paunch and more than a little gray in his mustache, was leaning in the doorway. Harlan nodded to him.

"What can I help you with, friend?" the shopkeeper asked.

"I'll be wantin' a few things. Got a list, uh, I think I got it here someplace." Harlan poked two fingers inside one shirt pocket, then the other. He patted his pants pockets and reached inside the right-hand one. "Well, I did have me a list. Seem to've lost it. I tell you what. I want t' stop over to the bank for a minute. I'll be right back an' pick out the things I'm needing. Would it be all right if I was to leave my horse here?"

"Sure thing. I'll keep an eye on it for you. Not that anybody would bother it anyway. You go ahead. Take your time."

Harlan smiled at him. "Thank you, sir. I appreciate the kindness." He touched the brim of his hat and ambled down the dusty street toward the bank.

Chapter Six

Harlan hunkered down beside the fire and reached for the can. He used his kerchief to hold on to the rim so he would not burn himself and tipped a little freshly boiled coffee into his cup, then set the can back onto the coals and with his free hand motioned for the boys to join him.

"Lemme finish brushing Ol' Paint here," Danny said. Every horse Danny rode was named Old Paint after the cow horse in a popular lament. This particular Old Paint was a seal brown that did not have so much as a single white hair on it, at least none that Harlan had ever noticed.

"Old Paint can wait a few minutes. Come listen while we're all awake an' paying attention for a change," Harlan insisted. He smiled when he said it but he meant it nonetheless. He wanted their attention and he wanted it now. He did not want to wait while everyone attended to camp chores.

Danny stuffed his dandy brush back into his saddlebags and came to join the others beside the fire. "All right, boss, what'd you find in the bank today?"

"Easy pickings, I think," Harlan said. He took a swallow of steaming hot coffee and grunted his approval. Little Jim reached for the can and poured some for himself, without bothering to protect his fingers from the heat of the thin metal and without showing any evidence of pain.

"The bank is in the middle of the block," Harlan said.

"Third store in from Fourth Street. Around the corner on Fourth are a shoemaker, a haberdashery and a barber. Me and Little Jim will go inside, just like always. Carl, you an' Danny paw through the merchandise inside Jolly's General Store. If Ezra Jolly asks—which he likely won't but in case he does—you're looking at ladies' brooches, trying to pick out something for the little woman back home."

"Why are we looking at brooches?" Carl asked.

Harlan grinned. "Because the display case is right smack in front of the window. Gets better light there, I suppose. It also makes it easier for you boys t' see if there's any commotion at the bank. I don't expect any trouble but if there is, you'll be in position to spot it an' help out. Otherwise, o' course, if everything goes the way it should, you finish your looking, maybe buy some tobacco or something, pay for it an' nice and slow come back here where Little Jim an' I will join you.

"That's if there's no alarm raised an' we can get in and out quiet. The bank is laid out with two teller windows but only one teller. There isn't even a door between the front and the tellers, just a gate. I think the gate is just latched closed but even if there's a lock on it we can step over it. There's a man who sits at a desk behind the teller cages. He's in front of a Victoria and Wiler floor safe. Good safe, but they leave it standing open during the day so it'll be dead easy to clean out.

"There's a door in the back wall leading out to the alley. That's the way Little Jim and me will go out when we're done. We go in the front, both of us showing pistols. If there's any customers we put them under the gun too. Little Jim will hold them an' the bank people while I clean out the teller's drawer and the safe. Currency and gold coins only, no silver."

"No silver dollars even?" Little Jim asked. "I could carry them. I don't mind the weight."

Harlan shook his head. "I don't think so. We want to be in an' out fast. Light too. Silver coins are just too damn heavy to bother with."

"Whatever you say," Little Jim said.

"When we're done we'll put everyone on the floor. Make sure they got no guns. Then slip out into the alley. We'll leave our horses tied in front of the barbershop. The alley comes out right beside it. If all goes the way it should, Little Jim and me will ride hell-for-leather past Jolly's store. When you boys see us flash past that window, you know you can pay for whatever you're shopping for an' come nice an' slow out here to join us."

"That sounds easy, all right, but is it fat?" Danny asked.

"The haul won't be terrible much, I'd think. Mind you, I didn't ask if I could count what they had, but the shelves of that Victoria and Wiler didn't look all that full. There was stacks of currency but I'd expect most o' that to be small bills. Not that we should complain. It's free money, right? Which one of you made this coffee?"

"I did," Little Jim said. "You got a problem with that?"

"Nope. It's good." He grinned. "For a change."

Carl grunted and stood. He stepped away from the fire and returned moments later with his cup, then knelt and poured for himself. Like Harlan, he used a kerchief to protect himself from being burned by the lip of the coffee can.

"Any questions?" Harlan invited.

"Nope."

"Not me."

Little Jim only grunted and drank some coffee.

"Tomorrow?" Danny asked.

"Ayuh, tomorrow. We'll give you fellas a half hour or so start on us, then ride in and get this thing done."

Chapter Seven

"The thing is, Sheriff, me and Tyler here," the man pointed down to a small gray and black terrier at his feet, "we was out tramping the woods, thinking to bring home a mess of squirrels. Tyler is a right good squirrel dog, you understand. Best I've ever owned. Anyway, me and Tyler was out here thinking to shoot us some squirrels but he got distracted. Kept digging and pawing at that log you see there. Trying to get under it, like. That isn't like him. Tyler likes to hunt squirrel just about as much as I do." The man fidgeted with the shotgun he was holding, as if he suddenly did not know what to do with the long-barreled old gun.

Sheriff Dougal McColm nodded and reached for his pipe and tobacco. He did not rush the witness.

"When I got up close I could smell it, of course, and I got to wondering if there was a coyote den under there. Because of my sheep I don't like coyotes. Don't like to have them around and I'll kill them every chance I get. So I was thinking if this was a den I'd kill whatever pups was in there before they could grow up to be sheep killers and chicken thieves. Or if there wasn't no pups I could come back with traps and some bait.

"Anyhow, I found that limb . . . the one laying there . . . and used it to prise the log up and tip it over. It was covering . . . it was covering what you see there." He looked down and grimaced. "I wasn't real sure at first that it was even a human thing, it being so rotted and pressed flat. By the weight of the log that was laying on it, I suppose. Then I looked close and seen the ring on its finger. That's when I realized that it was a human person laying there. Do you . . . do you got any idea who it could be, Sheriff?"

McColm struck a match and held the flame over the bowl of his pipe, sucking in until he got the pipe properly lighted. Then he looked at John Newcomb and said, "There's been some reports lately of young women going missing. Their families killed but their bodies not found. I suppose this could be one of those."

"I couldn't even tell this was a female thing. What makes you sure?"

"Now I don't say that I am sure, John. Not for certain. But the length of the hair, that suggests it was a woman. Did you look around? There might be some clothes discarded nearby, or something else that would help me get a handle on who this might have been."

"No, sir, I didn't look for anything like that."

"That's all right. I can do it later." McColm sighed. "God knows there's no reason to hurry." He paused to draw on his pipe, taking comfort from the taste of the smoke.

"Any idea how long it . . . she . . . might've been here, Sheriff?"

The sheriff shook his head. "Could be weeks or it could be months even, what with her laying underneath that log so the body was protected from carrion eaters. Out of the rain too. Maybe there's people who could examine her, if it is indeed a her, and tell you how long she's been here, but I wouldn't know about that sort of thing. It's been quite a while anyway. Whoever put her here didn't want her found, not right away, or maybe he was burying her, respectful like. Like taking care of her after she died." McColm shrugged. "Truth is, John, I just don't know."

"Do you think she was somebody passing through and just died or would you say she was murdered?"

"God, John, I got no idea about that sort of thing. I think what I'm gonna do is go back and get a wagon so I can carry her in to Dr. Weymouth. He can take a look at her and maybe come up with some answers." The sheriff pursed his lips and thought for a moment, puffed on his pipe twice, the smoke trickling out of the sides of his mouth and filtering up through his mustache. Then he said, "I'd best bring a wide plank too so I can slide her onto it and lift her into the wagon that way. Otherwise she's apt to fall to pieces when I try to pick her up. I'd like to take her in whole if I can manage it.

"John, I'd like you to stay here until I get back. Now that the log has been rolled off her and she's exposed, there could be vermin come around thinking to eat on her. Most of them will stay away if you're here. If anything, crows or whatever, if anything comes close, you shoo them away, please. I won't be long. Just long enough to get a buckboard from the livery stable and get back here with it."

"I guess . . . all right, Sheriff, I guess I can do that for you."

"No promises, you understand, but I'll talk to the board of commissioners, see if they'll pay you something for your services to the county. Staying here and keeping a crime scene safe ought to be worth fifty cents, I'd think."

Newcomb received that suggestion with delight. "Fifty cents cash money, that would be a big help to me, Sheriff."

"I don't guarantee it, remember, but I'll try and get it for you." He puffed on his pipe again and said, "I won't be long, John. Be back here quick as I can."

"Yes, sir, uh . . . would you mind if me and Tyler looked around for some squirrels while we're waiting on you?"

McColm smiled for the first time since he'd seen the thing that had been lying beneath that log. "Go right ahead, John, and good luck to you."

The sheriff turned away and started walking back toward town.

Chapter Eight

"Damn, Little Jim. You look almost human."

"I scrub up pretty good, don't I?"

"That's a fact." Harlan Breen bent, picked up the soot-blackened can they used to boil their coffee, then kicked dirt over what was left of the fire. The gang would not be coming back to this spot again. He scowled down at the can and said, "That's what I shoulda told the boys to get while they're in Jolly's store. A proper coffeepot."

"I got room to carry that if you like," Little Jim offered.

"Yeah, sure." Harlan handed the battered can to the big man and turned to his horse, checking that the cinches were tight and its hooves free of stones.

Toomey opened his saddlebags, rummaged inside and pulled out a rag. He checked to see there were no coffee grounds still inside the can, then used the rag, which had once been a shirt, to carefully wrap the can so it would not leave soot on the other contents of that saddlebag pocket. That done, he untied his bedroll from behind the cantle, unrolled it and removed the pale duster that he carried there, rerolled and tied the bedroll, and finally put the duster on over his newest and most colorful outfit.

By the time Little Jim was done with all that, Harlan was already in the saddle, ready to go. Breen too wore a duster buttoned to the throat to completely conceal his clothing.

"I'm ready," Little Jim announced as he swung onto his horse.

Harlan gave the brim of his Kossuth a tug and kneed his bay into motion.

They made the ride into town at a nice, easy walk. It would have made no sense to use up a horse that might need stamina as well as speed after the job was done. A bunch of Kansas farmers would not likely be instantly prepared to mount a chase. It probably would take some time for them to grab guns and horses. But it was only sensible to be prepared for something more immediate.

Harlan did not so much as glance toward the front window of Jolly's when they rode past a little while after breaking camp, but he had confidence that Danny and Carl were in there. It seemed a shame he couldn't stop and ask them to buy a coffeepot. That would just have to wait for another opportunity.

He turned the corner, Little Jim following, and stopped in front of the barbershop. There was only one other horse, a scrawny roan wearing a scuffed and ugly McClellan saddle, tied there. Harlan dismounted and draped the bay's reins through a ring on the post nearest the alley. Little Jim had to take his to a post on the other side of the roan. His animal too had been laboriously trained until it would stand tied without pulling back on the reins. There were times when fumbling with a bulky knot was simply not advisable. When men with guns were coming after a person, for instance.

An old man wearing a white apron came to the door of the barbershop. "I'll have a chair open for you in five minutes," he offered.

"Thank you, sir," Harlan said, touching a forefinger to the brim of his hat. "We'll step around the corner to the bank while we're waiting. We need t' go there anyway."

"I'll keep your place open," the friendly barber said.

"Nice man," Harlan commented over his shoulder, as he and Little Jim Toomey walked the few paces to Main and turned the corner toward the bank. As he walked he unfastened the middle two buttons on his duster and glanced around to see that Little Jim was doing the same.

They reached the door leading into the bank and paused there. Both men dipped their fingers inside the necks of their dusters and pulled up bandanas to cover their noses and the lower part of their faces. Both drew their revolvers as they stepped inside.

There were, Harlan was glad to see, no customers in the bank at the moment, just the bank's own personnel.

In a loud, clear voice Harlan announced, "Good afternoon, people. This is a holdup. I'm sure you know what to do."

Little Jim knew what to do also. While Harlan was advancing toward the teller's cage, Little Jim locked the front door and pulled down the rolled blinds. It was too early for the bank to close, but with luck no one would notice.

There was no lock on the gate that separated the teller's area from the lobby. Harlan unlatched it and swung it open. He held his Colt pointing in the general direction of the bank manager. His finger was on the trigger. Likely it would not be noticed that the revolver was not cocked. He would shoot if he had to. But only if he truly had to.

"Against that wall, please. No, facing it. Thank you, that's much better. Hands on your heads now. If you lace your fingers together your arms won't get so tired.

That's nice. Now just stay like that until I tell you otherwise."

Harlan motioned for Little Jim to join him in the cage, where Toomey took over the job of watching the bank people. Harlan pulled a cloth bag from the pocket of his duster and stepped to the teller's window. A drawer beneath the window held a slotted metal tray containing both coins and currency. He took the currency and shoved it down into the bag, then scooped out the handful of gold coins in the tray and dropped them in on top of the currency. Finally he turned to the floor safe standing open by the back wall.

He stripped the shelves of the neatly piled currency there too, and picked up a small box from the same shelf as the paper money. The box was unusually heavy for its size. Harlan put it in his bag without taking time to open it. He ignored several bags of coins on the shelves below the currency.

"There now," he said. "Wasn't that easy? An' nobody got hurt. Keep that in mind if you want it t' stay that way."

He went to the back door and slid free the bolts that secured it. "All set here," he said.

"Don't be showing yourselfs, neither one of you," Little Jim warned in his deep, gravelly voice. "Thirty minutes. Don't neither one of you stir for thirty minutes."

Harlan slid his Colt inside his duster and into its holster and took a moment to tie a knot in the neck of the now-heavy bag of loot. "Let's go," he said.

Little Jim kept his revolver in hand until they were in the alley. He followed Harlan toward Fourth Street and emerged beside the barbershop.

"I have that chair open now," the barber said.

"Thanks but we got t' run some errands first. We'll

be back later," Harlan said. He transferred the sack to his right hand and tugged the bay's reins free. He sorted them quickly and stepped into his saddle. Little Jim was doing much the same and got onto his horse at virtually the same time, both men moving with deliberate speed that would not call undue attention to themselves.

Harlan reined away from the barber's and headed down the street to Main. He held the bay to a trot as they crossed in front of Jolly's window.

There was not any reason to run. Yet. And if his luck held . . .

Chapter Nine

"Knee high by the Fourth of July? Bullshit!"

"Mind your tongue, Curtis. You have daughters, you know. They don't need to be hearing that sort of language."

"Sorry, darlin'."

"You don't sound like you really mean that."

The lean farmer's only response to that was a shrug and a grin. Curtis Womack was tall and sinewy, his face and arms as tan as leather, although he was fishbelly pale where the sun could not reach. He wore denim overalls that once had been blue and a red undershirt with the sleeves pushed back to his elbows. His hat was a cheap Kossuth, battered and dusty, the base of its crown crusted white with dried sweat.

Womack was in his early forties, with graying hair and a two-day stubble of beard from his habit of bathing and shaving on Saturday nights, a pattern he maintained even though the Womack farm lay too far from a Catholic church for the family to attend Sunday services.

Irina Womack was a dry little woman who at thirty-seven looked like she was in her sixties. She might once have been pretty but that was a long time ago. She wore a shapeless dress, pale from many washings, with neither petticoats nor shoes under it.

"You know what? I think that sonuvabitch at the store cheated us. I think he sold us some bad seed.

Left over from last year maybe. Just look how spotty it's coming up. It ain't worth spit."

"We will manage, Curtis. With God's help, we will manage."

"Praying ain't gonna make that seed good," Womack grumbled.

"How would you know? You've never tried it," Irina shot back at him.

"All right, you win. We'll do this like we do everything else then; we'll do it together."

Irina was not convinced. But then she knew her husband. She waited for him to continue.

"You pray," he said. "Me and the girls will hoe."

"Don't be silly, you old man. If you are out in the sun with a hoe in your hand I will be right beside you."

"Damn, woman, I knew there was some reason why I like you s' much." He bent down and planted a quick peck on her wrinkled cheek.

"Curtis! Someone might be watching." But she sounded pleased.

"Go see if the girls are done washing the dishes and fetch them out here if they're finished. I'll get a start on it." Womack glanced toward the sky and shook his head. They needed rain if there was to be any hope that this corn would come in.

He grabbed a heavy, broad-blade hoe from the shed. A lighter hoe was easier to use, but weight was needed to break through the stubborn Kansas soil. The ground here tended to bake rock hard in the heat of the sun day after day after day, and the unwieldy big hoe was needed to break it apart. Once Curtis finished with cutting through the crust, the girls could come along with their light little hoes to complete the job.

Womack looked again toward the sky and sighed. The question of whether to break the surface or leave it be was not a simple one. Logic told him that exposing the good soil beneath the crust would only allow the sun to more readily evaporate away the scant moisture that lay there. But if he left the crust alone so as to protect the subsurface moisture, the rain, once it did come, would be unable to penetrate to the roots of his crop and would only run off as waste water.

Whatever he chose to do was a gamble. A guess. And the future of his family depended on his ability to guess correctly enough times that they could make a living here.

Curtis Womack had failed once before in his life. He did not want to do it again.

The sound of young voices, bright and cheerful, drew his attention in the direction of the sod house—house? it was as much dugout as house really—that they had built when they first got here. His girls. His beautiful girls. He smiled when he saw them. He could not help himself. They were just so very beautiful.

Then he very softly laughed. To him they were the most beautiful creatures ever to grace the earth with their presence. To others . . . well, they should be beautiful to strangers also.

Meggie was in the lead. Sweet, freckle-faced, impetuous Meggie. She came skipping and laughing and looking back over her shoulder to talk—jabber, really—at her sister. Meggie was nine, the youngest of Womack's brood. She had reddish brown hair done up in pigtails and huge, clear blue eyes, and her knees and elbows were perpetually scabbed from headlong falls and mischief.

Behind Meggie was her big sister Liz. If Meggie was the apple of her daddy's eye—as indeed she was—then Liz was his joy.

At fifteen Liz was as pretty and vivacious as her

mother had been at that age. And much more outspoken. Liz had pale, soft hair that fell to her waist when in the privacy of home and family she shook it out of her customary braid to brush or wash it. A woman's hair was her crowning glory. Womack knew he had heard that although he could not recall if the sentiment came from the Old Testament or the New. It was biblical anyway, he was certain of that. And about Liz it was a fitting comment.

Not that he would admit his elder daughter was a woman. Not yet. She was still his beloved child and he was in no hurry for her to be thought a full-grown woman. What she might think of herself . . . that was another matter entirely.

She was his beauty though and his pride. Lizzie—no, he had to remember to stop calling her that as she already declared herself too old for a childish name—Liz was tall. Taller than her mother, indeed taller than most of the very few boys her own age she had ever met, in town or in church or back home in Tennessee. She held herself straight and proud and her figure, well even a father could see the reason why boys would find Liz of interest.

The girls were too far away for Womack to hear what they said but Meggie started toward the field. Liz stopped and spoke to her. Meggie looked back but did not stop, so Liz snapped at her. Something sharp judging from Liz's expression. From Meggie's too, for that matter.

Meggie stopped and sulked her way to the shed where she waited for Liz to join her. Each girl selected a hoe and then, Meggie in the lead again but not skipping and prancing this time, headed toward the cornfield.

Womack pretended not to have noticed any of this.

Lord, he did love those girls.

Chapter Ten

"Not a great haul but better'n a poke in the eye with a sharp stick," Harlan Breen said. He and the three members of his gang were seated around a table in a room at the Watsonian Hotel.

"What's it all come to?" Danny Hopwell wanted to know.

"Give me a minute to finish counting, will you? It's, um, it looks like $932."

"So divided four ways that would be. . . ."

"Like I said. Not great. But not rotten neither," Harlan said. He grinned. "Enough to buy us a couple bottles and a woman, anyhow."

Carl Adamley nudged Little Jim and said, "If all we can afford is one damn woman to take care of the bunch of us, then make sure I don't hafta get in line behind Jim here."

"That's because you know you can't measure up to a real man," Little Jim taunted his friend.

"No, it's because you always leave a stink on them. Why don't you wash more often?"

"Why don't you watch your damn mouth?"

"Settle down, children," Harlan said calmly. Bickering among the gang members was common enough, especially when they were feeling good, as they always did once the dangers of a job were past.

There was a peculiar excitement to the game of robbing people. Harlan felt it too. Always had. He figured if he ever found that he did *not* get a lift out of holding a gun on people and taking their money, well, that would be the time to quit the business and go do something else.

When he walked into a bank or a store, gun in hand and steel in his voice, he always felt taller and stronger and . . . well . . . better. Better than anyone in that bank. Better than he himself ordinarily was.

The money wasn't bad either, he reminded himself with a grin. The money came quick and easy, and a man didn't even have to work up a sweat to collect it. He might get a bullet for his troubles, but that was just part of the gamble. Robbing made a man's blood run quicker and the air taste sweeter. It was better than liquor, better than sex, better than just about anything.

It was not the money that was the best part of it though. The best part was the feeling it gave at the time of the actual robbery. Oh, the planning was fun and the spending more so. But it was the exhilarating feel of the robbery itself that addicted a man.

"Are we gonna lay out an' spend this for a while," Carl asked, "or go on right away?"

"We'll go ahead on," Harlan said. "Over to Wainwright, then Bufford and Plainfield, I think. We'll make a sweep an' take the little banks in each o' those places, then break back down into the I.T. where the law can't follow. That should put a nice, healthy haul in our pockets. Enough so we can be comfortable all through the winter. Then by spring the law will've clean forgot about us so we can go right back to work."

"Spring?"

Harlan shrugged. "Or sooner if we feel like it."

"Pass me that coffeepot, will you?" Little Jim asked.

Eleven days later, their pockets considerably heavier with other people's money, Harlan gathered his gang on the east bank of a rock-filled, loud-chuckling stream. Ancient trees overhung the west bank while shafts of sunlight slanting through the foliage danced on the water surface.

"We got time for a pot o' coffee?" Little Jim wanted to know.

"We got all the time in the world," Harlan said. "I dunno about you boys, but I'd say it's time we took ourselves a little vacation from all this hard work." That brought the expected round of laughter from the other boys. Every job they pulled this time around had come off smooth and easy.

"We each of us got more than a thousand dollars in our kick. That should be plenty enough to carry us through for a spell."

"Let's not wait all the way until spring though," Danny said. "One bad run o' cards and we'd have to tighten our belts. Or, shit, break down an' get a job."

"Now wouldn't that just be the day," Carl said. "I'd pay good money to see you with a shovel in your hands."

"How much money?" Danny shot back at him. He laughed. "I can shovel shit with the best of 'em."

"With your mouth maybe."

"Will you boys settle down, please? You sound like a pair o' old women squabbling over an old man. The point is here, it's time we split up for a while." Harlan pulled out his pipe and began absentmindedly loading it. "Whatever law is after us is looking for a gang. Two at the least and maybe somebody's figured out that there's the four of us. So it's safer if we split up, go have a nice time and then meet up later when we're ready t' go back to work."

"If you say so," Little Jim said.

"I think it'd be for the best," Harlan told them. He struck a match aflame and applied it to the bowl of the pipe, drawing deeply on the tobacco until he had a good coal built. He tipped his head back and blew a few near-perfect smoke rings, then said, "I agree that carrying over to spring is too long. Let's say . . . two months. Two months from today."

"Where?" Danny asked.

Harlan shrugged. "Red Bear's store on Bird Creek, over near Skiatook."

"I remember it."

"Aye."

"Me too."

"Red Bear's place it is then. In two months' time. We'll meet there an' take a little ride back up into Kansas. In the meanwhile each of us is free to go an' do whatever he pleases, and if it pleases you to join up with some other outfit or to stay on your own or get out of the business, whatever, nobody will hold it against you. No hard feelings is what I'm saying, though far as I'm concerned we fit together pretty well."

"I got a question," Little Jim put in.

"All right, ask it."

"Who gets to keep that new coffeepot with him while we're apart?"

"Jeez. Who's got it now? You, Carl? Give him the damn pot before he gets the shakes or something, will you?"

Harlan flipped his near stirrup onto the seat of his saddle and began tightening his cinches. The other boys could wait here to boil coffee if they liked. He wanted to go find a bottle and a woman. Perhaps not in that exact order.

Chapter Eleven

"He's a good horse, sound and decent mannered," Harlan Breen said, slapping the bay on the rump, "but you know how it is. I don't have work right now an' might have trouble feeding myself, never mind feeding him too. I'll keep my kak, o' course. I'll be needin' that soon as I can find me a job riding for somebody. But I reckon the horse has t' go."

The man at the livery was of middle years with dark, greasy hair curling over his collar. He had sharp, pointed features and needed a shave. Not that Harlan was in any position to criticize on that point, as he himself had not had a shave in five days.

Harlan did not much care for the idea of getting rid of the bay, but that was his policy. The horse had been seen at too many holdups. It could well be mentioned in a flyer being passed around among lawmen. One or possibly two series of robberies sweeping out of the Indian Territories and a horse had to go, no matter how much he liked it.

The livery man walked around the bay. Picked up each foot to examine the hoof and feel of the tendons. Peered into the mouth and each nostril. Peeled back an eyelid to look more closely into the bay's increasingly nervous eye. The horse threw its head and blew snot to show its displeasure.

"Six years old, you say?"

"I didn't say," Harlan told him, "but I'd put him closer to ten."

The livery man grunted to himself and continued his inspection of the animal, running his hands over its back, feeling of the chest and belly.

"He ain't skittish, I got to give him that."

"No, sir, he's never been goosey."

"He's sound, you say, not wind broke."

"He has good wind and a decent handle on him. Try him out if you like. I'm not in a mood to lie about him."

"No, I believe you. I just wish I could afford to buy him."

"Make me an offer," Harlan said. He would get rid of the bay here if he had to simply turn the animal loose to fend for himself, but it would be better if he could find a buyer.

"Mister, I ain't gonna lie to you. A horse like this is worth thirty-five, forty dollars or thereabouts. I can't afford anything close to that. Lord knows how long he would stand here eating my hay before I could move him along to a buyer. This is buggy horse country or heavy pulling horses. Does this fella drive? I might could use him if he drives because he's a handsome enough thing."

"I don't know if he's ever been in harness. He might take to it just fine or he could as easy blow up complete, I just don't know."

"Tell you what. I like the looks of this horse. I'll give you ten dollars for him."

"Twenty," Harlan countered. He had paid fifty for the bay, but he considered that he had gotten his money's worth out of the horse. A business expense, so to speak.

"Twelve."

"Fifteen."

The livery man shook his head. "Twelve is as far as I can go, and that's pushing it."

"Twelve it is then," Harlan agreed. He untied his bedroll and saddlebags and set them aside, then began loosening the cinches on his saddle.

Harlan dropped his gear on the floor and leaned on the hotel desk. A sour-faced woman, with her hair done up in a bun so tight it almost pulled the wrinkles out of her face, emerged from a tiny office and looked him over. Harlan would have bet that her ass cheeks were clenched as tight as her lips. She had that look about her.

"How may I help you?"

"A room," he said.

"And for how long?"

"A night, maybe two. How often does the stage run through here?"

"Tuesdays and Fridays," she said. The woman had bad teeth, he noticed. She was a walking example of why he was glad he had never married.

"An' what day o' the week would this be?"

"Wednesday."

"Until Friday then. How much would that be?"

"One dollar. In advance. That does not include meals. Meals, if you want to eat here, would be extra. Remove your boots before you lie down. I'll not have my bedclothes ruined by them. No drinking in the rooms. This is a family establishment. And I do not permit unmarried women to visit gentlemen in their rooms. Any infractions of these rules and I shall ask you to leave. Without any refund."

"Infraction," Harlan mouthed. "That would mean like breakin' a rule, is that it?"

"That is correct." She produced a register and opened it. "Sign here or you can tell me your name and make your mark."

Harlan bent and picked up his saddle, it and his bed-roll, saddlebags and carbine all wrapped into a tight, heavy bundle. "You can take your rules an' shove them up your ass," he said on his way out the door.

Surely there would be a whorehouse somewhere in this town. Two nights there would be a damn sight more fun than that hotel would have been anyway.

Chapter Twelve

"We left things just exactly the way we found them, Sheriff. We talked it over and figured you should see it just like it is. Maybe you can figure out what happened here."

The young sheriff nodded his thanks and peered thoughtfully around Curtis Womack's sod house. He had been here before and he knew that Irina Womack kept her home as clean and tidy as it was possible to maintain a house with a dirt floor and sod roof. The interior of the house was anything but tidy now.

"It looks to me," the sheriff said, "like whoever did this was invited to the table as a guest. See there," he pointed, "places set for Curtis and Irina and for each of the girls, plus an extra plate at the foot of the table."

"Mrs. Womack was a good cook. She didn't have much to work with but she always made whatever she had taste good. I've eaten here many and many a time when I'd come by to help Curtis or to ask him to help me. They were good people. Good neighbors."

The sheriff grunted. "The son of a bitch finished his dinner before he killed them. Cleaned his bowl right up." He stepped to the door and looked up toward the sky. "Are they what brought you over to see?" he asked, still staring at the buzzards floating gracefully overhead on unseen air currents.

"My brother saw them first. He's a mite timid, you know. He got me and dragged me over. Then after we saw we talked it over, like I already told you, then we flipped a coin to see who should stay here to sort of keep watch to make sure nothing got inside, foxes or coyotes or whatever, and which of us should drive into town and fetch you." He shrugged. "I lost."

"Yes, so I gather," the sheriff said dryly, returning his attention to the horror inside the soddy.

"They are all inside. How do the buzzards know? Do you have any idea about that, Sheriff?"

"It's the flies. The birds have remarkable eyesight. They see the flies swarming. That's how they know there is carrion."

"That's an awful ugly thought, isn't it? This whole family. Now they're carrion, or would be, if the damn birds could get inside."

"Ugly indeed." The sheriff stepped back inside. He moved around the room, careful to avoid stepping in the mud that had formed where blood soaked into the dirt floor.

"To judge by the bodies, I'd say they have been dead about three or four days."

"Three then. I saw Curtis four days ago. He came over to return a saw he had borrowed. That and to share a nip of whiskey with me and my brother. He did that every now and then. Irina doesn't . . . didn't, I mean . . . Irina didn't approve of spirits. She didn't like for Curtis to have them anywhere on the place so he would come over now and then and have some of ours. He was good about it though. A couple times he bought a pint and sent it home with us, so it wasn't like he was mooching off us or anything."

"Four days, you say."

"Yes, sir. In the evening that was, after supper. It was coming dark and me and my brother were fixing to go to bed. We sat up with Curtis and shared a drink. Then he went home. That was the last I saw of him."

"Three days dead, then." The sheriff frowned. "Whoever did this is a good enough shot, but then he wasn't far from his target. Just at the other end of the dinner table, I'd say. See the way Curtis is lying there, his chair tipped back from the head of the table and a neat hole drilled through his forehead. I'd say they were all still at the table. Our murderer finished his meal, then pulled out his pistol and killed Curtis.

"He got that one shot free, you might say. No one was expecting any sort of trouble. Curtis wasn't threatening him. The son of a bitch just up and shot Curtis. After that it wasn't quite so easy. See here? Irina was shot in the back, probably while she was at the stove to do something there. Fetch more food or put coffee on to boil. Something like that. Then Curtis was shot and Irina turned, like to get away. That's why she was shot in the back. Through the lungs would be my guess. She might've tried to run, but she had nowhere to get away. The man with the gun was between her and the door.

"Then he shot the girls. The little one . . . Meggie, was it? Cute little thing anyway. Her and finally Liz." The sheriff squatted down beside Liz's body and looked closer. "Her hands," he said.

"What?"

"Liz's hands. They're all bloody." He picked one up and inspected it closely. "If you look real close . . ."

"I'd rather not, if it's all the same to you, Sheriff."

"Fine, but if you did look close you could see that there's meat caught under her nails. I'm betting that Lizzie put up a fight. That would be the killer's blood on her hands. Whoever did this got scratched up pretty bad before he killed Liz." The sheriff pursed his lips in thought, then grunted. "I got to ask you something."

"Yes, sir?"

"When you got here, did you move anything? I mean anything at all?"

"Like, um, Lizzie's dress, you mean?"

"That is exactly what I mean."

"I guess we pulled it down to cover her. Her dress was pulled up and she wasn't wearing any drawers. She . . . it looked like maybe she was violated. There was, you know, shiny stuff on her flesh."

The sheriff looked around the little place. "I don't see any discarded drawers, do you?"

"No, sir. I hadn't thought about that, but no. There doesn't seem to be any sign of them."

"So the killer took them with him for some reason. Maybe to stanch the bleeding from where he was scratched."

"That could be."

The sheriff sighed. "Or maybe he wanted a trophy or maybe there was some other of a thousand possible reasons. I'll have to catch the bastard if I want to find out for sure."

"How will you do that, Sheriff?"

"I'll send out flyers with what little I know or figure out or just plain guess. Now help me get these bodies outside, will you? We'll put them in Womack's wagon and carry them to town. Let me hitch his . . . what does he have? A horse? Mule? Doesn't matter. I'll hitch up his wagon and we can carry them in that."

Half an hour later the sheriff hissed between his teeth and stood up, letting go of Irina Womack's wrists.

"What's the matter, Sheriff?"

"There. In the dirt. It looks like it took a little while for Irina to die. She rubbed something in the dirt. A name. Jesus! It must be the name of the killer."

"Aye. It's . . . Harlan . . . is that a name? And, uh . . ."
He shook his head. "I can't make out the second name.
But the first is definitely Harlan."

"I don't know anybody around here named Harlan,
but somebody, somewhere is bound to. Thank you,
Irina. We're going to find the man who did this to
your family. I promise."

Chapter Thirteen

Harlan Breen woke up in . . . he *was* awake, wasn't he? This couldn't be some sort of dream. A nightmare, if it was. His head felt like someone was squeezing it in a vice. And some other son of a bitch was pounding on it with a hammer. Two hammers, one for each throbbing temple. He was dizzy and sick to his stomach and his mouth tasted like somebody had shit in it. Man, to feel this bad in the morning he must have had one hell of a fine time last night.

He rolled onto his side, took a moment to work out that he was not going to puke—at least not immediately—and felt around for the girl he had been with last night. Girls, actually. At least he was pretty sure there had been more than one.

All he felt now was . . . cold metal? Where the hell had that come from? What had happened to his bed? Where was he if . . .

Oh!

It was starting to come back to him now. Sort of. He had been partying with, uh, whatever their names were. Two of them. Drinking. Screwing. Generally having a good time. Until they ran out of liquor. The girls had tried to go get some more but they were too drunk to walk, the stupid bitches, so he had manfully volunteered to go.

He'd ended up . . . he was not entirely certain but he sort of thought he'd gone out of the whorehouse and down the street looking for whiskey. Which would have been all right except that he'd been wearing his hat and his shirt. And nothing else.

Harlan sighed.

He sat up. It took him three tries but he managed to push himself more or less upright on the side of the bunk where he had awakened.

The movement made his head pound all the more, and for a moment he was sure he was going to throw up but forced the impulse back. He swayed dizzily, clinging to the side of the metal bunk with both hands as if afraid he would fall off if he let go. After a minute or so he opened his eyes.

Bars. And bricks. He was in jail. Damn! And he had been having such a nice time too.

Was the stagecoach due to come through today? Or had that been several days back?

Not that it mattered. He was in no condition to travel. The thought of bumping and swaying in the back of some mud wagon . . . just the thought was enough to make his already queasy stomach roil and churn. No. Not today, thank you. Maybe not tomorrow either. As soon as he got out of this damn cell he would have to check the stagecoach schedule. And until then he would just cut back on the partying. A little. Just enough so that he could remember how much fun he'd had.

Harlan took a deep breath, then several more. He rolled his shoulders and—gently—twisted his head. Released his grip on the side of the bunk with one hand and ran it over his face. He badly needed a shave. That was no surprise. The good news was that he had feeling in his cheeks and his nose. The drunk was wearing off. He did not try to stand up though. He was not ready for that much movement yet.

He swallowed back the bile in his throat. Swallowed

more. And more. Experience told him to quit swallowing or he would get sick on his own saliva, but it kept running and running and he spit instead. There was no cuspidor so he spit on the floor. Better some clear spit there than puke.

He shuddered and concentrated on breathing, then lifted his chin and called out, "Hey. Turnkey. Is anybody there?"

He had to shout three more times before finally a voice responded, "Hold your damned horses, I'm coming." The voice sounded annoyed.

An older man who was missing his left arm and whose face was badly scarred came into view. "What is it you want, mister?"

"Out. What the hell d'you think I'd want? Let me out of here."

"That ain't up to me, mister. I'm just the jailer. It'll be up to the marshal to say when you can go."

"Fine. Tell the marshal that I want to see him."

"Can't. Not right now. Marshal's on his dinner break. Likely he'll stop in to check on you before he makes his evening rounds. I'll tell him then an' maybe he'll talk to you. I can tell you one thing though. He won't turn you loose until you see the magistrate, and that won't be possible until tomorrow morning. Maybe not until Monday."

"Morning? What time is it? Hell, what *day* is it?"

"It's Saturday evening."

"So I've missed the stage," Harlan grumbled.

"There will be another come along. You can count on that."

"Look, can't I just pay a fine and go? What am I in for anyway? What charges, I mean. I know I was drunk in public. I admit that. I'll pay the fine and be on my way."

"I already told you. You got to talk to Marshal Glass about that, but I don't think he'll let you out before you see Judge Ramsey."

"And the charges?" Harlan reminded the man.

"Drunk and disorderly. Assaulting a peace officer. Public lewdness. I think those mostly cover it. Oh, and misappropriation of services. I almost forgot about that one."

"Misappro . . . what the hell is that supposed to be about?"

"Miss Vera told the marshal you left there owing her money."

"Like hell I did. I paid her. I paid that girl."

"She said you paid her for one girl but you took two."

"No, I paid the other girl too. I remember that much. I paid the madam for the first girl and paid the other girl in my room. I . . ." Harlan stopped, puzzled. "Wait a minute. I'm dressed. How's come I have my britches and things? I thought I walked out of there without them."

"Miss Vera brought your things with her when she came to file the charges against you. Me and the marshal stuffed you into your pants so you wouldn't shock any ladies that might come in. The rest of your things are out here. Your boots and gun and saddle and things. It's all here. You can have them back after you're let go."

"Well, at least there's that," Harlan conceded. "Listen, if I fall asleep again, please wake me up when the marshal gets here. I'd appreciate it."

"Sure. I don't mind. And I'll tell him that you're behaving decent. You just don't know how awful bad some prisoners talk to a jailer. Like it's my fault they're in here. You haven't done that, and I'll for certain sure tell Marshal Glass that you're being a gentleman about the whole thing."

"Why, thanks. Thank you very much."

"Now that you're awake would you like some dinner? You're entitled to two meals a day and you haven't had anything yet."

The thought of food . . . "No, thank you. I'm not hungry just now."

The jailer chuckled. "I bet you aren't. Maybe in the morning you'll be wanting something. In the meantime there's a bucket of water and a dipper hanging on the wall outside here, where you can reach them from inside the cell. If you need the outhouse let me know. I can take you out back, but I'll have to shackle you first. That's the marshal's rule."

"All right, thanks. And be sure an' tell the marshal when he gets in, will you?"

"I'll tell him. Now if you'll excuse me, I'll be getting back to my own dinner."

Chapter Fourteen

Bang!

Harlan winced as the sound of the gavel shot into his aching head. He was feeling considerably better this morning. That did not mean he was feeling good. He still felt like he had been dragged through a cesspool, stomped by a mule and hung up to dry. And that was an improvement. Lordy, the things a man put himself through in the interests of having fun.

"In accordance with your plea, Mr. Breen, I hereby find you guilty of public drunkenness and indecent exposure. As part of your plea agreement the other charges are dismissed."

The gavel came down again. Harlan opened his mouth and breathed deeply, trying to ignore the pain in his head.

"Do you have something to say, Mr. Breen?"

"No, Your Honor. I'm just . . . I still don't feel so good." The chain that linked his iron wrist bracelets rattled when he reached up to scratch an itch at the side of his nose.

That brought a hint of a smile to Judge Ramsey's lips. "No, I am sure you don't." He set the gavel aside and leaned forward, crossing his arms on the dais before him. In a much softer voice the judge said, "I am told you are well behaved, Mr. Breen, so I will be lenient with you. Normally you would be fined twenty-five dollars for the offenses you committed, but Marshal Glass has a good opinion of you. So I will make that only a fine of five dollars or, uh, five days in our jail. You can pay five dollars, can't you?"

"Yes, Your Honor." Harlan smiled. "I can handle that." He ought to have . . . he was not sure of the exact amount, not after the good time that had landed him here, but it ought to be somewhere north of twelve hundred dollars. Probably closer to fourteen hundred. Yeah, he could manage five dollars. Then, what the hell, back to the whorehouse until that stagecoach came through and he could get shut of this shitty little burg.

This was, what? Sunday. The stagecoach wasn't due again until Tuesday. So he could go back to partying tonight and tomorrow. But no whiskey. Lord, no. He'd had enough of that to last him for . . . for another few days anyway.

He wondered if he could get Miss Vera or someone at her whorehouse to make him some coffee. The coffee they made at the jail was terrible stuff. Weak. Since hooking up with Little Jim Toomey, Harlan had come to like his coffee stout enough to have hair on it. Damned if Little Jim hadn't ruined him.

"What, Your Honor? Sorry. I was lollygagging there."

"I said I hope you have learned your lesson from this incident."

"Oh. Yes, Your Honor, I surely have." That was what you were supposed to say. He knew that. It was bullshit, of course. Better to play their games, though, than to sull up and call undue attention to himself. Right now these yokels were thinking of Harlan Breen as just an out-of-work cowboy and he wanted them to keep right on thinking it. He wanted no questions raised that could make them suspect the way he came by his money.

"Marshal Glass, please take Mr. Breen back to the jail where he can pay his fine and be on his way." Somewhere outside a bell began to ring and the judge stood. Ramsey pulled his watch from his vest pocket and glanced at the time. "Dammit, I'm going to be late for church. Not your fault, of course, not your fault. Go on, Marshal. Call me if you need me." And the judge was gone from the small courtroom.

"This way, please." Glass took Harlan by the elbow and guided him out of the otherwise empty town hall and across the street to the jail.

Harlan paused on the board sidewalk in front of the jail and took a long, deep breath, not to settle his stomach this time but simply to enjoy the taste and the feel of the fresh, clean air.

It was funny how being locked up made the world seem smaller, somehow even made the air smell different. It was going to be good to be free again. And that was after just a couple nights with a jailer and a town marshal who were friendly. How much worse would it be in a prison?

Harlan had never been locked away in prison. He had no intention of ever allowing himself to be, despite the risk he took every time he and his boys took down a bank or robbed some out-of-the-way store. That just made him feel all the more alive. It was exhilarating. Exciting. But prison? No, thank you.

"Come along inside, Harlan, and we can finish this. I have a Sunday dinner to get to, and I'm sure there are things you would rather do than sit in my cell."

"Yes, Marshal, I reckon there are." A thought of that plump little blonde whore came to mind. Betty, was it? He thought so. Thought he would try her this time. He hadn't been with her yet. At least he did not remember if he had. Yeah, tonight he would ask for Betty.

The marshal opened the door and waited for Harlan to go inside, then followed. The turnkey, Gordon Dobbs, was sitting behind the marshal's desk. He stood when he saw Harlan and Marshal Glass come in. "Everything go all right?" he asked.

"Just fine," Glass said. "Get the key, Gordon, and take these chains off our guest, will you?"

"What's your fine, Harlan? Twenty-five?"

"Just five, thanks to you and the marshal here," Harlan said. He held his hands forward so Gordon could unlock the irons on his wrists.

Dobbs produced a key from the top drawer of the marshal's desk and removed Harlan's chains, handling key and manacles deftly, despite the handicap of having only one hand to work with. He laid the manacles aside and replaced the key in the drawer.

"Feels good t' get those off, I can tell you," Harlan said.

"I'd think so."

Marshal Glass took a large bound ledger from a shelf and leafed through it until he found the last entry. He laid the ledger open on his desk, took out a pen and bottle of ink and uncapped the ink. He dipped the nib of the pen into the black fluid and said, "If you'll hand over the five dollars, Harlan, we can conclude this business and get you on your way." He winked. "And get me home before my dinner gets cold and my wife along with it."

"You bet, Marshal. Where is, uh, where's my poke?"

"Your what?"

"My poke. My purse, Marshal. Where is it?"

"I don't have it."

"Yes, you do. It's in my saddlebags. Where are they?"

"Your things are all in the cabinet over there, Harlan, but there is no money with them."

"Sure there is. In the saddlebags." Harlan crossed the room and pulled the cabinet door open. His saddlebags lay on top of his saddle, which was crammed into the cabinet too.

"No, there isn't," Glass insisted. "When your things were brought over from Vera's place, Gordon and I inventoried everything in those bags. There is no money in them."

"Marshal, are you telling me that I've been robbed?"

"Of course not. Whatever you had when you came here, you still have. But there was and is no money in those saddlebags."

"Then, dammit, Marshal, I've been robbed."

"Not in this jail, you weren't."

"By Vera then, or one of her whores."

"Pay your fine, Harlan, and I'll go with you to talk with Vera and her girls."

"Marshal, I don't have five dollars in my pocket to pay the fine. I have a Mexican dollar and a few smaller coins. Less than two dollars total."

"Oh, my." The marshal thought for a moment, then said, "I think what we had best do is for you to go back into your cell until I can get this straightened out."

"But dammit, Marshal, I'm supposed to be getting out of here. The judge said so."

"Judge Ramsey said five dollars or five days, and that is what it has to be. Now, I already told you I will talk with Vera's girls. I know Vera would never steal from a customer. She has a good reputation here, and that would disappear if she were to begin stealing from the customers. Her girls might have taken what they shouldn't, however. I will find out. But in the meantime, Harlan, you have to wait in the cell. Either that or pay your fine, which you say you cannot do."

"No, I can't."

"Then, Gordon, put our guest back into his cell and find him something to eat."

"And you'll be talking with Miss Vera and her whores?"

"I said I would, didn't I?"

"Yes, sir."

"And so I shall. I'll go over there right after I have my dinner."

"Can't I go with . . . ?"

"No!" The marshal's voice was sharp. Sharp enough to suggest that Harlan not push the issue any further.

"Come along, Harlan. You know the way."

"Dammit it anyway, Gordon."

"I know. Come along though. It will all get straightened out."

Chapter Fifteen

Harlan was pissed off. Well and truly pissed off. Seething. The idea that *he* had been robbed made him furious. He had risked his neck—literally; there were places where he would be hanged if ever he were caught—to get that money, only to lose it to some bitch wearing nothing but perfume and rice powder.

What the hell was he supposed to live on for the next couple months until he got his gang back together?

And the worst part of the deal was that he had to play the mister-nice-guy role around Marshal Glass and Gordon. Had to be careful what he said about the money, lest someone get to wondering where a supposedly down-on-his-luck cowboy got it all.

He had to be careful just how much attention he called to himself. There were plenty of lawmen who wanted him and plenty of towns where he dare not show his face again.

A few days in jail was one thing. He could do that. Had done it often enough in the past for things like being drunk or celebrating a little too much. But he did not want to risk prison. That was a whole 'nother thing.

While he was here too it was only sensible to stay on the good side of the two people who would be responsible for taking care of him for the next few days. After all, that responsibility included things like feeding him—there was a world of difference between the pork chop and scrambled eggs he'd had for breakfast today and the bread and water that he could have been served instead—or deciding whether or not they wanted to bother allowing him out back to the crapper. All of which meant that he had to be careful how he acted. They would expect him to be angry, but Harlan did not want them to see the true extent of his fury. That he had to hide. Dammit.

It was evening—after a very good roast beef dinner—before Marshal Glass got back.

"Did you get my money back, Marshal?"

"Now what do you think? Of course not."

"You did go to Vera's place like you said you would?"

"I did. I spoke with Vera and I talked to a girl named Agnes."

"Agnes? I don't think I know her," Harlan said.

"I believe she calls herself Frenchie."

"Oh, uh, maybe I do remember someone named Frenchie. Big tits? Small waist? Has a tic under one eye?"

"That's the one. Her real name is Agnes."

"And what did she say?"

"Pretty much the same thing that Vera said. She didn't know anything about a missing purse."

"It isn't a proper snap purse," Harlan put in. "It's more like a pouch or a little leather bag about this big." He demonstrated the size with his hands. "Surely one of them saw it. It was in my saddlebags. The near side bag."

"Both women claim they didn't," Glass said. "Vera was quite distressed to think something might have been taken by one of her girls."

"Well if this Agnes didn't take my money, Marshal, it must have been the other one. Or somebody else who works there. The saddlebags were layin' there in the room where I was, uh, partying. What about that other girl, Marshal? Did you talk t' her too?"

"I asked for her, of course, but she has, um, left Vera and moved on. Vera didn't know where she went or if she will come back. She didn't say."

"Damn!" Harlan moaned.

"You seem really upset by this, Breen. Just how much was in that poke of yours anyway?"

Twelve hundred dollars, you fat idiot, was what Harlan wanted to shout.

"I'm not exactly sure how much I had left in there, Marshal, after the, uh, partying and all. I'd guess maybe, oh, fifty or sixty dollars."

The marshal whistled. "No wonder you're upset. Two months' wages gone. I don't blame you."

What he would have said had he known the true extent of the loss, Harlan could only guess. Certainly that would have raised the marshal's suspicions though. Surely he would have wondered how a drifting cowboy could have come by such a wad. It would almost have to be something illegal. An excuse that it had been won in a poker game *might* work. But maybe not. No, Harlan figured he was better off not raising any questions in the marshal's mind.

"You tried t' chase it down for me, Marshal. I'm beholden to you for that, and I thank you for trying."

"I wish I could have brought you better news, but I hope you weren't expecting me to succeed. The odds of that were somewhere between 'fat chance' and 'no way in hell.'"

"Yes, sir. I understand."

"If it makes you feel any better, Harlan, Judge Ramsey sentenced you to five days. He didn't specify so I think it is reasonable to say the time you've already been here should count against that sentence. That leaves you with only three more days."

"That's nice o' you, Marshal."

"I do want to caution you about one thing though. I already know how much money you have in your pocket, and that is not enough to buy any of Vera's girls. That means you have no legitimate excuse to go over there. I'll expect you to stay well clear of Vera's house once you are released from jail here. If you show up there looking for your money or just wanting to cause trouble, I will arrest you and put you right back in here. And this time I will not be asking Judge Ramsey to go easy on you. If I catch you at Vera's again, I can pretty much promise you a month behind bars. I hope you understand me. I am quite serious about it."

"Yes, sir. I understand. I'll not be going back to Vera's looking for my money."

Unless it's to rob the bitch of all *her* money, Harlan silently added to himself.

Which certainly was an attractive thought.

Imagining that cunt Vera trembling under the muzzle of his revolver and handing over the contents of her safe would give him something to enjoy over the next three days, Harlan thought.

He wondered just how much cash the madam might have on hand. Twelve hundred dollars maybe? More? Why, Harlan could practically smell that money.

Of course he would have to steal a horse before he hit the place. He could steal back the bay he'd sold so cheap to that stable operator. He knew how strong the bay was, how good its wind. More importantly, the bay already knew him. He could walk up to it in the night, and it would not set up a ruckus. And his cinches were already a proper length to fit the bay.

Yeah, that was what he would do. Slip over to that

stable at night and bring the bay horse out. Saddle it ready to go. Then hit Vera for whatever cash she had in the place.

Oh, he had a power of planning to do over the next three days. Harlan helped himself to a dipper of water from the bucket on the wall beside his cell, then stretched out on the hard bunk and tipped his hat over his eyes so he would not be bothered while he was planning his next robbery.

Things would all work out, he assured himself. They always did.

Somewhere between the livery and Vera's place, Harlan drifted off to sleep.

Chapter Sixteen

Well, just shit! Harlan woke and sat upright on the hard jail cell bunk. Sometime during the night it had filtered into his mind that there was no way he could hit Vera's place. They knew his name here. Marshal Glass knew him by name and likely Vera did too by now, and Harlan did not like the idea that he might be wanted by name.

Up until now he had been wanted in a good many places, sure, but only by vague description. When he robbed someone he wore a duster and respectable clothes, and his victims were not likely to connect that gentleman robber with the unkempt drifter that Harlan presented himself as most of the time.

Besides, when he and the boys hit a place he mostly used Little Jim as his backup, and between Little Jim's size and the threat of the revolver he waved at them, most witnesses paid scant attention to the fellow with the bag who actually collected their money.

That was deliberate and so far it had always worked. Hell, Harlan had seen some of the flyers posted about him and his boys. The descriptions given on them did not sound anything at all like him. Little Jim Toomey they had pretty well nailed on those posters, but Harlan, Carl and Danny were unrecognizable from the few words allotted to them.

But, dammit, if he robbed Vera now he would be putting the hounds on his tail. At the very least he would have to start living under a different name, and he did not want to do that. He would if he absolutely had to, of course, but it was not something he looked forward to.

Harlan looked up at the sound of someone approaching his cell. It was the jailer Gordon, whose snoring had been reverberating through the jail the whole night long.

"Mornin', Harlan. Do you need a trip out back before breakfast?"

"I could use one. Thanks."

Gordon began fumbling at the lock with the cell key. "Bring that thunder mug with you when you come. You can empty it in the shitter before you wash up." He finally got the lock open and tugged the door wide. "Look here now, Harlan, if you give me your word you won't run, I won't bother putting these irons on you."

"Of course you got my word about that. I'm not going anyplace." He laughed. "Hell, I got no place to go nor any money to get there. And you feed awful good here. No sirree bob, you got my word about that."

"Come along then." Gordon stepped back. Harlan picked up the thunder mug, careful not to spill any of the cold piss he had deposited there, and headed for the back door. He knew the way.

Chapter Seventeen

Harlan yawned and stretched. He had never been addicted to hard work but he had never been quite this inactive, and it seemed the less he did—and what was there to do inside a jail cell anyway?—the more sluggish he became. It was getting so he was taking naps after breakfast, after lunch and before dinner too.

At least it passed the time.

Now he woke, rubbed the sleep from his eyes and reached for his pipe. Then, remembering, he pulled his hand back.

"Gordon. Hey, Gordon. Next time you go out do me a favor, will you? Buy me a nickel bag of cut tobacco and a penny's worth of matches, okay? Gordon? Did you hear what I said, Gordon?"

The one-armed jailer appeared beside the cell door. He was holding a sheet of paper. He looked in at Harlan and said, "You son of a bitch!"

Harlan's feelings were hurt. "Why'd you say a thing like that, Gordon?"

"You lying, miserable, murdering son of a putrid bitch," Gordon snarled. "You bastard."

"Gordon, I don't understand."

"Listen, you prick. The law says you got to be fed. All right, you'll be fed. Twice a day. Bread and water. Don't ask me for nothing else. Marshal Glass says there's a law as says you got to have your thunder mug emptied every day. Fine. You'll be let out once a day so's you can do that your own self. If you don't feel like taking

a shit when I feel like taking you out back that's tough.
You'll just have to wait till the next day. Don't look for
no favors either. There won't be no tobacco nor anything else, so just shut up."

"Why? For God's sake, why?" Harlan stood and
took the two steps to reach the cell bars. He stood in
front of Gordon, close enough to touch the man. Gordon moved a pace back so Harlan was not so close.

"Bastard," Gordon hissed.

"What did I do, dammit?"

By way of an answer Gordon wadded up the paper
in his hand and threw it at Harlan. It hit the bars, came
partially open and fluttered to the floor. By the time
the paper came to rest, the jailer had turned and gone,
out of sight in the marshal's office.

"You sure know how t' wake a fella up," Harlan
muttered to himself. He knelt and reached through the
bars to retrieve the paper Gordon had thrown at him.
He carried it back to his bunk, sat down and smoothed
the paper over his knee.

When he read what was on it the blood drained from
his head and he felt a sudden rush of dizziness. His
breath became shallow and for a moment he was certain he would pass out cold.

WANTED FOR MURDER. REWARD. Unknown
fugitive. Murderer of family of four including two
young daughters. No description but first name
known to be Harlan. No last name. REWARD.
Sheriff Brandon Bates, Dowdville, Corleigh County, Kansas. REWARD.

"Jesus Christ!" Harlan whispered.

Murder. Four dead including two young girls. No
wonder Dobbs had acted the way he did.

But what . . . why . . . ? Harlan shuddered.

Murder like that was a hanging offense. No question about it. Once whoever did it was caught he would be strung right up . . . except . . . shit, it was obvious, obvious to Gordon Dobbs, anyway, that *he* was the unknown person called Harlan who had committed those murders. He was the one who would hang for them.

Marshal Glass. Sure. Marshal Glass was smarter than Gordon. He would understand that Harlan hadn't done those murders. Just having the same first name as a murderer, why, that didn't mean anything. It wasn't proof.

It was going to be all right. Marshal Glass would take his side of it.

Harlan would do his time in the jail here and then be released, just like the judge had said.

Thanks to Vera and her ladies he didn't have enough money to take a stagecoach out of town now and had no idea where any of the boys were, so he could not wire them for money. He would just have to steal the bay horse back from the livery and skedaddle. He could pull a stickup or two along the way to finance some travel until it was time to meet the boys and put the gang back together.

It would all work out. He just needed to talk with Marshal Glass, that was all.

Once he got that worked out in his mind, Harlan felt considerably better. He did wish he could get some more tobacco, though, and some matches.

Chapter Eighteen

"Marshal Glass. Sir? Could I talk t' you for a minute please? Please, sir?"

Glass scowled but he came closer to Harlan's cell. The marshal leaned against the wall, one thumb hooked in his belt close to the buckle and the other draped over the revolver that sat on his hip. It was unusual for Marshal Glass to wear a gun inside his own jail. He had not bothered to carry it even when he'd escorted Harlan to see Judge Ramsey, but now he was armed.

"Sir, I . . . Dobbs showed me that poster. Marshal, I don't know where Dowdville, Kansas, might be, but I never been there. I sure as hell don't know nothing about those murders. Lordy, I done a lot of bad things in my life but I've never shot a gun at anybody. Never, not my whole life long." Harlan wrung his hands and paced back and forth along the wall of bars that separated him from Marshal Glass. And freedom. "Sir, I know every man that comes in here charged with something would tell you he's innocent. I'm sure they do. But I really am, Marshal. I never done any such thing as kill anybody. Never."

"That isn't for me to decide, Breen. I've sent a wire to Sheriff Bates over in Corleigh County. He responded right away. He's sending two deputies to escort you back to Dowdville to stand trial. Your guilt or innocence will be decided there. I have nothing to do with it."

"But Marshal, that flyer only gives a first name.

There's no description. It could be anybody that done the murders."

Glass shrugged and stood upright, one hand still on the holstered revolver on his hip. "Let me ask you something, Breen."

"Yes, sir?"

"Have you ever known any *other* person named Harlan?"

"I, well . . . I was named for my mama's grandfather. Not that I ever actually knew him, you understand. He died before I came along. But his name was Harlan. Harlan Copeland from Greenback, Tennessee. So you see there's others with the same name as mine. Just . . . not a lot o' them maybe."

"Uh huh." Glass pulled out the makings and began rolling a cigarette. "That's something you prob'ly ought to tell the judge over there in Corleigh County. Bates's deputies are supposed to be here sometime tonight. They aren't waiting for the stage; they're bringing their own prison wagon. Borrowing one from Wichita or some such place. I expect they'll make a quick turnaround, likely start back first light tomorrow. That should put you in Dowdville tomorrow night and in front of a judge there come the next day."

The marshal finished making his quirly, dragged a match across the wall to strike it, and touched the flame to the cigarette. "My best guess would be that you'll hang along about next weekend. That will give them time to draw a crowd. Everybody loves a hanging, you know."

Glass blew a stream of white smoke into the stale air, then turned and walked out toward the office part of the town marshal's office.

Harlan felt sick. He felt hollow and emptied of breath, worse than if he had been kicked in the belly by a horse. He stumbled backward and dropped to a seat on the unyielding bunk in his cell.

Hanging. Jesus! He hadn't . . . he had done robberies, sure. Hell, he *liked* robbing. It felt good and the money was fine. It let him have liquor and women and control over men. But murder? No. Never.

And now . . . hanging.

He could imagine all too clearly the feel of the rope tight around his throat. He wondered if the fine hairs of the hemp would tickle. Now wasn't that an ugly thought.

He could imagine the sensation in the pit of his stomach when the gallows trapdoor dropped out from underneath his feet. Could imagine the fall. The sudden jolt when he reached the end of the rope and the noose pulled tight.

The thick knot was supposed to snap a man's neck so he died instantly. But did it work that way really? How much would he feel? Would he hear the snap when his neck broke? Would he feel the stretch of the rope and the little bounce when it jerked upward a foot or so after it bottomed out?

Would he foul his drawers and piss all over himself?

He had seen men die. A few. By accidents and fevers and whatnot. Once by hanging even. Sometimes men pissed themselves when they died. They shit their britches.

Would he live long enough to know if he did or not?

For some reason he did care. When he died—God help him, it should be a long time before that happened—when someday he died he hoped he died clean and shaved and with people he knew and cared about to grieve for him when he was gone.

Sitting there in his cell, perched on the edge of a steel bunk, Harlan felt his heart race and his breathing quicken. He felt lightheaded and woozy. He wanted a drink. Or at the least, a pipe of tobacco.

Lordy!

"Gordon? Gordon. I know you're out there, dammit. I need some pipe tobacco. I got money to pay for it. Just some tobacco, Gordon. An' some matches. That's all I'm asking."

Harlan could hear a low murmur of conversation coming from the office and the sounds of people moving around. Dobbs was sure to be out there. Probably Marshal Glass too. No one answered. No one came. Whoever was there ignored him completely. As if he were already dead and out of mind.

Harlan wrapped his arms tightly around his chest and began to rock back and forth, very softly moaning so only he could hear. And which he would have heatedly denied had he been asked.

Hanging. He could not believe he would hang. He had done nothing he should hang for. Never. Jesus!

Chapter Nineteen

Tonight. The deputies were supposed to arrive tonight. Then start back tomorrow and be in this Dowdville place tomorrow evening.

Deputies, Marshal Glass had said. That meant two of them. Or maybe even more. Enough to keep watch over him every second. Could be they would sit in here through the night even, watching over him with shotguns. Shotguns were worrisome. They could do cruel things to a man. Harlan shuddered. So could ropes.

His gut rumbled and churned and he felt as if he were going to be sick. He had to get away from here. Somehow. He had to.

Harlan leaned against the steel bars and listened to the talking that was going on out in Glass's office. He could not follow the conversations but he could tell there were at least three voices out there. He could make out a word now and then, a phrase or even a short sentence. He wondered if they were talking about him and about those murders and about the likelihood of a hanging. More than likely. He closed his eyes and concentrated on listening.

"All right, Gordon. Me and Walter are going to dinner. I'll be back directly, but if those deputies from Dowdville show up, tell them I'm . . ." The marshal's voice became faint and then faded altogether. Harlan heard a door close, then footsteps. That would be Gordon Dobbs keeping watch over him until the marshal got back or the deputies arrived.

Harlan felt a fluttering sensation low in his belly. He took a deep breath.

He slid the porcelain thunder mug out from under the bunk and removed the lid, laying it aside. Then he began dipping water out of the pail that hung on a nail just outside his cell, industriously carrying the dippers to the piss pot and emptying them into it. When he could get no more water out of the pail he replaced the dipper and moved the nearly full pot toward the front of the cell.

"Gordon. I got to take a crap, Gordon."

It took a while before Dobbs answered. When he did he said, "Use the pot."

"I can't, dammit. It's near full."

"How'd you piss all that much?" Dobbs said, reluctantly moving closer to the bars.

"I didn't. I puked in it. My whole damn breakfast came up. Last night's supper too prob'ly."

"I won't be sorry when they haul your ass out of here. I might even take some time off and go see you hang."

"I don't suppose there's any point in telling you again that I ain't done those things."

"Save your breath, you piece of shit."

"If you don't let me go out back I'll just have t' shit on the floor and you can clean it up after I'm out o' here," Harlan snapped back at him.

"All right, damn you, but you're wearing irons. An' if you make one false move I'll be shooting your ass. Do the world a favor if I was to do that too."

"I know the rule. But I really got to go. An' you can see for yourself that the pot is near about full."

Dobbs peered through the bars, then grunted. He turned and went back into the office, returning a few moments later with his ring of keys, a set of leg irons, and a revolver stuck into the waist of his trousers. "You know how to do this," he said.

"Right. No problem."

The jailer passed the heavy irons through the bars to Harlan. The irons were connected by welded steel chain strong enough to hold a horse, much less a man. Harlan took the irons, knelt and put the clamps around his own ankles, then stood and placed his back against the bars while Dobbs bent down and locked the clamps in place.

"Do you want me t' put the bracelets on too?"

"No need. It's broad daylight and you can't run in those anyway. You aren't going anyplace."

Harlan bent and picked up the thunder mug. Dobbs unlocked the cell door and took a few steps back. Carrying the heavy jar of piss and water, Harlan shuffled awkwardly out of the cell, through the office and out the back door on the now-familiar route to the outhouse.

Tonight, he kept telling himself. Tonight they were coming to hang him.

Chapter Twenty

Harlan's breath came quick and shallow. He could hear a roaring in his ears that sounded much like falling water. Jesus! This was a bigger rush than when he robbed a place. Not that he hoped to repeat the experience, but still . . .

"Mind you don't spill that shit on the floor," Dobbs grumbled. "If you do, you'll be the one who cleans it up."

"I'm being careful, but it's hard to walk in these shackles, y'know."

"Stand still there. I'll open the door. No, back up a little."

Harlan backed away half a step and waited while Dobbs pushed in front of him, unlatched the back door and stepped aside for Harlan to go through. Dobbs followed a pace behind as Harlan slowly and carefully negotiated the path past scraggly weeds, rusting tin cans and an equally rusty bedspring discarded in the lot behind the jail. The outhouse was small and weathered. The malodorous stink of it filled Harlan's nostrils the moment he pulled open the door.

"You can go in, but don't pull the door all the way closed and don't latch it shut from the inside there," Gordon Dobbs instructed.

"All right, dammit, hold your horses." Harlan edged inside the smelly structure and held his breath while he emptied the heavy crockery thunder mug into the hole. The contents of the jar splashed somewhere below the board seat, and a foul, fetid odor rose from the hole.

"What was that?" Dobbs called from a few feet away.

"You don't wanta know."

"Well hurry it up. I ain't had my dinner yet."

"I got the jug emptied. Now I got t' do what I came here for."

Now that he was here Harlan discovered that he really did have to take a dump. He set the thunder mug down, unbuttoned his britches and turned around. The wood of the seat had been worn smooth from the application of hundreds of butts over the years. He did what needed to be done and looked around for some paper, corncobs, any damn thing to wipe himself. There was nothing. "Damn."

"Now what?" Dobbs asked impatiently.

"I didn't bring no paper and there's nothing here."

"Tough shit. I sure ain't going back inside while you wait here for me, so button up and come on out of there."

"All right, but I'm not happy about this."

"Maybe the marshal will let you wash yourself before those deputies come to take you to your hanging."

"Now that's a comfort."

"Come on out."

"I'm coming, dammit, I'm coming."

Harlan buttoned his trousers and tucked in his shirt, then picked up the now-empty crock, holding it dangling in one hand, where before he had had to hold it very carefully in both hands. He elbowed the door open and stepped out of the outhouse.

The chain securing his ankle clamps rattled as he seemed to lose his balance. Harlan tottered forward, his free hand flailing.

"Hey, watch yoursel . . ." Dobbs did not have time to finish the sentence. Harlan swung the heavy crockery jar in an arc, slamming it into the side of Dobbs' head. The jailer was knocked off his feet, sprawling onto his back with his arm flung out wide.

Harlan dropped to his knees beside the jailer and quickly rifled his pockets for the ring of keys. They were in the second pocket he tried. He snatched them out and began frantically working on the locks at his ankles.

Dobbs groaned and lifted his head, so Harlan picked up the crock and bashed him with it again. That was hard on Dobbs, who had really been pretty decent to Harlan, at least until Harlan had been accused of multiple murders, but it came down to Dobbs or himself and there was just no contest there. Harlan did hope, though, that he hadn't killed the man.

The left ankle clamp fell away and he began working on the other one. That took only a few more seconds, and he was free.

More or less.

He was free to move but he still had to get away.

Harlan grabbed hold of the revolver stuffed behind Dobbs' belt and pulled it free. It was not much of a revolver, a little Ivor Johnson .32. Not his own good .45 but better than nothing. A hell of a lot better than nothing.

Now for the rest of what he intended.

Chapter Twenty-one

Harlan ran to the mouth of the alley but stopped short of going out into the street. He stopped there, took a deep breath and peered around the corner of a store building. There were two saddled horses and several wagons in sight. Harlan chose the more capable-looking horse, a pale roan with an ugly head but a wide chest and broad rump. The other animal was cat-hammed and bony and likely had no stamina.

He walked boldly into the street and ducked under the hitching rail in front of what he now could see was a law office. Not that he needed a lawyer. There was no way he was going to trust his life to some SOB he didn't even know. Better to get the hell away from there and let the law and the lawyers work things out however they pleased.

Harlan took a moment to flip the near stirrup up onto the saddle seat and check the cinch on the center-rigged outfit. It would have been more than a little annoying at a moment like this to try to mount and have the saddle end up underneath the roan's belly. Satisfied that the cinch was tight, he tugged the reins loose and swung onto the saddle. Damn but it felt good to be out in the sunshine with a horse between his legs again.

He pointed the roan down the street without being particular about which direction they went—all he wanted was a fast exit from the town limits—and

put it into a lope. Once he reached the edge of town
he kicked it up into a run.

No one was shooting at him.

Yet.

But a posse would be coming soon enough.

In a few minutes Gordon Dobbs would wake up
and sound an alarm. Or Marshal Glass would come
back from dinner and find that his prisoner had
flown the coop. Either way they would be on his
trail shortly.

And if they caught up with him, they were as likely to shoot him as to take him back to the jailhouse.

Harlan put his heels—his spurs, like his .45 and
his hat, were back in Marshal Glass's damn jail—to
the roan horse.

"Perfect," Harlan muttered to himself, pulling the
roan to a halt.

A tangled copse of runty cedars and wild grape
lay close by the north side of the road. Sometime in
the past few years a forest fire had come through,
leaving the thicket littered with dead, fire-blackened
saplings along with the newer, healthy growth.

"Just perfect," Harlan repeated.

He took down the rope the owner of the roan had
left on his saddle, shook it out and dropped a loop
over one of the dead cedars. He tied the rope tightly
to the saddle horn and led the horse forward until
the spindly cedar pulled free from the loam where it
had grown until fire destroyed it.

Harlan led the horse into the middle of the road
and then, smiling, he gave the roan a sharp whack
on the butt accompanied by a shout just as loud and
sharp as he could make it.

The horse bolted forward. When it came to the end

of the rope, the dead cedar bounced high in the air. The terrified roan damn near turned itself inside out trying to get away from the thing that was so malevolently chasing it.

Horse and cedar went tearing off into the distance, going just as hard and fast as the roan could go. Harlan figured this parade would not come to a halt until the roan was completely exhausted or the dead wood pulled free, whichever came first.

And with any kind of luck the posse that was sure to be tracking him would find where he'd dismounted, see the scrape marks left by the cedar and believe Harlan was pulling a drag in an attempt to hide his tracks. They would ignore the human footprints and follow the drag marks and hoofprints instead.

With any kind of luck, that was.

Harlan slipped deep into the thicket and wriggled into the middle of a tangle of grape vines. He made himself as comfortable as he could and settled down to wait.

Chapter Twenty-two

For men chasing down an escaped murderer, these fellows were not very quick. Harlan judged that it took the better part of an hour before the posse came along. He snorted and very quietly chuckled to himself when it occurred to him that these boys might not be wanting all that bad to catch him. After all, he did have Gordon Dobbs's little pistol in his pocket now.

He could hear the voices well before the first of the pack reached the spot where he had dismounted and rigged that cedar onto the roan.

"Here. Right here," someone called. He thought it sounded like Marshal Glass's voice but he was not sure about that.

Harlan was no hand at calculating the sizes of posses—he had never had any of them get this close before—but it sounded like half the town must have turned out for the fun of running down another human being. From the way they were laughing and cat-calling and talking back and forth, it sounded more like a holiday than a manhunt. He resisted an impulse to move closer so he could get a look at the bunch.

As it was, he was lying in a depression with a solidly leafy green wall of wild grapes between himself and the road. He could not see out and he was sure the men who were hunting him could not see in. He saw no point in tempting fate by moving around and perhaps disturbing the canopy of vines that covered him.

He was not near enough to make out much in the way of individual voices, but he got a word here and a phrase there, enough to tell that they had indeed found the spot where he'd pulled up the burnt cedar and dragged it behind the horse. The posse seemed to be falling for the idea that he was trying to cover his tracks. For sure none of them suspected that their quarry was lying there only a few rods distant, listening in on all this.

Someone called from the back of the bunch, "Hey, wait, I gotta take a piss," and there was a general stirring within the group as more of them decided this would be a good time to take a leak.

Harlan could hear the slap of leather as cinches were adjusted and the sharp crack of rein ends on horseflesh when one of the mounts acted up and had to be set straight.

Twigs crackled as some fellows came to the edge of the wood to unbutton and piss away from the public eye, although what they had to hide Harlan did not know. For a moment he worried that some shy son of a bitch might walk in deeper and spot him, but no one came any farther than the side of the road.

"Hurry it up, dammit," a voice called. "He's getting away."

There was more crackling of brush and some grumbling and cussing and then the hoofbeats moved off down the road in the direction the roan had fled.

Harlan picked a pair of fat black ants off his forearm, then stood and brushed himself off.

When he took stock of his situation it was not all that good. He was a hundred miles from anyone he might consider to be a friend. On foot. No hat. Less than two dollars in his pockets. With only a miserable little five or six—he released the catch and broke the revolver open to take a look—with only a little five-shot .32 with which to defend himself.

That was looking at the negative side of things. On the positive, he was free. That had to count more than anything else. More than everything else, really.

And what the hell, the .32 in his pocket might not be much of a gun, but nobody wanted to be shot with one. Once he thought about it he realized he could rob someone just as easily with a .32 as he could with his own .45.

He could steal whatever he needed. Horse, hat, clothes or whatever. Now that Marshal Glass's posse had rushed on into the distance, Harlan could go wherever he pleased and do whatever he wanted.

Of course he would have to change his name if he did that. Quick as that posse got back to town without him, there would be warnings flying all over the damn telegraph lines telling lawmen everywhere to be on the lookout for Harlan Breen. Description included.

Shit!

He did not want to have that weighing on him. It had always been a point of pride to him that he could walk the streets—most places anyhow—and give his own name when he did it. No one had ever been looking for him. Not him in particular, that is.

This could change all that.

Besides, anyone who would rape and kill a pair of young girls was one sorry son of a bitch. Harlan hated the thought that anyone might believe that of him.

Whoever the bastard was, he was giving Harlan Breen a bad name, damn him.

Harlan wondered if just maybe he should do something about that.

Where was this place where the murders had taken

place? Dowdville, that was it. In Corleigh County, wherever the hell that was.

Harlan could not remember the name of the sheriff there, the one whose deputies would now be going back empty-handed. But he thought, what the hell, maybe he should give that man a hand. And clear his own name in the process.

He picked a few more ants off himself, took a deep breath . . . and started walking.

Chapter Twenty-three

"Would you care to sign our guest register, Mr., uh, Mr. . . . ?"

"Jarrett," he said with an easy smile. "Harlan Jarrett."

"Thank you, Mr. Jarrett." The desk clerk, who looked to be still in his twenties but whose blond hair was already receding, gave the gentleman an ingratiating smile in return, opened the cloth-bound register to the appropriate page and spun the book around to face Harlan Jarrett. "Here, if you please, sir," he said, needlessly pointing below the last name listed.

The clerk set an inkwell on the desk, uncapped it and handed Jarrett a pen with a coarse steel nib.

Jarrett accepted the pen but only to lay it aside. He reached inside his coat and drew out a leather wallet with his initials embossed in gold leaf. He opened the wallet and removed a pen with an ebony shaft and a fine-pointed gold nib. Using his own pen, he signed "H. Jarrett III."

"Very good, sir, thank you. And have you any idea how long you will be staying with us, Mr. Jarrett?"

"A week perhaps. I don't have any definite plans at the moment." He held the point of his pen down on the blotter to remove any remaining ink and replaced pen in wallet and wallet in coat.

"Yes, sir, very good, sir." The clerk smiled and bobbed his head, then turned and in a louder voice called, "Donnie. Front desk, please."

A teen with lank hair and acne responded. He looked as if he might have been the desk clerk's younger brother.

"Take Mr. Jarrett's bag to room three, Donnie." To Jarrett he added, "I put you at the front in case you would like to view the street. Donnie will show you the way, sir."

"The street view will be fine," Jarrett said, although he had not been asked.

Donnie picked up the two bags that the boy from the livery had deposited in the lobby of the best hotel in the city. "This way, Mr. Jarrett."

Jarrett followed the bellboy up a flight of stairs and to the right. Room number three was on his right.

Donnie set the bags down, pushed the room door open and moved aside for Jarrett to enter first. Once the guest was inside, Donnie followed with his bags. He set them onto a bench at the foot of a broad bed and went to the window. He raised the roller blind and tugged the casement window open to allow a little air into the room.

"If there is anything else you need, sir, anything at all . . ."

"I'll let you know if I do." Jarrett frowned. "Is there no bellpull?"

"No, sir, but if you just call down the stairs someone will hear."

Jarrett's frown deepened. He absolutely was *not* going to make a spectacle of himself by shouting in public as if he were calling hogs. In the unlikely event that he wanted anything from these people, he was perfectly capable of walking down the stairs to ask, quietly and calmly.

The gentleman removed a small purse from his pocket, selected a nickel and handed it to Donnie.

"Thank you, Mr. Jarrett. And remember, if you need anything, anything at all . . ."

"I shall ask. Yes, of course." Jarrett ushered the boy out of the room and closed the door. The room was a little stuffy from being closed, so he opened the transom above the door to allow air to flow through, then turned and took stock.

The room was ordinary at best. Plain, cream-colored wallpaper. Plain white curtains that fell below the windowsill but short of the floor. Soft bed—he sat on it to find out—but noisy springs. Bedspread but no dust ruffle. Small pine wardrobe stained to imitate rosewood. Small chest of drawers that also served as a washstand. One single chair. But at least it was a rocking chair and had a stuffed pillow on the seat. Braided rug. Two mounted wall lamps, one on either side of the room. Cheap brass spittoon beside the bed.

And this was the hotel's finest?

Harlan Jarrett sighed. It would do, he told himself. It was only temporary and it would do.

Chapter Twenty-four

"It is the next street over and five blocks down," the desk clerk said.

"In which direction would that be?"

The clerk pointed.

"Thank you."

"May I call a hansom for you, Mr. Jarrett, or would you like your own rig hitched and brought around?"

"No need for that. It looks to be a fine morning. Besides, I need to walk off some of that good breakfast." Jarrett touched the head of his walking stick to the brim of his hat by way of a salute and strolled outside.

It was a fine morning indeed. The sky was nearly cloudless and at this early hour the air held a hint of the crispness that fall would soon bring. Jarrett was glad he had worn his waistcoat and gloves.

He sauntered along, in no hurry whatsoever, enjoying the sights and the sounds of a city that was not his own. Harlan Jarrett enjoyed encountering the new and the different. New places. New people. New sensations. Wonderful.

He paused to admire the display of small goods in a druggist's window, for the most part patent medicines and such nostrums, the boxes and jars and tins arranged in an attractively colorful pyramid. On a whim he stepped through the wide-open door. A man in sleeve garters stood behind the counter. The fellow was thin but Jarrett noted that his forearms were thick with muscle, probably from years of using mortar and pestle to grind the ingredients for his pills.

"May I help you, sir?"

"You have laudanum, I'm sure."

"Yes, sir, of course."

"I need to have some made up in the form of boluses."

"The liquid won't do for your needs, sir?"

"No, too bitter. A bolus works much better, I think. Use your own judgment what to mix it with, but something sweet would be ideal. Horehound, perhaps."

"That's an unusual request, but . . ." The man stared toward the ceiling for a moment in thought, then smiled and nodded. "Yes, I'm sure I can come up with something. Perhaps even something quite tasty."

"Wonderful." Jarrett's enthusiasm was genuine. He had used laudanum and other opiates in the past, but he had always had to force them down the, um, subjects. But if a chewable form of the drug could be created, particularly in a tasty form that would not be resisted . . . that would be wonderful indeed. "Yes. I like it."

"I'll need some time for this. I may have to experiment a little, in case the horehound doesn't work."

"I'm not in a rush. Better to do things right than quickly, I always say."

"Yes, sir, I quite agree. And how many will you want?"

"However many will fit into a tin like that one," Jarrett said, pointing toward a flat, pocket-sized tin of cough lozenges. "But bigger. And the laudanum bolus should be bigger than a normal lozenge too. The dosage, I mean. It should be something suitable for emergency procedures when one is in the wilderness," Jarrett said, answering the questions the druggist had not yet asked but could be expected to in the near future. A man, especially one who was neither a doctor nor a veterinarian, would not normally want a chewable opiate with a flavor agreeable to the tongue.

Gracious. Now that Jarrett thought about it, if he could keep his subjects sedated, yet capable of some feeling, he might even be able to expand his field of opportunity. If he could keep them from making too much noise, he could play in closer proximity to others.

He would have to conduct some experiments first, though. It would not do to arouse an entire countryside. But this . . . this might work.

"Now that I think about it," Jarrett said with a smile, "make up two tins of those for me, would you please?"

"Of course, sir. Check back with me in a day or two."

Harlan Jarrett was whistling when he left the pharmacy. Now he needed to go find that telegraph office so he could get a wire off to dear Mother, lest he run out of funds.

Oh, he was glad he had stopped here and happened to come up with the idea of a laudanum bolus. Ever so glad.

Chapter Twenty-five

Harlan Breen lay at the bottom of a shallow irrigation ditch—thankfully dry now—and watched as a red and gold sunset darkened and became night. He had been in the ditch for most of the afternoon, ever since coming across the small, isolated farmstead.

He was cramped and hungry, and now that the sun had gone he was beginning to get cold too. His coat, his slicker, practically everything he owned was back in Marshal Glass's damn jail cell, and the more he thought about it the angrier he got. It would be one thing to be locked away for the thousand and one things he had actually done. But to be jailed for somebody else's crime, that pissed him off.

Still, he was in for it now. The remaining question was, could he do anything about it?

For certain sure there was no chance for him to recover his former happy life, as long as he was wanted for raping and murdering young women.

While sitting in that cell his first thought had simply been to get away. Now that he was out and running, though, he realized that that was not enough. He was still being hunted.

They knew his name. That would be easy enough to change. A man was whatever name he chose to call himself. But Glass also had his description and that he could not much change.

Besides, rape was about as rotten lousy a crime as there was. It galled Harlan to think that a rapist might get away with his crimes just because the law was looking for a man named Breen. He did not want to see that happen.

At the moment, though, what he wanted—needed—was something to eat and a way to keep warm.

He lay where he was, shivering and miserable, keeping watch on the farm, until the candle glow he saw through cracks in the shutter covering the lone, unglazed window of the cabin disappeared. The lanky, bearded fellow who lived there, a bachelor to judge by the little movement Harlan had noticed during the afternoon, apparently followed old Ben Franklin's dictum of "Early to bed and early to rise makes a man healthy, wealthy and wise." Harlan had no idea about this fellow's health or his wisdom, but the man sure did not appear to be wealthy. The farm was a hardscrabble affair. Harlan doubted that the farmer saw twenty dollars cash money in a year's time. Harlan could spend that much on whiskey and whores in a weekend. Or on either one of those alone, if the other were not available.

Not that Harlan intended to rob this fellow anyway. Pilfer a little, perhaps. But not actually rob.

After the light disappeared he waited a little longer, just to make sure the farmer had plenty of time to drop off to sleep. Then he silently came to his knees and brushed himself off a bit before rising to his feet and getting out of the ditch for the first time in hours.

He stood there for a moment, shivering, regaining the use of cramped limbs before starting off.

There was no moon—it was not due to rise for a few hours more—but the cloudless sky was pale with starlight. A very light breeze blew, and the soft sound of clucking hens came from a shed close by the low barn.

Harlan walked slowly across the yard, painfully

aware of the crunch and grind of his boot soles on gravel and of the night silence that surrounded him.

He stepped over a scantling fence that would likely be enough to keep chickens out of the garden but surely would not stop anything else. From the ditch he had not been able to see what the farmer was raising in his garden, but what Harlan was hoping for was something that he could eat without cooking, as he had no matches or a store where he might buy any with the few cents in his pockets.

What he found was not encouraging. It seemed his friend the farmer favored okra—the thought of raw okra made Harlan's stomach lurch—and peas, which were tasty enough raw except these plants had long since been picked over and were now dried and dying.

He found some tomatoes, not his favorite but acceptable in a pinch, and slipped three of those inside his shirt. Some beans had been left on the vine to dry. Harlan filled his pockets with bean pods.

At the far side of the garden he found twin rows of potato hills. That was more like it. He threw the tomatoes away, heaving them into the night and hoping the farmer would not notice them on the ground come daybreak, and stuffed his shirt full of potatoes, unmindful of the dirt that clung to the pale-skinned tubers. Those he could enjoy raw.

He thought about raiding the hen house in the hope of finding some eggs, but the thought of raw eggs was almost as distasteful as raw okra. And besides, chickens were notoriously loud if something disturbed their roosts at night. Harlan did not want to bring the farmer charging out with a shotgun in hand, expecting to find a fox or a coon, and coming nose to nose with a thief instead.

Thief. That was a damned ugly word to Harlan's mind. It was . . . dammit, it was petty.

Now a robber, that was something a man could be proud of. Robber was a word that had hair on it. It implied courage and danger and a devil-may-care way of looking at things.

There was nothing petty about a robber. But any fool could be a thief. He did not mind being called a robber. If anything he took it as a compliment. Harlan Earl Breen had his pride. It grieved him to think that now he might be considered a common thief.

There was nothing for it though but to keep on. He needed to get a good distance behind himself before he risked pulling a proper robbery so he could outfit himself and then get on with life.

After that, well, after that he would see what could be done about this situation.

Chapter Twenty-six

Now Harlan knew why God had invented horses. His feet hurt and he was dead tired after walking the whole night through.

Dead tired. But not dead. As he surely would have been if those Corleigh County deputies had carried him off to Dowdville. Tired feet beat dead all hollow.

Harlan did not know where he was, but there had to be a town nearby because he had been walking past plowed fields and darkened farmsteads for quite a while, and lately he had been passing smaller holdings. Houses with garden patches rather than actual farms. And dogs. He had aroused the interest of all too many barking dogs in the past half hour or so. It was time, he figured, that he find a place to hole up for the day.

The night sky was beginning to turn pale, the smaller stars winking out completely and even the bright ones fading. In several of the houses he passed lamplight was beginning to show as people woke and began to prepare for the day ahead. That was fine as long as catching escaped prisoners was not in their plans. As it was, Harlan intended to sleep through the day and walk on again come nightfall.

Travel at night was not a problem, he had learned, as long as he stayed on the roads. At first he'd tried walking cross country. That had not been the best idea, as he had concluded about the third or fourth time he'd gone sprawling facedown from tripping over unseen obstacles. On the road he stumbled now and then when he stepped into a rut, but at least he had not gone completely down again. And he made much better time on a road than he could by walking through field and forest.

The road he was now following reached a tiny run of live water. It was hardly big enough to be called a creek itself, more like a feeder from some spring that flowed into a proper creek somewhere else. It was big enough for his purposes though.

Harlan followed the little rill upstream away from the public road a hundred yards or so, pushing his way through sumac and horseweed and into a thicket. West of the brook there appeared to be little or no vegetation. It was still too dark for Harlan to see well, but probably there were cleared fields, either crops or pasture. No houses in the immediate vicinity though. He was sure of that. And no barking dogs to call attention to him either.

There was no sweet grass to lie on, but as tired as he was he was convinced he could have stretched out on a bed of nails and broken glass and gone to sleep.

He knelt beside the thread of cold water and drank a little, picking it up in his cupped hands and first drinking, then rubbing his wet hands over his face and the back of his neck. A prickly sensation there told him that he was already burned by what sun he had exposed himself to by being without his hat.

He washed his face a little and slicked his hair down, then pulled one of the potatoes from his shirt—he still had five left not counting that one—and washed the dirt from it as best he could. He picked a more or less clear spot and gratefully sank down to the ground.

The potato tasted as good as beefsteak, hunger being a fine sauce. When he was done dining Harlan lay down, the soon-to-rise sun now putting color into the sky toward the east.

Harlan draped an arm across his eyes to keep the sun out of them and dropped quickly into sleep.

Chapter Twenty-seven

"Hello, mister."

Harlan wakened very slowly from a deep, dreamless sleep. He was groggy, his head feeling like it was stuffed with cotton. His mouth tasted vile and when he opened his eyes they stung. Judging from the position of the sun he had been asleep no more than an hour, possibly less. For a moment he could not remember what woke him.

"Why are you sleeping in the woods?"

He managed with some effort to focus his eyes. A little girl was standing beside his head. She was blonde and perhaps five or six years old. She was carrying a small basket.

"Are you all right, mister?"

Harlan groaned and sat up. His head spun. "Who are . . . what are you doing?"

The child turned and shouted, "Mama! There's a man here."

Her voice pierced the fog in his head and made him wince. He heard leaves crackle and crunch underfoot, and a grown female came up behind the little girl. She too was blonde and carried a basket, hers somewhat larger than the child's. She wore a faded housedress and a white apron with frills on the shoulder straps.

Harlan climbed slowly to his feet. He swayed a little, still half asleep. He bobbed his head. "Ma'am."

"What are you doing here?" she demanded.

"Sleeping, ma'am."

"So far off the road?"

"I didn't want nobody t' come upon me while I was asleep, ma'am." He shrugged and gave her a wry grin. "Reckon that idea didn't work out too good."

"Where is your horse?"

"Don't have no horse, ma'am, nor money t' buy a ticket on a coach."

"You need a shave," she said accusingly.

"Ma'am, I need more than that. I need a bath, a shave, a hot meal and them's just for starters. I'm sorry if I frightened your little girl."

"You did not frighten me, and I am not little," the child put in.

"Sorry," Harlan said. "I thought you were. It's good t' know that I was wrong."

"Where is your hat?" the kid demanded. "Everybody wears a hat. Boys, I mean. Girls don't have to."

"I lost it."

"You don't have much of anything, do you?" the mother said.

"No, ma'am."

"Do you have anything to eat?"

"Yes, ma'am. I got me some 'taters here." He patted the bulge in the front of his shirt. "If you an' the little . . . I mean, you and the young lady here . . . if you're hungry I'd share with you."

The woman tilted her head and peered at him for a moment, then nodded. "Come along. We can give you a meal. We don't have much but I won't see anyone pass by in hunger."

"That's mighty nice o' you, ma'am. Your husband won't mind you havin' a stranger to table?"

"He won't mind." To the child she said, "Sarah, run on ahead and tell Daddy."

"But what about the berries?"

"This afternoon. We'll come this afternoon and pick berries."

"All right. What do you want me to tell Daddy?"

"Just tell him about the man."

Sarah whirled and went skipping toward the fields west of the tiny creek. Her mother motioned for Harlan to join her and followed in the same direction Sarah had gone.

Once they broke clear of the thicket Harlan could see a farmhouse and outbuildings not more than a hundred yards from where he had been sleeping. The house was made of logs, the other structures from sawn lumber. Sarah was already halfway across the field of stubble left from some crop that had already been harvested. She was running pell-mell toward a man seated at a grindstone set beside one of the smaller buildings.

"Our name is Jesperson," the woman said. "You've met my daughter Sarah. The man you see there is my husband Nels."

"A pleasure, Miz Jesperson." Harlan grinned. "I'd tip my hat except for not havin' one. But I would if I did have one."

"I am sure you would, Mr. . . . . ?"

"Oh, I, uh . . . Jones," he said. It was a lame answer, he supposed, but the only name he could think of at the moment. "Uh, Johnny Jones." Why the hell hadn't he prepared for such a question? Never mind that he hadn't intended to talk with anyone. Or be seen. He was in for it now, and he should have thought about so simple a question before now. "I've, um, had a run o' bad luck. That's why I'm on my way now t' visit some friends. See if they can help me get back onto my feet."

"What is it that you do, Mr. Jones?" Mrs. Jesperson

seemed to accept his story so far. Her question now sounded like polite interest rather than suspicion.

"Cowhand," he said. "Wrangler. Post-hole digger." He grinned. "I ain't proud. I'll do 'most anything if it pays an honest dollar." Honest. Yeah, sure. He fleetingly wondered what she would have said if he told her he robbed banks and caroused for a living.

Ahead of them Sarah had reached her father and was speaking with him. Nels Jesperson stood and set aside the scythe he had been sharpening. He wiped his hands on a rag, ruffled Sarah's hair and came to greet the visitor who had been sleeping in their woodlot.

Johnny Jones, Harlan kept reminding himself. *I am Johnny Jones from . . . where the hell am I from? Beeville, Texas. Sure. Why not tell the truth there? That way there won't be so much to try and remember. And I was between jobs. Laid off after a cattle drive. No, make it horses. Me and some other boys drove a bunch of horses from north Texas to, um, where'd we drive the horses? Fort Leavenworth. To sell to the army, that's what. Then I got into a card game. In, oh, make it St. Louis. Sure. I intended to take a steamboat downriver to New Orleans but I got into a card game and got skinned. So I started walking. And I've got friends in . . . make that Dowdville. So that's where I am bound. To see my friends and see can they give me a stake.*

Harlan felt considerably better once he had a story in mind, something he could tell to this Jesperson fellow without stumbling all over himself.

He was smiling and had his hand out to shake when he reached Nels Jesperson.

Chapter Twenty-eight

"I would give you work if I had any," Nels Jesperson said over the rim of his coffee cup, "but my crops are all in for this year, and I never have anything that a cowhand would be interested in anyway. I wish I could help."

"You and Miz Jesperson are sure enough helping," Harlan said. "This meal . . . best-tasting thing I've had in a while."

Since walking away from that jail, actually. Mrs. Jesperson was a thoroughly nice person and the family was eager to share what they had, but what they had was chicken boiled until it felt—and mostly tasted—like gum rubber, leftover turnip greens and cold corn pone. None of those, with the possible exception of the cornbread when it was hot and covered in sweet butter, was much to Harlan's taste.

Still, Harlan appreciated the family's generosity. And he sure as hell had been hungry. Raw potatoes filled the belly but by themselves did not really satisfy.

"Would you like more coffee, Mr. Jones?"

"Yes, ma'am, I surely would, thank you."

The lady refilled first her husband's cup and then Harlan's. "Mother," Jesperson said when she was done, "I just had a thought. Do you remember that cap your brother gave me for Christmas two years ago?"

"Of course."

"It's a nice enough cap and it was fine of him to give it, but you know I'll never wear it. Perhaps Mr. Jones here would like it. It might help to keep the sun out of his eyes. Do you know where it is?"

"I think so, yes."

"Get it for him, please."

Mrs. Jesperson smiled and disappeared behind the draped sheet that hid their bed cubicle from the rest of the cabin.

"Would you like another pone, Mr. Jones?"

"I'm full up, thanks. What I really could use now would be your outhouse."

"You know where it is. Go ahead."

Harlan excused himself and went outside. He did his business, stopped at the washstand for another dab of soap and water, then returned to the house. Mrs. Jesperson and Sarah were both grinning at him, and Sarah held one of the soft, flat caps like Harlan had seen on the heads of miners and draymen and the like. There was not much of a bill to the caps, but Jesperson was right; what there was should help to keep the sun from his eyes.

"See if it fits, Mr. Jones."

The little girl handed the gray tweed cap to him. It was a trifle large but a few twists of tall grass stuffed inside the headband would take care of that. Harlan tilted it to a jaunty angle and said, "How's it look?"

"Like it was made for you," Jesperson said.

Harlan looked at the lady and said, "Ma'am, I kinda think that sometimes your husband lies. But I do thank you for the hat." To Jesperson he said, "I been walking the whole night, tryin' to get there and get back on my feet quick as I can. Would there be someplace where I could stretch out for a few hours an' get some sleep?"

"Of course. You can bed down in my shed. I don't have a cot or anything but we can give you the loan of a blanket to lay down. When you wake up come find one

of us. We'll give you something more to eat and a few
things to carry along with you. And Sarah, mind you,
stay away. I don't want you pestering the gentleman
while he's trying to sleep."

"You folks are awful kind," Harlan said.

"Just doing our Christian duty. No more than that."

"I'm thanking you. I don't . . . I have more'n a dollar
here. I'll be glad to pay you for what I've took."

"You will do no such thing, Mr. Jones," the lady
quickly put in. "We are just glad we could help a man
in need."

Good folks indeed, Harlan thought. He smiled. "Sarah, can you show me where to lay that blanket your pa
was talking about?"

The child seemed delighted to be asked for her help.
She jumped up and darted behind the bedroom curtain for the blanket.

Chapter Twenty-nine

Harlan was feeling pretty damn good as he hiked along that afternoon. His belly was full and so was the ratty old gunnysack he carried on a stick over his shoulder. The Jespersons had insisted that he take more cold pone and a dozen hardboiled eggs. They'd added a paper of salt—he hadn't realized just how very much he missed salt on his food—and most of a box of matches. All that and they refused to take so much as a penny for their kindness. There were times when Harlan just plain forgot how kind people could be. And him a complete stranger.

He was as full right then of goodwill toward mankind as he was of the grub Nels and . . . come to think of it, he never had heard an actual name for Mrs. Jesperson. But whoever she was, he was grateful to her.

In that mood, sauntering along fat, dumb and happy, he damn near reached the end of his rope. Literally.

He was approaching a covered bridge above a narrow darkwater creek, cap atilt and whistling a gay tune. He passed into the shade of the bridge roof and felt the chill of the coming evening here where the sun could not reach. His footsteps rang hollow on the planks underfoot, and for a moment he shivered. Someone walking over his grave, they used to say when he was a kid. Harlan stopped whistling and increased his pace.

As soon as he stepped out from inside the bridge someone shouted, "Hands up" into his right ear, and someone else leaped out of the bushes on his left, brandishing a double-barreled shotgun. The gun, Harlan noticed, was not cocked, but that gave him scant comfort. Odds were that a charge of lead pellets could travel faster than he could run, so there seemed no point in running.

"Boys, I got nothin' but a little food here and about a dollar in my pockets. You're welcome to it all. You don't have t' shoot."

"What the hell do you take us for?" the loud one on his right demanded. That one was wearing a close-cropped beard while the other was clean shaven. Apart from that, the two could have been peas from the same pod, both lean, dark men with unkempt hair and pale eyes. Crazy eyes, Harlan sometimes thought of anything that pale and watery. He guessed the two were brothers but likely not twins, as the one with the beard was a good three or four inches the taller of the two.

"You're robbing me, ain't you?"

"Hell, no, we ain't no robbers. There's a murdering sonuvabitch on the loose 'round here and we aim to collect us the ree-ward for the bastard."

"A reward, you say?"

"That's right. Two hundred dollars, cash money. That's what's posted on every town hall and saloon door in east Kansas an' western Missoura," the one with the scattergun proclaimed. "And do we turn you in we'll be picking that up, I'm thinkin'."

Harlan scowled at first one of them and then at the other, taking his time and giving each a thoroughly evil look. "Do you turn me in, what you'll be getting is a lawsuit, for I'll file papers against you on a claim of false imprisonment. Whatever you got, I figure to take. Mark my words an' don't be messing with me, you hear?"

The two brothers exchanged glances and the tall one, who Harlan took to be the older of the pair, cleared his throat and looked away. They were a long way from being convinced of his innocence, but at least he had created doubt in their minds.

"Now look-a here," Harlan said, pressing whatever small advantage he might so far have, "I don't know who this murderer is that you're looking for, but my name is Johnny Jones from Beeville, Texas. If you want to check on me, you can ask my friend Nels Jesperson an' his lovely wife."

"You know Nels an' Coleen?"

"Well, I wouldn't give them for my bona fides if I didn't, now would I?"

"I s'pose you wouldn't at that." The younger brother sighed and dropped the butt of his shotgun to the ground beside his foot. Bare foot, Harlan noticed now. Neither one of them was wearing shoes. "Shit, we was hoping to fall into a fortune. We been waiting by this stinking son of a bitch of a bridge 'most all the day long."

"I dunno about you, Jimmy, but I'm commencing to get cold an' hungry an' I want to go back to the house," the tall one said. To Harlan he added, "I'm sorry if we gave you a scare there, mister."

"You ain't no sorrier than me, I can promise you that," Harlan told them. "I like to shit my britches when y'all came out from beside this bridge an' shoved a gun up my nose. You say this fella you're looking for is a murderer, is he? An' with two hundred cash dollars on him?"

"In gold, the flyers says."

Harlan whistled. "Man, I sure as hell could use me two hundred dollars. In gold or greenbacks or sacks of damn pennies, I wouldn't mind."

"Yeah, I don't know about you, but I've never seen two hundred dollars. Not all to once I haven't."

"You, Jimmy?"

"You know I haven't. How's about you, Mr. Jones?"

"Matter of fact, I have. Me and my pards came up from Texas with a herd of horses. We sold them to the army. That was for cash money. Currency not coin, but it was cash nonetheless. Got more than four thousand dollars for them. Of course there wasn't much of that mine. Most of it went to the owner of the outfit, then the next largest share to the foreman and finally to us hands. But I seen it when they paid off. Oh, it was a fine, brave pile, it surely was."

"You been to Texas, have you?"

"Bred an' born there. But I been lots o' places, trailing beeves and horses and whatnot. Why, once me and some fellas paid off in Bozeman, up Montana way. We come down past these stinking sulfur springs where the water tasted like rotten eggs and come out o' the ground hot enough to boil stuff. Wasn't no fish there but if you caught a fish in one of the creeks around those parts you could cook it by just leaving it on the hook and dropping it into one of them hot water springs."

"No!"

"It's the truth, cross my heart an' hope to die. I seen it with my own eyes." Harlan ran his forefinger back and forth across his chest in the general vicinity of his heart. Or where a heart was supposed to be; there were those who disputed the notion that he had one. Their claim was supported by the fact that his yarn about Montana was only that. A yarn, although one he had heard once from a waddie who returned from the north country and told everyone about the strange sights up there. Harlan did not believe the hot water and fish thing himself, but he did admire a good lie when he heard one, and was especially fond of that one because of the sincerity in the young cowboy's face and voice when he told it. Harlan had always believed that a man who could fake sincerity was sure to go a long way in life.

The three of them walked along together for twenty minutes or so until they came to a rutted lane that led off the road for forty or fifty yards to a farm that had a dilapidated cabin, something that might barely pass for a barn, and a fenced trap holding a pair of milk cows and a rib-thin old horse standing hipshot with its head hanging.

A black and white dog came barking and growling out of the barn. It approached the men with its tail held low. With good reason, it seemed. The closer of the two gave it a kick in the ribs that sent the cur yelping back into the barn. Harlan did not like that. Did not like these two men either. But he did have a fondness for dogs.

"I don't suppose I could talk you fellas into giving a stranger an invite to dinner," Harlan said.

"You suppose right, mister. We don't take in no tramps."

"I understand. No hard feelings." Harlan smiled and offered his hand, which the brothers grudgingly took. "Good luck to you," Harlan told them.

"Sure. Same to you, Jones."

Harlan was whistling again and his step was light as he moved on down the road, head swiveling from one side to the other as he searched for a place to settle down this evening.

Chapter Thirty

Harlan napped until well after dark, then took a corn pone out of his sack and ate half of it. The other half he put—carefully, lest too many crumbs and crumbles fall off—inside his shirt. He stashed his bindle and stick beside the road and laid a branch out in the right of way so he could find the spot again in the dark. Then he walked back to the farm owned by the inhospitable brothers.

He was whistling under his breath as he walked up the lane. He felt . . . alive. Exhilarated. Filled with zest. This was without question the best he had felt since the last robbery he and the boys had pulled. This was *living!*

The dog he had seen earlier in the day came growling and barking out of the barn. Harlan stood his ground. The dog continued to bark and to dance around him but did not come close enough to be kicked and so could not offer to bite. After a minute or two a harsh voice came from the cabin: "Shut up, damn you, or I'll come whup your ass, dog."

The dog whined and quieted at the sound of the man's voice. It slunk belly down and tail stiff, following Harlan as he moved slowly and calmly to the side of the lane.

Harlan hunkered down and reached inside his shirt for the piece of corn pone he saved from his supper. He pulled off a small piece and tossed it to the dog. The animal first shied away but soon came slinking back to sniff the bit of pone and quickly gobble it. Harlan pulled off another piece and threw it. This time the dog ate the offering without first darting away. Harlan hoped this would not take long; he would soon run out of pone.

By the time the last morsel of pone was gone, the dog was flat on the ground in front of Harlan's feet. It whined and rolled onto its back. Harlan scratched its belly and under its jaw. When Harlan stood upright the dog jumped to its feet and wagged its tail. Harlan grinned and bent down to pet the animal and rub it behind the ears. When he walked to the barn it followed.

It took him a while fumbling around in the dark inside the rickety barn to find and identify the items he wanted. Those included four empty feed sacks. A snaffle bit with the long driving reins removed, rolled and tucked inside Harlan's shirt. And a ball of twine.

He also found a rusting tin can half filled with old nails. The can still had its lid attached but cut open and peeled back. Just what Harlan needed. He bent the steel disk back and forth until the metal became fatigued and broke off in his hands. Harlan slipped the resulting piece into his pocket, gathered up the rest of his loot and left the barn. The dog was still with him so he took a moment to pet it some more, then walked to the fenced trap and slipped through the rails.

The two cows moved warily to the far side of the enclosure while the horse whickered and plodded toward him in search of a handout.

Harlan ran his hands over the horse's neck and flanks and withers. He picked up each of its feet, tapped on the frog a couple times, then set the foot down again, opened the horse's mouth and then scratched beneath its jaw.

The horse took to being handled without complaint. Harlan smiled. It would do very nicely, he thought.

He took three of his four empty feed sacks and smoothed them over the horse's bony spine. Several wraps of twine around the animal's barrel served to secure the feed sacks in place like a bareback pad. He cut the twine from the ball with the sharp edge of the can lid he took from his pocket.

More twine cut to length became reins. When he had more time he intended to cut the leather driving lines down to proper size for a ridden horse, but with only a can lid to work with, that would likely take a good while and he did not want to take that long.

The horse accepted the snaffle bit without quarrel. Harlan led it to the gate, took it outside with the dog still at his heels and tied the horse to a fence rail.

He went back inside the trap and walked to the far side, then began hazing the cows toward the gate. Once it saw what he was doing the dog helped, nipping at the heels of the slow-moving cattle and forcing them into a trot.

When the two cows were outside, Harlan untied the makeshift reins from the fence, retrieved the fourth gunnysack, which now held only the remainder of that ball of twine, and hopped onto the horse's back.

The horse swung its head around and gave him a critical look, but it did not buck and did not even pin its ears back. It was obviously more curious at being mounted than it was angered.

Harlan nudged it in the ribs with his heels and pulled its head around, reining with the light twine. He suspected he would have to plow rein the animal even after he got the shortened leathers back onto the bit, because the horse very likely had never been taught to neck rein.

Riding again, like a man should, he set off down the road to retrieve his poke of food that the Jespersons had given him.

The black and white dog trotted along beside the horse. Neither animal gave any indication of regret at leaving that farm.

Chapter Thirty-one

Dowdville was a pretty enough town, laid out around a parklike central square. A three-story stone courthouse stood on the north side of the square with businesses arranged around the other three sides. The park was filled with shade trees, their leaves beginning to change color at this pleasant time of year. Benches and hitching posts were placed around the perimeter, and in the center was a pedestal bearing a statue of an infantry soldier, his long bayonet just slightly tilted out of line with the barrel of his lead rifle. Lead for sure because it weathered gray, while more expensive bronze took on a greenish cast with age and exposure. Dowdville was proud of her boys but was just a little bit cheap too.

On an impulse Harlan dismounted and walked over to the statue. He made his way around it, admiring it from all sides, and began to grin before he was done. On the north side of the monument, facing the courthouse, there was a cast bronze inscription honoring the town's sons who had fought for the Union army. There were—Harlan counted—twenty-three names there.

On the south side of the same monument was another inscription, just as lovingly done, to honor the eight local boys who had chosen to fight for the Confederacy.

The east and west sides had benches rather than plaques.

It was a warm afternoon so Harlan took a few minutes to sit on the west side of the soldier, enjoying the sun and giving some thought to how he might handle this. He idly petted the black and white dog. It had stayed with him through last night and all day today, and if he did not watch himself he was going to start liking the animal.

He needed another name, having given the John Jones moniker to those sorry-ass brothers who used to own the horse and the dog.

Earl seemed reasonable since it really was his middle name. And . . . oh . . . Woods would work. Or Fields. Woods then. He liked the sound of Earl Woods. That took care of that, then. As soon as he stood up from this bench he would be Earl Woods from . . . Tilden, Texas, which used to be called Dogtown but had been renamed in honor of the presidential candidate of that name a few years back.

Earl Woods was here in Dowdville because, um, he'd heard there was a reward posted for the fellow that killed some folks. Sure thing.

He gave the dog a few more scratches behind its ears and stood. He pushed the soft cap back on his head to let a little hair hang down onto his forehead, and cleared his throat a few times, reminding himself that when it came to avoiding suspicions, stupid beat smart all hollow.

Harlan first untied the horse and led it to another side of the square where he saw a public water trough. He gave the animal time to drink, then took it half a block down so it would not block the way if someone else wanted to use the water. He secured the horse to a hitch post and slapped his thigh to tell the dog it could follow, then went across the street and up the stone steps to the courthouse doors.

A slender young man wearing a green eyeshade and

black sleeve protectors told him, "Sheriff Bates's office is downstairs in the basement. You have to go back outside and around to the east side of the courthouse. There's steps. You'll see them there."

Harlan thanked the fellow and followed the instructions. A sign over the basement steps showed where he should go.

He went down the stairs to a closed door. He felt something of a chill at the bottom, but whether that was the temperature or a bout of apprehension he really was not sure.

The hell with it. He reached out, thumbed the latch and pulled open the door.

From now on, dammit, he had better be Earl Woods because otherwise he was walking straight into the hornet's nest.

Chapter Thirty-two

Inside the sheriff's office, Harlan pulled a pushpin out of the corkboard that hung on the wall just to the right of the door. He took down one of the flyers advertising for his capture and peered at it for a while, holding it out at arm's length and moving his lips as he did so.

"Is there something I can help you with, mister?" the handsome young man behind the desk asked.

Harlan grinned at him. In a slow drawl that came from low in his throat, he said, "I'm here t' see the sher'f. Is you him?"

"Sheriff Bates is not in at the moment, but I'm his deputy. You can talk to me."

Harlan shook his head. "No, sir. I'm here t' see the sher'f. I'll state my business t' him, I'm thinking."

"I don't know when the sheriff will be back. It could be a while."

"That's all right. I ain't in such a big hurry." He eyed the pair of wooden ladder-back chairs placed beside a side wall, then walked almost to the deputy's desk and looked at the chairs from that angle too. He squinted his eyes nearly shut and tilted his head back and forth, then eased himself down onto the chair closer to the front wall. There was no difference between the two. Harlan held the Wanted poster in his lap and every so often smoothed it over his right thigh.

The deputy dropped his eyes to something lying on his desk and seemed entirely willing to forget that Harlan was in the room.

"Say, could I ast you a question?" Harlan said, after a few minutes of silence had passed.

The deputy looked up again. "I suppose so, sure."

"This here poster." He held up the item in question for the deputy to see. "It says there's some kind o' ree-ward for catchin' this fella. What can you tell me about that, hey?"

The deputy shrugged. "That flyer says pretty much everything we know. A man name of Harlan killed a family out east of here. Curtis and Irina Womack and their two daughters Meggie . . . she was nine or there-abouts . . . and Lizzie. Lizzie was fifteen, I think. Sixteen. Somewhere around there. Liz was, um, violated, if you must know. They were killed but not robbed. The murderer, this Harlan fellow, just left them lying there. We didn't find them until they were three days dead."

"You did'n tell me anything about the ree-ward," Harlan reminded him. "That's the part I'm wantin' to know."

"Three hundred dollars," the deputy said.

"Cash money?"

The young man nodded. "Any way you want it. Gold, currency, bank draft, whatever. But you have to qualify for it."

"What's that mean?"

"It means you have to catch the murdering son of a bitch and bring him in."

"Alive?"

"He doesn't have to be alive, but the sheriff and the judge would have to have some way to know for sure he's the one that done it. Better·if he's alive, I'd say. May I ask you something now?"

"Ast away. I got nothin' to hide."

"Why do you want to know all this?"

"'Cause your sher'f is gonna drop that three hundred cash money into my pocket, that's why." Harlan cackled and slapped the poster that lay on his leg.

"You, uh, do you have information about this killing?" The deputy was leaning forward on his chair now.

"That's for me t' know and the sher'f to find out."

"You have information about the murders?"

Harlan put a stubborn expression on his face, lips pressed tightly together and chin jutting forward. He said nothing.

"Excuse me for a minute, will you? I'll be right back." The deputy practically leaped out of his chair. He crossed the room in three strides and was out the door in a heartbeat.

Harlan stayed where he was. It was not particularly warm in the sheriff's office, but it seemed awfully close and he found it a little hard to draw breath in there. He fanned himself with the Wanted poster in his hand, wondering as he did so if it had been a good idea to come here when he could have headed straight for California. Or Canada. Australia. Lord knew, anyplace would be healthier for him than Dowdville, Kansas.

Except, dammit, he had his pride and whoever that son of a bitch Harlan somebody was, he was messing with Harlan Breen's peace of mind.

Chapter Thirty-three

Sheriff of an entire county, now that was a pretty exalted position, or so Harlan had always heard. Worth quite a bit of money too, what with salary and collecting fees plus whatever, like any good politician, the fellow could steal. Sheriffs tended to be imposing men with the ability to remember names, to shake hands, to smile and to give stump speeches in loud, booming voices. Sheriff Brandon Bates did not fit that mold.

For one thing, he was young. Harlan would have bet the man was not yet out of his twenties. He was slight of build and wore an ordinary brown hat with a narrow brim and pinched crown. He had short dark hair parted in the middle and slicked down with some sort of grease. He was clean shaven and dressed like a church deacon. He wore neither a gun nor a badge, at least not that Harlan could see. He had a gap between his two front teeth and that, combined with his small stature, made him look like a kid who had not yet started to get his growth.

Harlan looked at Sheriff Brandon Bates and felt a twinge of fear. Never mind what the man looked like, Bates had not gotten to be sheriff of this county without having abilities that went way beyond the obvious.

It was too late to pull out now, so Harlan painted a lopsided grin on his face. He stood, stumbled over the dog that was sitting pressed against his lower legs, righted himself and stuck out a hand for the sheriff to shake. Which the man did.

"It pleasures me t' meet you, Sher'f."

"My deputy said you may have information as to the whereabouts of the murderer Harlan Breen. Is that correct, Mr., uh . . . ?"

"Woods, Sher'f. My name is Earl Woods from Dogtown, Texas. Well, Tilden, they're calling it now. Used t' be Dogtown though. 'Cause of all the dogs. Like this'un here." He pointed at the black and white dog. "Real heavy brush down that way, y'see, an' the best way t' chase cow-critters out to where they can be roped down is with dogs. Lots o' brush, lots o' cows an' lots o' dogs, y'see."

"That is interesting, I'm sure, Mr. Woods, but tell me what you know about this Breen."

"Why hell, Sher'f, I come here so's you could tell me about him." Harlan patted himself on the chest and declared, "I figure t' catch him for you, Sher'f. Your man says the ree-ward is three hunnerd dollars hard money. Is that right? Three hunnerd?"

"I thought you said you had information about Breen, Mr. Woods," the sheriff put in.

"Now, Sher'f, I never said any such of a thing. I prob'ly did mention that I figure t' bring him in for you. Now I prob'ly did say that 'cause it's e-zackly what I intend t' do. And I'm right sure that I said you all should get the ree-ward together 'cause I aim t' collect it." Harlan grinned and cackled. "But I reckon I got t' catch him first. I's hoping you can tell me a little more t' go on here. But don't you worry. I got me a pistol here. See?"

Harlan pulled Gordon Dobbs's little revolver out of his pants pocket and showed it to Sheriff Bates.

The sheriff's expression suggested he had a bad taste in his mouth. He was polite enough though. "I see, Mr. Woods, and I thank you for coming by. Now if you will excuse me . . ."

"Ain't you gonna help me t' find this fella for you, Sher'f?"

"That will be up to you, Mr. Woods. Now, please. I need to get back to what I was doing. Excuse me. Please."

Bates turned and disappeared into a back room. He did not offer to shake hands again.

Harlan hid a bit of a smile. He thought that had gone well enough, everything considered.

He slapped his thigh again to summon the dog and went back up the steps into the sunlight.

He still needed to get directions to the Womack farm. That was something he had intended to do inside the sheriff's office, but once he saw Bates he had changed his mind about that. Any man who could gain public office as a lawman and look that mild and inoffensive was very likely someone to walk wide around.

Chapter Thirty-four

There were two mercantiles in Dowdville, Hanratty's on one side of the square and Isaacson's opposite it. Harlan left the horse where it was and walked over to Isaacson's, which was slightly closer. The dog ambled along at his side.

Inside the store he was surrounded by shelves and tables and tidy piles of merchandise, most of it devoted to the home and the stomach rather than to farm implements or livestock. The shaded interior was easy on the eyes, and the place had a warm, homey smell, a combination of smoked meats and naptha soap, peppermint candy and furniture polish.

Harlan stopped beside the store's counter. He slapped his leg and the dog came closer and sat beside his right foot.

"What can I do for you today, young man?" The proprietor was in his fifties or thereabouts, Harlan thought. He was small, with a neatly trimmed gray beard and a sharp, prominent nose. He had bright eyes contained behind the shiny glass of wire-rimmed spectacles and wore sleeve garters. He was going bald, his hairline racing to join the back of his head.

"I, uh, there's a couple things I could use, but I got to tell you square. I ain't got much money. Hardly a'tall in fact."

"We will think about your money after you tell me what you need."

"Yes, sir, well, I'm needing me some matches. 'Bout

two cents worth, I'm thinking. And, um, some extra-long boot laces if you got such a thing."

The storekeeper glanced down. "Your boots do not take laces. They just pull on."

"That be true, but it ain't for lacing up boots that I need the boot laces."

The man tilted his head and thought for a moment. "Would you do me the favor to tell me why you say you have little money but want boot laces when you do not wear lace-up boots?"

"I don't mind that a'tall, Mr. . . . . ?"

"I am Benjamin Isaacson."

"An' I'm Earl Woods, Mr. Isaacson. Yes, sir. I'm thinking to cut a piece outa the tail of this here shirt an' make me a slungshot with them boot laces. I used t' be a fair hand with a slungshot when I was a button. I'm thinking I can use one now t' knock down some rabbits or birds or such. You know. Something t' cook over the fires I figure t' start with them matches."

"Thank you for that explanation, Mr. Woods. I appreciate you humoring me, and I will do you the courtesy of not asking how you come to be without funds when you are so obviously used to more comfortable circumstances." Isaacson paused for a moment, then chuckled. "You needn't look so stricken, Mr. Woods. I am a merchant, you should remember. I have an eye for quality goods. Your shirt and your trousers are very nicely made. Your boots and your belt were expensive items once. Anyway, it is none of my business what brings you to my door. Whatever the cause, I shall be glad to be of whatever service I can. Now, can you afford four cents for the matches and the laces?"

"Yes, sir. I can handle that."

Rather than pulling Harlan's purchases from the shelves, Isaacson disappeared into a back room with the admonition, "Don't go away. I'll be only a moment." He returned several minutes later with a small parcel wrapped in heavy brown butcher paper.

He handed the package to Harlan and very crisply said, "That will be four cents, please."

Harlan dug out his coins. He handed Isaacson a nickel and got back a shiny penny in return.

When he was a boy, Harlan's mother had always told him that a shiny new penny was a lucky penny. He hoped that was true.

"Thank you, Mr. Isaacson."

"I wish you a good day, Mr. Woods."

Harlan snapped his fingers. The dog jumped to its feet, wagging its tail. It followed him out into the street. It seemed to be interested in the package of matches and boot laces.

Harlan ignored that and retrieved his horse. Now what he needed, he thought, was directions to the Womack farm. Likely the people at the Dowdville Farm Supply Co. would be able to provide that.

Chapter Thirty-five

"Howdy, neighbor. I just came up from Arkan-sar and I was wonderin' if you could help me with some-thin'." Harlan gave the man an aw-shucks smile, peered down at his toes and said, "Two somethin's actu-ly. First off I'm looking for my cousin Curtis. I know he lived aroun' here someplace but I don't know how to find his farm. I figger he oughta likely do business with you, so you oughta likely know how I can get there. Second thing, I come a long way. I could sure use a gallon o' grain for my old horse out there. Could you sell me that? I ain't got much money but it's a poor sort as won't take care of his livestock, I always say."

"You say this Curtis is your cousin?" The man at the farm supply store had some age on him but he had a blacksmith's powerful muscles, with arms thick as young trees and legs like old oaks. He wore his hair greased and slicked down like some sort of dandy.

"Yes, sir. Curtis Womack, that would be. Him and me are connected through my mother's people on her grampa's side. We ain't what you would call real close kin but close enough to visit back and forth. Can you tell me how t' get to his place, mister?"

"I have bad news for you, I'm afraid. Very bad news."

Harlan managed to hold back his tears when he heard—again—his cousin's fate, this version embel-lished with considerable detail that the sheriff's deputy had left out. Or was fabrication, bad news having a tendency to grow with each retelling.

Either way, Harlan received the sad news with manful restraint.

"They're buried in the St. Francis of Assisi Catholic Cemetery over in Winnock, the whole family." The man shook his head sadly. "All of them," he repeated.

"I'll hafta go pray over 'em," Harlan said solemnly. "I'd 'preciate it if you could tell me how to get to their farm an' then from there to this . . . St. Francis, did you say? Get from the farm to the cemetery. If you'd be so kind."

"Aye, I can do that. Do you need a poke to carry this gallon of grain? Which by the way will be ten cents. Normally I'd just put the dime on Curtis's account, but you can understand that I won't be collecting . . . say! I just had a thought. You're the man's cousin. How's about you pay his seed bill? He owes me, uh . . ." The fellow grabbed a ledger and began thumbing through it.

"I'm sorry," Harlan said quickly. "I'm near about broke m' own self. I can pay you for the grain but I don't have no extra to settle Cousin Curtis's account. When I get home though I'll pass the hat among the rest of the fambly an' see what I can come up with. I'll send you whatever we can. That's only right, Curtis being our kin and all."

Harlan dug a dime out of his dwindling supply of small change—he had less than a dollar remaining—and gave it to the farm store man in exchange for a burlap sack of mixed oats, barley and milo. "Thank you, sir."

"And don't forget now. You take the left-hand turning when you get to the stand of pecans I told you about. Curtis's turning is only a mile or so past that. A little lane taking off to the left. There's no signpost but the last time I was out there, there was a busted wheel laying in the weeds beside the lane. You can find it by that if the wheel is still there."

"Much obliged," Harlan said, placing a forefinger to the side of his cheek in salute.

Chapter Thirty-six

Harlan found "Cousin Curtis's" place after getting lost only twice. Which wasn't bad, considering. The lane looked as if it had been never improved and rarely been used. Fortunately the broken wheel was there, its hub and most of the spokes broken and its iron tire salvaged and gone.

By that time it was nearing dark. The sun had already disappeared and the shadows were deep.

Harlan did not believe in haunts or goblins or any of that truck, but he could see no good reason to stumble around on a dead man's spread looking for . . . whatever.

The whole area was secluded. Plenty of forest, but few people here and few cleared fields for crops. There were hogs running free in the thickets, so he made a bed of ferns well away from any oak trees with acorns that might attract them. He laid a camp of sorts, then hobbled the horse and poured out the gallon of grain for it.

In the last lingering glow of daylight he opened the packet Isaacson had given him, intending to get the matches he'd paid for and start a fire so he could mix some cornmeal dough and bake some corn dodgers on a dingle stick.

The matches were there. Many more than two cents' worth. So were a pair of extra-long boot laces.

The storekeeper, however, had included more than the items Harlan had paid for. There was also a scrap of soft leather with holes already punched so he could easily fashion a slungshot. And in addition to those, Isaacson had put at least a large handful of dried jerky into the package.

Son of a bitch, Harlan thought. For the man to do all that, and him a total stranger with practically no money in his pockets . . . son of a redheaded bitch.

"You and me are gonna eat better than I expected," Harlan told the dog.

After a much better supper than he'd expected, he lay down on the rather sharp-scented ferns. He left the little revolver loose in his right hand in case any hogs came around to investigate, and pulled his cloth cap over his face to discourage amorous mosquitoes. The dog curled up tightly against Harlan's side, its tail curled and lying over top of its nose.

Harlan went to sleep to the sound of the horse pulling up the sparse grass that grew in the shade of the forest.

Chapter Thirty-seven

"Good evening, Mr. Jarrett. Please come in," the woman said, with a slight bob that might have been intended as a curtsy. She was dressed in blue silk, her skirts full and bodice modest. She wore a cameo at her throat. She was probably in her forties.

Harlan Jarrett removed his hat and stepped inside the large, comfortable house. "You know me?"

The lady smiled. "When a gentleman of quality arrives in town, a gentleman such as yourself, people take note. Before you ever appeared at my door I knew where you were staying, what your business at the bank would be . . . not the details, I hasten to add, but the general tone of your needs there . . . even how you treat the help at the hotel and at the restaurant. Frankly, sir, I am surprised you took this long to find your way here. Please be assured that you are welcome." Her smile grew wider. "And that I am the soul of discretion. Would you like a drink before we discuss business?"

"Coffee would be nice."

"I have some excellent brandies and a fair selection of wines."

"Just the coffee, thank you."

"May I take your hat? Thank you." The lady took Jarrett's beaver carefully in both hands, then turned and transferred it into the hands of a young black woman who appeared seemingly from nowhere to wait on her. "This way, please."

She led the way into a small but elegant parlor with flocked cream-colored wallpaper, brocade upholstery on the deeply cushioned chairs, and love seats and swagged draperies at the two windows.

"Please sit down. Make yourself comfortable. Would you like a cigar? No? Some powdered coca? My name, by the way, is Mrs. Adams, Mr. Jarrett." Mrs. Adams tugged a bellpull and the black girl reappeared with a silver tray bearing a coffeepot, creamer and sugar, and two painted china cups. The girl set down the tray and withdrew. Mrs. Adams poured coffee for both of them.

She chose a seat close to Harlan and took her time arranging her skirts and spooning sugar into her coffee before she said, "Our fee is ten dollars, Mr. Jarrett, payable to me in advance."

"Perhaps not," he said.

"Mr. Jarrett, I do not haggle. It is so unladylike, don't you agree?"

"You mistake me, madam. It is just that in fairness we should discuss a somewhat larger fee. You see . . . I have special needs . . ."

Her smile did not waver. "How special?"

"Do you have any, shall we say, disposable merchandise?"

"No. Absolutely not."

"How close to it might one come?" Jarrett asked.

Mrs. Adams absently sipped at her coffee while she pondered the question. At length she leaned forward and replaced the cup onto its saucer. When she straightened again she said, "I do have some who could use a little discipline. Your needs might serve as a reminder."

"Some?" he asked.

"Two, actually. Only two. And those may not suffer permanent damage."

"Whips?" he asked.

"Certainly. But no scarring. Belts or strops are preferable."

"Cutting?"

"Light cutting perhaps, but not deep. And clean edges only. Razors would be acceptable. Most knives would not."

Jarrett nodded.

"No bones to be broken," Mrs. Adams added.

"And your fee for this service?"

"Seventy-five dollars," the woman said quickly. The amount was three months' wages for an ordinary working man. Half a year or more for most farmers.

"Each," Jarrett said.

"Yes, of course."

"Let me see them, please."

Mrs. Adams picked up a silver bell that Jarrett had not noticed on the side table near her. She rang it once only and a moment later the black girl stepped into the parlor. "Bring Edna," she said, "and Betty."

"Yes'm." The girl withdrew. Jarrett could hear footsteps racing up a set of stairs. Soon other footsteps descended.

The girls were a little long in the tooth to be working in their chosen profession. Both wore kimonos loosely wrapped around themselves. One was dark, possibly Mexican, with black hair and dark eyes. She had a round face and squat, blocky figure. The other was a bleached blonde with dark circles under piercing blue eyes. She had a bruise on her left cheek.

"Let me see them better," Jarrett said.

Mrs. Adams gestured with her hand and both women loosened the ties of their kimonos and spread the garments open. They were naked underneath the Oriental silks.

Jarrett sat where he was, taking his time looking

them over. Finally he said, "That one," pointing at the blonde. "I'll save the other for my next visit."

He reached inside his coat for a wallet, carefully counted out the seventy-five-dollar price agreed upon, and placed the money onto the silver serving tray next to Mrs. Adams's coffee cup.

"That one is Betty," Mrs. Adams said. "Edna, take the gentleman down to the basement room, please. Betty, you may remain here for a moment while I have a word with you."

She stood, smiling, and said, "I hope you enjoy your visit, Mr. Jarrett."

"Thank you, ma'am. Now Edna, please lead the way."

onto a fence rail where his horse was noisily munching hay in the bunk. No more riding with nothing but a pad, thank you.

Since he was right beside it, he headed from there into the barn. By then the dog had finished its explorations and rejoined him.

The barn too, he discovered, had been picked over by the neighbors, quite reasonably so since there were no longer any Womacks to lay claim to whatever had been taken. After all, someone else might as well get some benefit from the things that had been left behind.

Judging by the droppings left behind, the Womacks had kept a few chickens and pigs and either horses or mules. Those were all gone, either to whoever had gotten there first or apportioned out among the family's friends and nearer neighbors. Their greed for the things and the animals that had belonged to the Womacks must have greatly allayed the grief of the multiple buryings. At least, Harlan thought, he was honest about his own greed.

All of the grain had been taken out of the bins, and the stored hay had been unloaded from the loft.

Womack's corn still stood in a field close to the house. Almost certainly someone would come along to harvest that crop in a few more months. He wondered if they would come from time to time to hoe and to weed as well. He doubted they would bother, even though they intended to receive the benefit of the crop.

In the barn Harlan did find a broken chisel with a sharp edge on what remained of the blade. He fetched the driving lines that had been on his horse's snaffle and used the chisel to cut them down to a manageable length, so he could use the leathers as ordinary reins. He removed the twine that had been serving that purpose and rolled the two long pieces. He stuffed those into a pocket and replaced the newly shortened reins on the bit. Those were sure to be much more comfortable to use. He tossed the chisel aside and went to investigate the house next.

Someone had put a padlock on the door, so Harlan broke out a window and went in that way.

Bloodstains on the floor, overturned chairs and dirty dishes still on the table showed clearly enough where the family had been killed and what they had been doing at the time. Four had died there. Five dinner places had been laid. The family had invited their murderer to dine with them. And the bastard had, enjoying their charity before he slaughtered them, one and all.

It chilled Harlan that he could still read the brown, barely legible scrawl left behind by one of the victims—the woman, had someone told him?—that read "Harlan." It was that, dammit, that had landed him in this mess. Otherwise he would be down in the Nations living a life of ease, with his pockets full and his prospects excellent.

Not that there was any point to whining about it now. Now he just needed to find a way to get out from under the burden of his own good name—well, such as it was anyway—slandered and of being pursued as a murderer.

The contents of the house had been picked over too, but only by men, he saw. The things belonging to Mrs. Womack and the two girls were virtually untouched, while all the clothing owned by Womack himself had been taken away.

Nearly all, that was.

Harlan's face split into a wide smile when he saw a battered and dusty Kossuth hat hanging on a peg beside the door. Obviously no one had wanted that.

Until now, that was. The black, versatile Kossuth had always been Harlan's preference anyway. He took this one down and tried it on. It was a little large but something stuffed inside the sweatband should take care of that. He hung his cloth cap neatly onto the peg and looked around for some paper or something to put inside the sweatband. In the past he had always favored dollar bills—or larger denominations when he was flush—for that purpose, but he didn't happen to have any of those at the moment. Anything paper would do though, or silk. Silk was good too.

Womack's things had been taken away but Mrs. Womack's belongings were intact. Surely she would have some paper in her things.

The lady of the house had had a small cedar chest located at the foot of the bed to hold her more personal things. Harlan took the blanket off the bed—it would make a decent bedroll—and lifted the chest onto the bed so he could go through it more conveniently.

Most of the lady's unmentionables in the chest were of no interest but he did find a silk scarf that he pocketed. Tucked away in the bottom of the chest was a leather folio that the previous visitors had missed finding.

It held paper, all right. Eight dollars in paper currency, a five-dollar gold piece and three silver dollars.

Harlan laughed aloud when he slipped those into his pockets.

The only other paper item in the chest was a carefully preserved certificate of marriage joining Curtis Womack and Irina Rostov in holy wedlock.

Harlan tore it in two and folded one section into an inch-wide strip that he tucked inside the sweatband of the floppy black hat. He tried it on again and grunted with satisfaction.

He had a similar reaction when he looked inside the cabinet that stood beside the kitchen range. The men who had cleaned out the place had not bothered to take the partially used tins of flour and sugar and lard.

The obviously useful things such as bacon and canned food were gone, but the loose flour was just as useful to Harlan. He mixed a paste of flour and lard and wrapped it inside a twist of cloth. He could add a little water and use the paste to bake a passable hardtack.

He made up another twist of roasted coffee beans and one of the dark, lumpy sugar.

On a shelf beside the range he found a sharp butcher knife that he slipped behind his belt and a palm-sized Arkansas stone that he put into the bedroll he was making up.

He used the twine that had temporarily been reins tied to the horse's bit to secure the blanket into a roll.

He considered the visit here to be a raving success as far as it went. But that, unfortunately, was not far enough.

He had hoped to find some clue to who this other Harlan was. In that he was disappointed. The murderer had left nothing behind, at least nothing that Harlan could recognize. Nothing that would easily lead him to the bastard.

The man raped and killed. That was the only sure thing Harlan knew about him.

Harlan took his finds and climbed back outside. He stopped for a moment and peered into the distance. The killer was out there. Somewhere.

Because of him, Harlan Breen was wanted as a rapist, the lowest of the low, and as a murderer.

The law was after either of them. Both of them.

But whoever and whatever the killer was, Harlan Breen knew a thing or two about being on the dodge.

He just hoped he knew enough to catch up with this son of a bitch before his own neck was stretched in the murderer's stead.

Chapter Thirty-nine

Harlan Jarrett was annoyed. All this fuss over a whore . . . it was unseemly. Really a great nuisance. The little bitch seemed to quite enjoy his enthusiasm the first time he had used her. This time he'd just gotten a little . . . carried away.

The black maid poked her head inside the room without bothering to knock. "Miz Adams, ma'am, the doctor, he here. I seed him out the window coming up the walk now."

"Well, bring him down, dearie. Bring him down here immediately."

"Yes'm." The girl withdrew and a moment later he could hear the clatter of her feet on the stairs.

The room door was standing wide open so he could all too clearly hear sounds coming down the stairwell. The chime of the bell at the front door. The sound of the door opening. The girl greeting the doctor. Dammit all anyway, Jarrett silently grumbled.

Behind him he could hear the blonde girl moaning and crying. If there was anything he could not stand, it was a girl who sniveled. It was one thing for them to howl when they felt the whip or the knife. After all, that was what he paid them for. But this incessant sniveling annoyed him.

He could hear footsteps on the stairs—if they were going to use this basement room, they really should carpet those stairs and make some improvements in the appearance of the place—and then a small man with a salt and pepper mustache and a rumpled black suit came in. He carried the traditional black clamshell bag and wore a dark gray derby.

Without bothering to remove his hat, the doctor set down his bag and opened it. He took out a stethoscope, put it around his neck and leaned over Betty, who lay sprawled, still whining and blubbering, on a bed stained with sweat and blood and perhaps a little urine too.

The doctor listened to Betty's heart and lungs, examined her visible wounds, and clucked softly to himself while he rummaged into his bag again.

"What do you think, Willy?" Mrs. Adams asked.

Willy—Jarrett thought the name most inappropriate for any doctor and especially so for this one—looked up. "Oh, she'll live all right, Sal. Those fresh wounds will heal in time. The older ones are already scabbed over. She lost a few teeth, of course, but nothing seems to be broken. It's too soon to tell if anything might be ruptured inside her. She reacted to my pushing and poking but she didn't pass out. If anything is seriously wrong inside they usually pass out. From the pain, you see."

"She's going to be all right then?"

"Oh, yes." He took a brown bottle out of his bag, selected a bit of cloth as well, and began unscrewing the top of the bottle. "I'll swab the wounds with carbolic and give her a heavy dose of laudanum. That will calm her down. Then whenever she starts to carry on again, just give her more laudanum."

"Will she be able to work again, Willy?"

"Ah, now that is another question entirely, Sal. The way she is torn up down there . . ." Willy shrugged. "It's possible. I wouldn't count on it though."

Sal Adams glared at Jarrett. "You are not welcome

here any longer, sir. I want you to leave. Leave right now, please, and do *not* come back."

"But you have the best . . ."

"*Leave!*" There was no mistaking that tone. "If she dies, I'll put the law on you, Jarrett. I know who you are. Everyone does. If Betty dies, you will be a marked man."

"Good Lord, woman. She's only a whore," Jarrett protested.

"True, but she is by damn *my* whore. Now get out. Don't come back."

The doctor stood there glaring at Jarrett too. So did the little black maid who was hanging around the doorway, looking as if she would like to slip a knife between Jarrett's ribs.

The hell with them all. He didn't care a fig what any of these rubes thought. And the woman had more or less said she would not be calling the law on him. Unless the whore died, she'd said. And the doctor said he expected her to live.

Unless there was something wrong inside her. Wasn't that what the man had said? Unless there was something ruptured in there?

He hadn't hit her *that* hard. Surely not.

And anyway he would be putting this miserable town behind him just as soon as his money came through. It had been too long already, and if this tardiness continued, he would have to have harsh words with his lawyers back there. Perhaps even take his trust fund away from Mother's control and put the whole thing in the hands of the lawyers.

One thing he was most assuredly not going to do, however, was to leave this wonderful field of opportunity and go back there where the damned police kept pestering him with their questions.

It was just a very good thing that the cops were so stupid while he himself was ahead of them every step of the way.

And such a delightful way it was too.

Harlan Jarrett was still enjoying himself so very, very much.

Out here he could let his imagination run wild. Here he could indulge every whim and fantasy.

Here there were no limits. None.

Despite the eviction from Mrs. Adams's whorehouse, Jarrett was whistling in happy anticipation as he sauntered back to his hotel. After all, it was a limitless future that lay ahead of him.

Chapter Thirty-eight

The farm was neither large nor grand but he could see that it had been put together by someone who intended to stay. It was no stopgap on the way to somewhere else. This *was* the somewhere else.

And of course it had been the Womack family's last place. Harlan felt sorry about that. Robbery was fun, but murder pissed him off.

He rode into the farmyard as if he had a perfect right to be there and slid down from the back of the plow horse he had stolen back there in . . . wherever the hell that had been.

He led the animal into a holding pen beside the barn and stripped the snaffle bit out of its mouth. There was still hay in the feed bunk so he turned the horse loose to eat. The dog went trotting off to explore all the new and presumably enticing scents it was finding.

Harlan began his own explorations.

Obviously the neighbors had been there in the days since the slain family had been discovered. A shed that must have once held tools and harness was completely empty, stripped of everything except the pegs on the wall and the bare shelves.

In a dugout that must have served Womack as a home until the family's house had been built, he found a jumble of broken harness, hames and—wonder of wonders—an ancient but still serviceable McClellan saddle.

Harlan immediately carried that outside and hung it

Chapter Forty

This was humiliating, dammit. He was a *robber*, not some lowly thief. He had standards. And he had balls. He was willing to stand in front of a man to take his money, then make a dashing, romantic getaway. But this, this was sad.

Necessary though.

Harlan Breen crouched in the weeds and patiently watched.

This afternoon when he had stopped to buy some grub, he overheard the storekeeper say he and his missus would be going to the city for church services in the morning and to place orders for the store stock he would be needing for the next several months.

That meant the place would be empty overnight. Once the storekeeper left, Harlan would have free rein inside his place.

Breaking in like that was not Harlan's normal style, but in this case it seemed necessary. For one thing he lacked the plain duster that would hide his clothing and keep a victim from giving a good description of him to the damned law. And the pistol in his pocket was a dinky little piece of crap that was more an embarrassment than a menace. He was not sure he could get anyone to be afraid of the silly little thing jailer Gordon Dobbs had carried.

Then there was the horse. It was an ungainly thing. The McClellan saddle he had found back at the Womack farm barely fit on the plow horse. It was big and

it was slow and it was positively painful to ride at a
trot, almost impossible to put into a run. It was not
exactly the sort of gallant steed a robber needs, and
Harlan did not have the wherewithal to pay for a re-
placement.

And pay he would. When finally he was able to find
a proper mount, he would pay for the animal and get
a bill of sale. A notarized bill of sale, thank you very
much. Horse theft tended to be taken very seriously.
Out beyond farm country, men hanged for that crime.

For sure, though, he was not going to pull an armed
robbery as long as he was mounted on the big, patient
old thing.

So here he was. Hiding in the damned weeds like
a common thief. Waiting for the storekeeper to hitch
up his buggy horse and head off to whatever town it
was where he did his churchgoing and his merchandise buying.

It was close to sundown—Harlan guessed it was six
or thereabouts—before the man finally came out of the
back of the store. Living quarters, obviously.

The man went to his shed and pulled the double
doors wide. He propped the doors with some lengths
of two-by-four and wheeled a snappy roadster outside. There was enough daylight left for Harlan to see
that the buggy was a deep maroon color with gold pin-
striping and red leather seats. Fancy.

The storekeeper sorted out his harness, then went
around back of the shed to a small corral. He led out a
long-bodied seal-brown horse that was narrow in the
chest and had a neck like a snake. The animal looked
fast and if Harlan had seen it earlier he might just have
stolen it and taken a chance on writing his own bill of
sale. Down in the Nations he knew a few folks who
for a dollar or two would cheerfully swear they had

sold him any horse he dragged in and would get him that notarized bill of sale. It was wonderful the things a man could accomplish in the Indian Nations, down where the law was a delightfully flexible thing.

He watched the storekeeper drape the brown with a harness that looked as flashy as the rest of the outfit. All patent leather and German silver doodads. Oh, it was a fine, handsome rig when the brown horse was secured between the poles of that roadster.

The storekeeper led the horse over close to the back steps and went inside. He was gone a good five minutes, which seemed like five hours to an increasingly impatient Harlan hiding in the weeds.

It was near dark before the storekeeper emerged, this time with a woman on his arm.

Harlan could not get a good look at her but he damn sure wished that he could. It had been entirely too long since he had been with a woman, and the storekeeper was treating this one like she was the Venus de Milo. But with all limbs and faculties intact.

All Harlan could really see was that she was wearing a dress with skirts that were so wide the storekeeper would have to be half buried in them once he got the both of them into the buggy. The dress was some pale color that Harlan could not make out in the dark, and she wore a very large bonnet thing that appeared to be the same color.

Good look at her or no, he got a hard-on just from watching the storekeeper help her into the roadster.

The woman settled into her side of the red leather seat and took her time about arranging those skirts. The storekeeper came around to his side of the rig but waited for her to get comfortably set before he climbed in beside her. He took a whip out of the socket, picked up the lines and spoke to the brown. The horse pulled away smooth as glass without jerking the lady behind him, and quickly found a spanking fine trot with his knees rising high and mane flowing.

It was as fine a thing as Harlan had seen in quite a while, to the point that he was almost sorry to see them leave.

Still, he had his work to do.

He waited until the storekeeper and his woman were well away, then rose to full height and brushed himself off.

It was time to get busy.

Chapter Forty-one

The side door was no problem at all. There was a lock but it was cheap junk, little better than pot metal. The front door, as Harlan had checked when he was in there to do his shopping earlier, was top-quality stuff that would defeat most burglars. But the side door was another matter entirely. Childishly so. Harlan simply selected a good-sized rock from the border of the flower bed beside the building, heaved it through a glass pane set into the door and reached inside. A twist of the wrist and the lock was open. He let himself in without a qualm.

He had to fumble around a bit to find his way in the living quarters toward the back of the building. There was a small vestibule where the family could deposit their coats and boots in winter. A lamp and block of lucifers was conveniently placed on a shelf above a washtub. Harlan found those mostly by feel. Quickly he peeled off a match, struck it on the bottom of the block and lighted the lamp. That was better.

The vestibule led into a kitchen and that to a tiny bedroom that smelled of some flowery scent. Woman stuff.

He had no interest in smelling a woman who was not close enough to touch, but the bedroom was definitely of interest. It was very likely that the storekeeper would keep his money there, a bedroom being the most intimate and protected room in any house.

Harlan poked through the drawers and rummaged

into a wardrobe that was hung full of women's clothing, all of it carrying that same scent of flowers. Lilac?
He thought maybe.

He found a small stash of loose coins among the
wife's things. He plucked out the few gold coins and
tossed the rest onto the unmade bed.

He tried on the storekeeper's sheepskin coat. It was
handsome but too small for comfort.

Finally, underneath a linen coverlet masquerading
as a side table, with a jewelry box and a lamp with a
painted globe on top, Harlan found what he was looking for, a Davis and Wilbourne Surety Co. safe.

He smiled. The D & W safes were impressive things,
with slabs of heavy black iron and bright gold pin-
striping much like that on the storekeeper's pretty
roadster. They carried three-tumbler combination
locks and weighed more than two strong men could
carry away.

But they did have one tiny flaw. The back panels
were cheap crap. Someone at the D & W factory was
cutting costs, it seemed.

Harlan laughed when he tipped the safe over onto
its face, lamp, jewelry box and all. The lamp broke,
spreading oil onto the floor and into an Oriental rug
lying beside the bed. If he'd wanted to torch the place
to hide his thefts . . . but no, that would be mean.

He carried his lighted lamp out into the store that
occupied the front half of the building. There were
some tools racked along the right-hand wall. He took
a mattock down and took it and the lamp back into
the bedroom.

One solid whack with the pointed end of the heavy
mattock was enough to give him a purchase point. He
used the flat end to prize up the light steel panel on
the back of the safe.

After that it was just a matter of reaching inside and taking what he wanted.

The money—it amounted to more than three hundred dollars in mixed gold and paper—went into the pockets of a duster that he took off the store shelves.

He also chose an only very slightly used .45 caliber Colt revolver and two boxes of cartridges, a 12-gauge shotgun, and one box of shells for that and some narrow leather strapping that he could use to hang the shotgun from his saddle. There was no gun belt for the revolver, but Harlan figured that was what God had made trouser waistbands for.

He found a gunnysack and put a few select foodstuffs into it, tinned sardines, soda crackers, ready ground coffee and the sugar and canned milk to smooth it out.

Hell, this was a fine way for a man to do his shopping.

He carried it all outside and carefully latched the door shut behind him.

"Thank you kindly," he said to the night sky as he swung into the saddle and headed off again at the big horse's slow, steady pace.

Chapter Forty-two

"He's sound but mind you that I don't gar-on-tee nothing. Go ahead an' ride him if you like. Take him down the road a piece an' back again. I think you'll find he has an easy way of going. Lope smooth as a rockin' chair, and you can see from the slant o' those shoulder bones, set just right at forty-five degrees, that his trot won't give you no headache. No sir, this here is one fine horse. Best I have in this here barn. I daresay he's the best I've seen in a long while."

Harlan tended to agree that the gray horse very likely was the best the horse trader had seen in some time. The animal had a delicate head but with wide nostrils to pull in air. That meant he likely had stamina. He had a good rump and wide chest. Short-coupled back. Small, expressive ears. Harlan always liked a horse that showed a man what it was thinking.

He had long since made up his mind to buy the gray, but of course he did not want the seller to know that.

"Mister, I dunno. Your price is awful steep for a impoverished ol' boy such as m'self."

"Forty dollars, friend. I can't go a penny less than that."

"I think . . . if he rides out sound, mind you . . . I think I could go thirty." Hell, Harlan would have paid a hundred if he had to. Especially now that there was the law after him, thinking he was the son of a bitch that murdered those folks. This gray looked like it could hold its own in a chase and there could come a time when that was the difference between living and dying. And living was sure worth a hundred dollars. Maybe even more.

"I couldn't go no thirty, mister."

"You got a saddle I can use? The bars on my McClellan is splayed out kinda wide from being on the big horse there."

"I think I can find an old one to strap on him."

Five minutes later Harlan was going down the road at a pleasant enough trot. Not so choppy as to rattle a man's teeth but not so springy that it suggested the horse was having to carry all the weight of horse and rider alike on sloping canon bones. It was Harlan's experience that a soft ride was often paid for in breakdowns of an animal's lower leg, and that was something he could get along without.

He touched the gray with his heel, and the horse lifted into a lope without having to be coaxed.

A squeeze of the knees and it pulled its ears back and commenced to run.

Harlan was grinning long before he turned the animal around and started back toward the sales barn.

He wiped the smile off his face when he got near and even managed a small, very slightly worried frown for the gentleman in the bib overalls. He stepped down out of the saddle, which was a damn sight more comfortable than any ball-busting McClellan, and dropped the reins.

Not that he trusted a so-called ground tie. Never. He figured no matter how much training had gone into a horse, a ground tied horse was still just a . . . loose horse.

For what it was worth, though, this one dropped its nose and gave a little shake to its head but did not offer to sidle away like many—most—would often do.

Yeah, this horse was worth something.

"The horse goes well enough," Harlan conceded. "I'm thinking if push comes to shove I could come up with another two dollars. Call it thirty-two."

"Thirty-six," the seller countered.

By then both of them pretty much knew where this would end up.

"Thirty-five," Harlan said, "and you throw in that saddle."

"What about your rig there? Are you thinking to make a swap?"

Harlan shook his head. "No, sir, I want to keep my brown for a pack animal. I'll use the McClellan too since I already got those bars mashed open a bit to accommodate the size o' him."

"Thirty-five cash money?"

"Ayuh. Cash money."

"Specie, not no paper?"

"If you like."

The horse trader stuck out his hand to shake on the bargain. "Friend, you got yourself a horse. Come inside an' we'll make out the bill o' sale. Then we can go over to the bank an' get it notarized. What name d'you want on it?"

"Earl Woods," Harlan said. "My name is Earl Woods."

"It's a pleasure, Mr. Woods."

Chapter Forty-three

Harlan was starting to feel like a real person again. He had some money in his pockets and proper weapons for when he ran up against that sonuvabitch other Harlan. He had a good horse and a fine pack animal. And a dog. Damned if he didn't kind of enjoy having the dog tagging along behind.

Best of all, though, most important of all, he had the bill of sale for the gray horse. That, written out to Earl Woods, would go a long way toward establishing his identity should anyone ask.

He rode into a small town that was more or less in the middle between farm country and ranch land. He had no idea what the place was called. Not unless it was named First Bank of Commerce.

Harlan rode past the bank with hardly a sideways glance. Without his boys along to help, he had no interest in bank robbery. And anyway there were other things that were much more pressing than picking up more cash. Like getting his own good name back. And like finding this murdering bastard other Harlan. And, come to think of it, like finding some way to turn that Harlan over to the law without bringing any of their shit down on him. That right there could be a problem, even assuming he did find the killer.

This day he went straight past the bank and drew rein at the wide alley that led through the center of the town's livery stable. An old man who had the look of a man who knew horseflesh was sitting on an upturned nail keg beside the entrance, a wad of tobacco in one cheek and a much-worn dime novel in his lap.

"Afternoon, son. What can I do for you today?"

"I'd like these two put up for a night or maybe two. I'll be wanting them grained as well as hay, and I'll be wanting a look at your hay before you fork any their way."

"You want them rubbed down and hoofs looked over?"

"No, sir, I'll do that my own self. It ain't that I don't trust you, just that some things a man wants to do for himself."

"It's a damn shame more young folks don't have that attitude. My price is thirty-five cents a head. That includes all the hay they can eat, which you are welcome to look over, of course, and a half gallon of mixed grain apiece per day. Without the grain it would be a quarter, if that's important to you."

"No, sir, the grain is more important to me than the dime would be. Two more questions then. Where do I put them and d'you mind if I dump my kak here while they're in your barn?"

The old fellow stood and it became apparent that he had one leg that did not point in the same direction as the other.

"I see you looking, son. This here happened on a drive up from the south of Texas back not too long after the war when they were still shipping Texas cattle out of east Kansas railheads. We got caught up in a lightning storm and the steers went to running. Us boys got after them and my horse ran smack into a coulee in the dark. Must've fell six or eight feet and came down right atop my leg here. We didn't have no doctor so the boys set the thing the best they could. This here is the result."

"You couldn't get it broke again and set proper?" Harlan asked.

The old boy shook his head. "They said not. Said by the time we got to a doctor the bone had growed together too well for that. Said it might break in a slightly different spot and end up worse than it is. Not that it matters now. I've learned to get along fine just the way it is. But that doesn't answer what you asked. Put your animals in the second stall along the left side there. Your gear, whatever of it you want to leave, you can pile over against the wall there. Mind though, there's mice and some rats around. If you got food along, and I'm assuming that you would, you might want to dig it out and let me take it inside. I got some tin-lined grain boxes that the varmints can't get into. I can put your grub in there until you want it again."

"That's mighty kind of you, sir. Now let me take a look at that hay and peek into your grain bin for a minute, then I expect I'll be unloading an' leaving things in your charge."

The old man nodded and stuck out his hand. "My name is Henry Dawson, son."

Harlan shook with him. "I'm Earl Woods, Mr. Dawson. I'm pleasured t' meet you."

"Say now," Harlan told the town's harness maker, "I just paid off from a job of work and there's something I been thinking on."

"Yes, sir?"

"Well, I been lugging this pistol gun around stuck in behind my belt, but that can be awful uncomfortable, especially when I set down. I been thinking that maybe I ought to buy me a holster. D'you got one that this thing would fit into?"

"Let me see it, if you don't mind."

Harlan took the Colt out of his waistband and handed it to the man. The harness maker was a heavyset fellow with curly side whiskers and small, delicate hands.

The man examined the revolver closely, measured the barrel length with his fingers, then laid the gun down on a piece of brown butcher paper. He took a stub of pencil and drew an outline of the pistol.

"I'm guessing you don't have anything in your shop that my gun would fit," Harlan said.

"No, but I can make something up for you easy enough. I can have it for you by midday tomorrow if you have the time to wait."

"I have the time," Harlan told him.

"Seventy-five cents for a plain holster. More if you want carving on it."

"No, no car . . . wait a minute. I would like some carving, I think. The initials E.W. Kind of fancy lettering, if you can do that."

"E.W., I can put anything on it that you want to pay for."

"The initials stand for Earl Woods."

The harness maker nodded. "E.W., it shall be then. Do you want the leather stained? Black would look good. Go with that hat you're wearing and make you look all together."

"I think I'd like that," Harlan said.

"With the carving and some stain and wax on top of it, I'll charge you a dollar for the whole works. Do you need a cartridge belt too?"

"No, sir, I've wore one of those once. They are heavy sons of bitches." Harlan shook his head. "Not for the likes o' me, I'm thinking. I'll just hang your holster on this belt I'm wearing right here."

"Then can I suggest a separate belt, at the least? You

put a holster onto the belt that holds your britches up, then you have to practically undress whenever you go into a place where you have to leave your pistol hanging. Like to church or a dance or in some towns or wherever. You might find it's easier to use a separate belt even if you don't put any cartridge loops onto it."

"That makes sense," Harlan conceded. "How much?"

"Another fifty cents and I'll stain it to match your holster."

"Dollar and a half total," Harlan said.

"That's right."

"An' the whole outfit will be ready tomorrow?"

"Ayuh. So it will."

"All right then."

"Let me measure your waist." The harness maker had a cloth tape marked out in inches like a dressmaker's measure. He took a wrap around Harlan's waist with it, grunted, and wrote the number down on the same piece of brown paper where he had drawn the outline of the revolver.

He handed the gun back and Harlan stuck it into his waistband again.

"No offense intended, but I'd like to get some money up front if you don't mind, seeing as how I don't know you."

"No offense taken. Now if you don't mind the question, would you happen to know if there's a whorehouse in town?"

The harness maker grinned. "Come out the back door here and I can point it out to you."

Chapter Forty-four

The place was not fancy but it was friendly enough. The madam was a fat woman wearing a curly blonde wig and a good pound and a half of powder on her face. But then with all that jowl, she had a lot of face that needed powdering.

"Come right in, darlin'. It's a little early for our kind of business, but you're welcome here, always welcome, come right in. I'm sure we can find a girl who will tickle your fancy."

Harlan stepped inside and removed his hat. There was a small parlor on his left, a closed door to the right and a hallway in the middle leading toward the back of the house. Other than the madam there was not a female in sight.

"What is it you have in mind today, darlin'?"

"Well, I just, uh, nothing special. A girl, that's all."

"Any particular sort of girl?"

"Oh, I dunno. A pretty girl. Long hair maybe. I'm partial to long hair."

"Black be all right?"

"The hair or the girl, d'you mean?"

"Either one actually. I got a Negro girl who helps around here and fills in for me when there's need or if a gentleman has a particular liking for that type of girl. Or I have a girl . . . she's on the skinny side, which some gentlemen don't like all that much, but she's pretty and she has long hair."

"Skinny is all right," Harlan said.

"My girls get fifty cents a throw. Same again if you want seconds."

"I'm thinking all night."

"That would be five dollars."

"Ma'am, it ain't seemly to argue over the price of a whore, but you've mistook me for a rich man." Harlan winked at her. "An' a stupid one too. All night should be two dollars. That's what I'll pay."

The fat woman did not seem at all offended by his bargaining. "All right. Two dollars but that won't include drinks. Will you be wanting anything to drink?"

"Sure, I'd like a bottle of whi—uh, make that a bucket of beer instead o' the whiskey." He was thinking about a certain other whorehouse experience that had left him broke and in jail. There would be no repeat of that, thank you very much. He would have his fun but had no intention of getting drunk this time. "And I'll want you to send out for a bit of supper too. I haven't had anything t' eat since early morning."

"Potatoes fried in bacon grease and hominy do for your supper?"

"Yes, ma'am. I ain't fussy."

"Then you can eat what my girls get for breakfast. Supper and the beer together will be another fifty cents. Or do you want to argue with me about that too?"

Harlan laughed. "No, ma'am. I'm sure that's fair." He dug into his pocket—not too deep as he did not want to give anyone here a reason to rob him like that other bitch had—and paid her.

"Come along then. I'll set you down to the table and you can have your supper while I go fetch Annie for you."

* * *

Harlan yawned and stretched. He sat upright and swung his legs off the side of the bed and reached for his trousers.

"Where you going, honey?"

"It sounds like folks are having fun out there. I thought you and me might go join them an' get us a drink." There were sounds of merriment drifting down the hallway from the parlor and someone had wound the player piano. "Put your dress on, girl. We'll go see what they're up to."

Harlan pulled on his shirt and began buttoning it, admiring Annie as he did so. She was not a bad-looking girl. The madam hadn't lied about that. She had silky black hair that came down to the small of her waist. Her eyes were perhaps a trifle too close together and she had slightly crooked teeth, but neither of those kept her from doing what she was paid to do and that was to do whatever pleased him. All night long.

She was, Harlan was discovering, a very agreeable girl. Flexible too.

Annie slipped into her kimono and tied the sash at her waist. Her hair shimmered in the lamplight when she tossed her head.

"Sit down, honey, so's I can help you with them boots." She knelt in front of him and reached for his boots, smiling all the while. Yes sir, he did like this girl.

Once they were both presentable Annie led Harlan out, closing the room door behind her and leaving a little carved wood medallion hanging on the outside of the door to indicate it was still in use. "This way, honey."

The parlor was not as full as the noise suggested. There were two men there and four girls, two of whom were sitting in the men's laps while one sat at the player piano and the fourth tried to sing along without actually knowing the words that went with the tune.

"Can I get you a drink, honey? It costs two bits extra if you want something. We got whiskey and brandy and wine here, but if you want more beer we got to send for it."

"Whiskey would be fine. One for you too, if you like."

He gave her fifty cents for the drinks. Annie handed twenty-five of it back. "I'll have a strawberry soda. That doesn't cost us girls nothing. Sit here now. I'll be right back with your whiskey." She got Harlan comfortably settled, gave him a smile and a mimed kiss and disappeared into the kitchen.

Out in the vestibule a bell tinkled, and a moment later he could hear the madam leave her lair and go to the door.

Harlan could not hear what was said at the front door but after a moment the madam appeared in the parlor entry with a tall man on her arm. The newcomer had a huge mustache, a Santa Fe–style broad-brimmed hat, and wore a pair of very large revolvers, one in a holster on his right hip and the other rigged for a crossdraw to the left of his belt buckle.

The fellow also wore a very large polished steel badge on his chest.

Harlan's heart dropped into the toes of his boots when he saw the madam point straight at him. He could not hear the woman's voice but he did not need to. He could plainly see her mouth: "That's him over there."

The lawman strode across the small room and stopped immediately in front of Harlan.

Chapter Forty-five

Son of a bitch!

Harlan's revolvers, both the .45 and the piece-of-shit .32, were back in the room where he had been sporting with Annie.

If they had been where they belonged, he would have damn sure made a try for a gun. He was no fast-draw artist, but at least with a gun he would have a chance. Against a hangman's rope there was no chance at all.

"I'm Marshal Julius Brandt, son. I heard there was a stranger passing through. Earl Wood, is it?"

"I, uh, Earl Woods, actually. With an s," Harlan corrected.

Brandt nodded as if he had known that all along and was just testing Harlan when he'd mispronounced the name. "Henry Dawson over at the livery mentioned you to me. Said you've been traveling some."

"That's right."

"Before I forget, Henry said that big horse needs both back shoes replaced and the front two reset. He can do the work but it will cost you two dollars and a half."

"Then I'd best have the work done," Harlan said.

"The saddle horse's feet are in better condition. Henry looked that one over too. Said he doesn't need anything."

"Thank you, Marshal. I'll get word to Mr. Dawson in the morning that I'll be wanting him to do that for me."

"That isn't why I dropped by to have a word with you though, Mr. Woods."

"I kinda thought it wouldn't be."

"The thing is, out on the road like you've been, you may have heard something about the murders and the rapes that have been taking place in this part of the country lately."

"I sure have," Harlan told him. "Killed an entire family over by Dowdville. Matter of fact, that's why I'm traveling. I'm looking for the man. There's a three-hunnerd dollar ree-ward out on 'im. I aim to collect it."

"More than that at this point," Brandt said. "More reward money . . . it's up around seven hundred the last I heard . . . and more murders too. Three folks dead over near Water Oak Crossing. Another two in Carter County. Mind you, we don't know the same man killed all of them as there were no witnesses left alive to tell the tale, but it seems likely. This is not a violent country. Not since those Texas cattle drovers stopped coming to this end of the state. That plus the fact that all the killings seem to have taken place much the same way. Close up, using a small-caliber revolver."

Harlan reminded himself to ditch the .32 the first chance he got. If someone—this town marshal, for instance—wanted to check him over, he did not want that sorry little excuse for a gun to point fingers at him.

"What I was wondering, Mr. Woods, is have you seen or heard anything that you might consider suspicious?"

"Marshal, if I did have any suspicions about anyone, they would've been marched to the nearest jail and turned over to the law. Like I told you, I want that reward money. I do figure to put it into my pocket. No, sir, I have not seen or heard anything. Do you know anything about what this killer looks like? Anything you can tell me that would help me find him and know him when I see him?"

"They actually had him behind bars at one point, Mr. Woods. Marshal Hugh Glass had him in on a drunk and disorderly charge."

"They had him and just let him go? Didn't they know who they had?"

"Not exactly. They identified him as the killer and were holding him for the Corleigh County authorities to come transport him back to Dowdville for trial, but he escaped. He got the best of a kindhearted jailer, the way I heard it. Beat the poor man senseless and took off running."

"He didn't kill the jailer?"

"They say the only reason that man lived was because this son of a bitch Breen didn't want to alert the town with a gunshot. Otherwise the jailer would have been dead for sure."

"That makes sense. What description do you have for him?"

"Nothing new, if that's what you mean." Marshal Brandt proceeded to give a reasonably accurate description of Harlan, down to and including the boots he had been wearing when he made his escape.

It amazed him that the marshal, who seemed to be sharp enough, could stand here face to face with the man he was hunting and not have any inkling about who "Earl Woods" really was.

But then generally speaking, a man was who he said he was. And if he wanted to change his name and go under some other, well, he was perfectly entitled to do that.

"When I find this Harlan Breen fella, Marshal, if he happens t' be somewhere around here, can I turn him over to you or do I have t' haul him all the way back to Dowdville?"

"You can turn him over to any law enforcement agency in the state. County sheriff or town marshal, that won't matter. The important thing is to get the man in custody again so he can stand trial."

"But the reward will be paid whether he's brought in dead or alive, is that right, Marshal?"

"That is exactly right, Mr. Woods. Not, you understand, that I countenance any man taking the law into his own hands. Execution should be a matter for a jury to decide. But if you have to kill him, don't think twice about it. A man who would rape a girl and murder an entire family so he can have her, a man like that does not deserve much in the way of the normal considerations. If you, um, understand what I mean, Mr. Woods."

Oh, Harlan understood that well enough to send a chill up his spine. Now that he had escaped once, even the lawmen around here did not really want to take a chance on him freeing himself a second time. No one would think a thing about it if someone recognized him and decided to simply gun him down. Hell, they would even celebrate the event. Another bad man bites the dust.

Except in this case the bad man would be an innocent Harlan Breen and the dust in his mouth would be bitter indeed.

He had done a heap of crimes in his time. But never that. Never murder. Never rape.

Brandt touched the brim of his sombrero and sauntered away to talk with the other customers taking their leisure in the parlor. Harlan turned to Annie and said, "Talk like that takes me out o' the mood for partying. Let's you and me go back to your room."

The girl took him by the hand and led him back the way they had come. As soon as they got there, Harlan waited until Annie's back was turned and retrieved the little .32 from under the pillow, where he had stashed it along with his .45. He slipped the little gun into his pocket and said, "Before we get back to what we was doing a while ago, I wanta make a trip to the outhouse. How do I get to it?"

"There's a thunder mug under the bed that you can use, honey."

"No, I want the outhouse if you don't mind."

The girl gave him a very small smile. Obviously she had learned over the years to be cautious about exposing her bad teeth. "I'll take you, honey. Come with me."

No one was likely to dig around in the cesspit for a small pistol, Harlan figured, and that was exactly where the .32 was going just as soon as he could get it there.

Chapter Forty-six

The desk clerk used a forefinger to push his glasses higher onto his nose. He bent over his calculations, moving his lips slightly as he figured. Then he straightened upright with a broad smile. "That comes to forty-six dollars and, um, fifty cents, Mr. Jarrett."

The smile disappeared, to be replaced by acute consternation. "Surely that can't be right. You weren't here but two and a half . . . now I see the problem. The monthly rate on that particular room is thirty-six dollars. Even. So it would only be fair to charge you for the month even though your stay has been shorter. I, uh, do hope your time with us has been pleasant, sir."

"It has been fine," Jarrett said. It was not entirely a lie. The room had been marginally acceptable. It was the town that was lacking. And of course he had been upset by the length of time it had taken for his money to come in.

Imagine. Western Union had not had sufficient cash on hand to pay out the transfer from back home. They'd given him a draft, the cheeky devils, and obligated him to go to the bank to convert the draft into cash.

Fortunately all of that was behind him now. Jarrett laid three gleaming new twenty-dollar pieces on the desk and said, "Please distribute the excess to your cleaning staff."

"Why, that is most generous, Mr. Jarrett. Very generous indeed."

"Have your boy fetch my buggy around, will you,

and load my luggage into it. I shall be having my
breakfast. I expect everything to be ready by the time
I am done."

"Yes, Mr. Jarrett. Indeed, sir."

Jarrett stepped into the hotel dining room, which,
like the room, was only marginally acceptable. He removed his dove gray, broad-brimmed planter's hat—
an affectation he had adopted during his travels, although there was no hint of the South in his accent or
tone of voice—and draped it on one of the arms of the
clothes tree beside the entrance.

It was already well past the normal hour for breakfast but he did not usually care to rise early. And this
way he did not have to take his meals in the company
of strangers.

He made his way across the room and took what he
had come to regard as *his* chair.

A small woman, probably not yet out of her teens,
with stringy hair and a mottled complexion, poked her
head out of the spring-loaded double doors leading
into the kitchen. She smiled when she saw him. "Good
morning, Mr. Jarrett."

"Good morning, Junie."

"Will you be having your usual this morning, sir?"

"No, not today. I shall be traveling today so I want
something more substantial. A breakfast steak, I think,
cooked medium well. Fried potatoes. And, um, three
eggs soft poached. Soft, mind you, or I'll be sending
them back."

"Yes, sir. I know how you like them."

"So you do, Junie. So you do."

The girl leaned over the table to pour Jarrett's coffee. The position stretched the cloth of her shirtwaist
and apron tight over her breasts, and Jarrett felt himself growing hard as he imagined what Junie's breasts

would look like. And how she would scream if he had the opportunity to slice them off. How her tears would flow and mucus run from her nose.

The fantasy made his breath come quick and shallow.

"Mr. Jarrett? Sir? Are you all right, sir?"

"Hmm? I . . ." He smiled. "Just fine, Junie. Thank you for asking."

The girl finished pouring the coffee and helpfully set a heavy cut glass sugar bowl within easy reach and an inelegant but useful can of tinned milk beside it. "Your breakfast will be just a few minutes, sir."

"That's fine, Junie. Just fine."

He watched her walk away. No hip sway. He wondered if that was deliberate, a way to avoid encouraging the dining-room patrons who might want overly much familiarity.

Jarrett wondered what Junie would think if she knew about his thoughts. Probably she had no concept of pleasures such as his.

But, oh my, it had been too long. Entirely too long.

He yearned for another . . . partner. Someone who would fulfill his every desire. One who would endure and not expire too quickly.

Some died almost before he had a chance to properly begin. Their hearts failed them, he supposed. He always regretted that. It seemed such a waste.

But . . . the next one. He was convinced of it. The next one would be the one he had been searching for. The next one would be his perfect partner.

All of a sudden he was anxious to get breakfast over with so he could get on the road again in search of the perfect girl to fill his need.

"Junie!"

"Yes, Mr. Jarrett?"

"I've changed my mind about breakfast. I want you to pack me a picnic brunch that I can take with me in my buggy."

"But your steak is already cooked. It's . . ."

"That's fine, Junie. Put it between two slices of bread or stuff it inside a roll. I can take it with me. But be quick about it, please. I'm in a hurry to get on now."

"Yes, sir. As you say, sir."

Jarrett could hardly sit still as he waited on the food to be brought to him. The buggy should already be out front, waiting for him.

And the whole wide world was open to him.

Chapter Forty-seven

Harlan woke up with a foul taste in his mouth. He had no idea what the time might be, but there was daylight beyond the thick cloth draped over the one tiny window. His head ached from too much liquor and his tongue . . . he really did not want to remember what that tongue had been up to last night. This morning. Whatever.

He sat up and winced, too many bad horses and hard knocks leaving their imprint on his joints.

Beside him Annie was still asleep. She snored. And she smelled kind of ripe.

For that matter, so did he.

He yawned and scratched and when he stood up he passed wind. But he felt better as he came more awake.

He supposed he was entitled to a morning tumble if he wanted one, but . . . looking at the girl, sweaty hair plastered tightly to her head and a bare hip that looked like a lump of suet, he was just not in the mood for it. Maybe later but not right now. He reached for his clothes and quickly dressed, pulled on his boots and stuffed the .45 into his waistband.

The .32, thank goodness, was safely disposed of in the stinking slop under the fat madam's outhouse.

He debated with himself for a moment, then reached into his pocket and fetched out a Mexican dollar. He laid that on the pillow beside Annie's head—she really had been an agreeable girl—and reached for his hat.

No one else seemed to be moving at this not-so-early hour, so Harlan let himself out the front door. The dog was lying stretched across the stoop, waiting for him. It looked up and wagged its tail when Harlan came outside.

"Come along, fella. Let's go get us some breakfast. Or lunch. Whichever."

He stopped first at the livery.

"Mornin', Mr. Woods. The marshal said I should go ahead and take care of the big horse's feet. Is that right?"

"Yes 'tis, Mr. Dawson."

The old man turned his head and spat a stream of brown juice, which landed on a half-dried horse apple.

"Good shot," Harlan said.

The hostler smiled. "Years of practice."

"What do I owe you for the work you've done so far and, I think, for another night's board?"

"Two and a half for the trim and the shoes. Seventy cents for the board. That comes to, uh . . ."

"Three twenty," Harlan put in for him.

"Right. That's right."

Harlan paid his bill and walked down the block to a likely looking cafe. He stuck his head inside the door and asked, "Are you still serving breakfast?"

A thick-bodied woman with dark hair and a hint of mustache said, "If that's what you want to eat, hon, that's what I'll fix for you."

"Can the dog come in too?"

"Sure. Most dogs are nicer than most people anyway. What's his name?"

"It's, um, Junior," Harlan said, improvising quickly. He hadn't given any thought to a name for the dog, not until that moment. Probably it had had a name at some time but there was no way Harlan could know what it might have been.

"You haven't eaten but how about him?"

"Nope. He hasn't either."

"Then set yourself down, mister. I'll get to you in a minute. First I have to give Junior something to eat. Does he like eggs?"

Now how the hell was he supposed to know that? Except of course Junior was supposed to be his own dog. "He likes eggs right well," Harlan declared.

"I have some here getting cold. Asshole said they were too hard. Said he wouldn't eat them and wouldn't pay for them neither. Huh! I ran his butt outa here. But I still got those eggs."

She took down a steel plate, piled four eggs on it, and then crumbled up some toast to serve with it. She added some scraps of ham and an only slightly scorched flapjack and set the plate down to Junior.

The dog liked eggs.

"Now, mister, what would you like?"

Chapter Forty-eight

Harlan felt much better with a hot meal nestled behind his belt buckle. Damn near human, in fact.

He spotted a barber's striped pole in the next block over from the cafe and headed for it. He had the inner man taken care of. It was time to do something about the outside.

"There's about a half hour wait ahead of you," the barber announced when Harlan came inside. The barber was a lean man wearing a white shirt, string tie and a spanking clean apron. He had gray in his hair but huge jet black eyebrows. His customers, Harlan noticed, did not look as if they had been butchered.

"Tell you what then. I need t' go find me a clean shirt an' whatnot so's I won't have to put these nasty things back on again when I get cleaned up. Hold my place here, if you would. I'll go down the block and see what I can find in the way of fixings."

"You'll be wanting a bath too, then?"

"Yes, sir, I will."

"I'll put more water in the boiler and have it hot and ready when you get here."

Harlan touched the brim of his hat by way of a salute and backed out of the place, almost stepping on Junior in the process. "Watch yourself, boy. We're goin' this way down here."

There was a men's haberdashery across the street, but Harlan did not want anything that fancy. Besides, a necktie would only remind him of a hangman's noose and he would rather avoid those.

He followed the directions given to him by a gent he passed on the street, and instead of the proper haberdashery settled for a general mercantile two blocks over.

"Got some sturdy clothes I might look at?" he asked the woman behind the counter.

"You have to leave the dog outside."

"Yes, ma'am."

"I won't stand for having any of those filthy things in my place, so get him out of here if you please, and be quick about it."

"No, ma'am, I understand," Harlan said, "an' I agree with you. I wouldn't want Junior in here neither. He might catch some disease in this stinking shithole."

Harlan spun around, Junior close on his heels, and headed off to see if he could locate another mercantile in town.

"I think this one should fit you. Turn around, please."

"What . . . ?"

"Please. Just turn. I need to hold the shirt up against your back."

"Lordy, I couldn't wear nothing as pretty as that," Harlan objected.

"Trust me. Once you feel this fabric on your body you'll never go back to wool or coarse linen. Here. Feel it."

"It's damn sure soft enough, but will it wear? I got t' have clothes that will hold up to a lotta use."

"Trust me. This will wear like iron but feel like heaven."

"If you say so." The shirt had pearl buttons and fancy stitching and long cuffs and looked like it belonged on someone in Buffalo Bill Cody's Wild West show, rather than a plain old robber from Texas.

"Good. Now about your trousers . . ."

Half an hour later Harlan had a paper-wrapped package tucked under his arm. He would carry the new things with him to the barbershop and dress only when he was clean and fresh. The clothes he was wearing now had been on his body—well, except for a few very pleasant hours—since before he'd been tossed into Marshal Hugh Glass's jail. This haberdashery stuff wasn't so bad after all, he had long since concluded. The clothes looked good. They fit. And a man got waited on like they were glad to have his business. He decided he was glad he had come in, even if he was going to look like a dude once he got into the new togs.

He accepted his change from the clerk—Daniel, he'd said his name was—and started for the door, then stopped again when he noticed the tall rack just to the left of the doorway.

"Those hats," he said. "Do you think . . . ?"

The beat-up old Kossuths he had been wearing for years had a purpose when he was robbing. So many men wore them that they were not really remarkable. But dammit, if he were going to be a peacock from his ears down, it only made sense that he put a proper hat on top of his head.

"Try this one on for size first," Daniel said, quickly appearing at Harlan's side once the likelihood of another sale showed itself. "These are all four-x grade beaver felt. They will hold up to any weather. And they will take any shape you want. Montana peak. Cattleman's crease. Whatever you like. First we will find a hat in the size that fits and a color you like. Then I will steam it and shape the crown for you. I can have it ready by the time you finish at

Stan's barbershop."

"How 'bout that," Harlan marveled. "Now that's damn sure service."

"We're glad to do it, believe me."

"And how much does one o' these here hats cost?"

"Twelve dollars and fifty cents will buy you any one of them, and the price includes shaping."

It took longer for him to select a hat than it had for him to buy the entire rest of his new outfit, but in the end he was mightily pleased. Despite all the money that had passed through his hands over the years, Harlan had never before had a hat this fine.

Why, he was beginning to feel like quite the dandy. "I'll see you when I'm done across the way," he said, after he paid for his new hat.

"And what initials would you like us to put in the sweatband?" Daniel asked.

"Initials?"

"It is a service we provide to our gentlemen. No charge, of course."

"You ink them in?"

"No, *sir*!" Daniel sounded indignant at the very idea. "We use stamping tools to emboss the initials into the leather. What may we put in your hat?"

"My, uh, my name is Earl Woods. So, um, E.W. would be just fine."

"Very good, Mr. Woods." Daniel's smile was broad. "I will try to have everything ready for you when you are done at Stan's shop."

"Thank you, Daniel. I didn't think I'd ever say such a thing, but I'm mighty glad I stepped in here a while ago."

Daniel seemed in very good spirits when Harlan excused himself and headed toward the barbershop again.

Chapter Forty-nine

Harlan felt like an entirely new man when he stepped out onto the street wearing all new clothes—top-quality duds at that—and a brand-new dove gray hat with his initials—well, they were *supposed* to be his initials—stamped into the sweatband. He had even had his boots blacked while he was in the bathtub.

His hair was cut and combed nice and fresh, and he practically reeked of Pinaud Clubman cologne. He still had his whiskers though. He'd had the barber trim all the spiky hairs from close around his mouth and underneath his nose—those bothered him to no end—but he had decided not to shave. He wasn't sure a beard would do him much good as a disguise, but it was worth a try. After all, there were folks who knew him as Harlan Breen. Those people might be right confused to hear he was Earl Woods nowadays. Earl Woods with a beard, that is.

If only the damn thing would quit itching. He had heard others tell that the itching only lasted four or five days. He surely hoped so. Otherwise he might claw his own throat open from scratching and bleed to death right where he lay.

Harlan adjusted the set of his handsome new hat and ambled over to the harness maker's shop, the dog following at his heels.

"Good afternoon, sir. Can I help you?"

"I've come for my holster if it's ready."

"What hol . . . say, are you the gentleman I talked to yesterday?"

Harlan chuckled. "Aye. That'd be me."

"You sure don't look like the same person but I guess I should have remembered that dog that's with you." The man laughed. "All that from just one visit to a whorehouse? I'd best get over there myself and see what they're serving. If I can get away from my wife for a few hours, that is."

"About my holster?"

"Oh, it's all done. Looks good too. It isn't a match for your hat anymore, but black goes good with gray too. I have it right here."

The harness maker reached underneath his sales counter and produced the shiny black belt and holster. The initials E.W. were carved into the leather in a script so curly it took Harlan a moment to see what the letters were.

"You do nice work," he said.

"Thank you, Mr. Woods. I'm glad you like it." He handed the rig to Harlan, who slipped his .45 out of his waistband and pushed it into the holster. It fit perfectly. Snug but not tight.

"I took the liberty of adding a safety thong you can keep over the hammer to make sure you won't lose your gun if your horse gets into a storm. You didn't say anything about that so I took a chance. I hope you approve."

"Sure. I should've thought to mention it myself." Harlan was not fast to draw and never had to worry about speed with a gun anyway. After all, he always had ample time to remove a safety thong before walking into a bank or a store.

Harlan strapped the rig around his waist. Swiveled back and forth. Rose onto tiptoe and banged down again. Moved the holster forward a little, then back. Finally he grunted, satisfied.

"All right?" the harness maker asked.

"Just fine," Harlan assured him. "Sure beats stuffing the thing down my pants. I don't owe you anything more, do I?"

"No, sir, you settled up yesterday. I haven't forgotten."

Harlan winked at him. "Neither have I." He extended his hand to shake and said, "I thank you for a good job. It's a right comfortable outfit."

The harness maker turned and pointed to a sign on the wall that said: IF YOU ARE SATISFIED TELL YOUR FRIENDS; IF YOU DO NOT LIKE OUR WORK TELL US.

Harlan touched the brim of his brand-new dove gray hat, adjusted the set of the pistol on his hip one more time and ambled out into the street again.

It would not be a completely bad idea, he thought, to get another bite to eat at that same cafe—call it a late lunch or maybe an early supper—and then head back to the whorehouse for another tussle with Annie.

"Come along, Junior." He slapped his thigh and the dog trotted along with him.

Chapter Fifty

Oh, it felt fine to be out on the road again. Harlan Jarrett clucked softly to his horse and spanked it with the driving lines. The animal increased its pace only a little, so Jarrett took the whip out of its socket and cracked it above the horse's ears. That did the trick. The animal picked up into an easy trot.

After all, they had miles to cover. And Jarrett was anxious to find a suitable location to exercise what he had come to think of as his peculiarity.

He smiled as he passed an empty field. And then another. The fewer houses, the better he liked it. He did not like to see neighbors close to the homesteads that were worth investigating.

An hour later he judged he had come a good seven miles from the town that had so delayed his travels. Things were better now, though. He had money in his pockets. The horse was rested and ready to travel. And Harlan himself was more than ready for more of that peculiarity.

He was passing large fields now, much larger than he was accustomed to seeing. They were full of some sort of stubble, suggesting that a crop had already been harvested despite the time of year. Jarrett had no idea what the crop might have been. He was not really very familiar with farming. Nor with ranching, for that matter.

He did value certain of the arts though. Writing, for instance. He very highly valued the writings of a

Frenchman from the previous century, the Marquis de Sade. He had collected most of the marquis's works and would buy more if only he could find them.

He had an interest in photography. One of these days he expected to take up the art of photography himself.

The thought of being able to capture images of his next . . . playmate . . . He felt himself stir and grow hard merely at the thought.

Oh, he had his memories. Of course he could remember each and every one of his partners. But to be able to see them again. End stage tableaux perhaps, carefully arranged and committed to photographic plates. Possibly even a sort of performance art, the photographs captured while the partner still lived. And still bled.

Now wouldn't that be something?

There might be a problem with the storage and transporting of the heavy glass plates. Surely he would want a great many poses showing each individual. And just as surely he looked forward to sharing his interests with a great many young women in the months and the years to come.

He would like to photograph them all.

What he needed to do, Jarrett concluded, was to exchange this light buggy for a larger, heavier wagon. A coach perhaps. And two horses to pull it.

Even so, the weight of that many plates was very likely to be a limitation. And it would not be possible to store the plates anywhere outside his direct control.

No, he thought, the better idea would be for him to capture the images onto the plates, print those images onto treated paper—that was possible nowadays—and then destroy the plates. He could easily keep and store the paper images. Those should not take up much space or add significantly to the overall weight of his coach.

He still would need a coach, though, in order to transport the camera, chemicals and other supplies required for successful photography.

At the next opportunity, he decided, he would seek a trade for such a coach. And he would look into the photography too. He would need the equipment but that was no problem. That was simply a matter of buying whatever was needed.

Determining what was needed . . . that was the problem.

Perhaps he could find a photographic studio in the next town he came to. Or in the one after that. Whatever.

The point was that he could pay the photographer to instruct him in the art and the science of his craft. Why, the man might even be induced to sell his entire equipment.

Yes!

Harlan Jarrett was doubly excited now. By the prospect of finding another playmate very, very soon and by the idea of being able to photograph the result of his encounters. He could have photographs to keep and to cherish. Photographs that he could look back on in great, unfading detail through the days and the nights when he lacked a subject for his desires.

Jarrett could scarcely contain himself. He was practically aquiver as he turned off the road into a lane leading to a ranch or farmhouse not far away. He could see the roofline peeking over a low rise in the ground.

There had to be someone living there.

With luck there would be someone for Harlan Jarrett to play long and happily with, before the screams finally faded away and she died.

Chapter Fifty-one

It felt good to be on the road again, never mind that Harlan Breen had no idea in hell where he should be going next.

It seemed he was learning something now that he probably should have guessed before but had not. That simple but terribly important fact was that every man had his own range of abilities, and expertise in one area did not signify a damn thing when it came to something else.

Harlan considered himself to be a pretty good robber. A superior robber even. He had been living high off the highwayman's trade for several years now. Knew how to do it and liked the doing.

But murder. Rape. He did not know shit about those things. Never had and never wanted to.

Now he was free. He was moving. But he did not have the first lousy idea where he should go now and what he should do.

Almost without conscious thought he found himself choosing south-leading paths whenever he came to a fork or a crossroads.

There was nowhere he could really call home but the Indian Nations were as close as anything these days. The territories of the Five Civilized Tribes was where he and the boys liked to spend their leisure time between jobs. It was a sanctuary where they were not wanted. Were careful not to pull any robberies down there, no matter how fat and tempting the targets.

Harlan had a half-formed notion that if he could find his boys and get them working on this with him, he might be able to come up with that son of a bitch other Harlan.

Just exactly how they would be able to do this . . . he did not have that quite worked out just yet.

However, lacking any better plan, this one would have to do.

Once he realized which way he was unconsciously guiding the gray, he made up his mind to do it in earnest.

Two days later he rode up to Charlie Alligator's trading post and dismounted. He unsaddled the gray, rubbed it down with a handful of straw, checked its feet and turned it loose in Charlie's corral, then shifted his attention to the plow horse he had stolen back in Missouri. He pulled the pack off its back and gave it a rubdown too. It pleased him to see that the ribs that had been so prominent when he'd acquired the horse no longer stood out like the slats on a xylophone, and the horse was not so stumble-footed as it had been either. Harlan was gladder than ever that he had taken the horse. He could not abide any son of a bitch who would mistreat an animal.

He turned the big brown creature into the pen also and forked a generous measure of hay into the bunk. There was already water in the trough but he worked the pump handle a few licks to add some fresh to what was already there, then chirruped to the dog and headed for Charlie's store.

"Hey, you ugly damn redskin, what d'you got to eat around here?" Harlan called out as he went in.

"You give me any lip, paleface, I'll have fried white man's liver on the menu," Charlie Alligator snapped back at him.

The two men glared at each other for a moment, then burst into smiles. "I would've thought they'd have hanged you by now, Harlan. Lucky you got back to the Nations before some Kansas lawman caught up with you, but don't think you're home free. You hungry?"

"I could eat a horse. Come to think of it, considerin' the way you are, whatever you serve might damn well be horsemeat."

"I got stew, or if you'd rather, you could have stew. That's if you're in a hurry. If you don't mind waiting a bit for the skillet to heat up I could cut you a steak."

"Cow?"

"Deer. Got a nice doe hanging in the spring house."

"How's about a bowl of stew for me an' another for my friend here." Harlan gestured toward the dog. "We'll have those while you cook us a steak."

"I can handle that." Charlie turned and shouted something in his own tongue—whatever that one was—then took two bowls down off a shelf. The stew was in a large pot on the potbelly stove, which showed the bright red of flame behind the door. Harlan had not thought it cool enough to justify a fire, but now that he was indoors he had to admit that the heat felt good. "Just one spoon, or does your friend use one too?" Alligator shoved a large spoon into one bowl and handed both to Harlan.

Harlan set down one bowl for the dog, then leaned against Charlie's counter and dug into the other bowl. "Good," he mumbled around the first mouthful. "Your old woman always could cook."

"Ugly as she is, you knew she had to be good for something," Charlie said with a twinkle in his eye.

His wife, Conception, was half his age and mighty good-looking. She became pregnant often enough but had never managed to carry children to full term. Charlie did not mind that. He had a flock of children by his other wives, but Conception went into deep funks about it every now and then.

"What do you hear?" Harlan asked, once his first bowl of stew had been deposited behind his belt buckle.

"I hear there's people after your white ass," Charlie said. "Murder, or so they say."

"Folks say a lot of things. That don't make them true."

Alligator grunted. "I ain't surprised. Murder, well maybe, especially if somebody gave you trouble during a robbery. But rape? I heard that too and it ain't easy to believe. You can be hard on whores, Harlan, but I never knew you to mess with a decent woman."

"I never have an' don't figure to."

"I wondered," Alligator conceded.

Harlan picked up the dog's empty dish and set both bowls onto the counter. "Got any idea where my boys are?" he asked.

"Not now I don't. Danny Hopwell and Little Jim Toomey came by a week or two ago. Said they was gonna go meet up with Carl Adamley and think about plans for the future."

"They said anything about me?"

"You wouldn't want to hear exactly what it was that was said. Point is, they don't want the kind of grief that you'd bring with you now. They'll be going off on their own from now on."

There went Harlan's notion about putting his gang together and getting them to help him find this other Harlan and clear his name.

"I expect you'll be moving south before long," Charlie offered.

"Should I?"

"Might be a good idea. There's a reward out for you, you know. Three, maybe four of them. They tote up to a pretty good amount. That's up in Kansas. The worse news, if you want it, is that now there's a federal warrant out for your arrest. Those asshole deputies riding out of Parker's court have got some sort of extra . . . extra . . ."

"Extradition?"

"That's it. What you said. Anyway, they're carrying paper on you, or so I hear. Any of them comes across you or anybody wants to collect a fee for turning them onto you, you'll be a dead man, Harlan. If they don't shoot you down for a dog right to begin with, they'll hang your ass quick enough once they got the 'cuffs on you."

"Shit!" Harlan frowned. "You, uh . . . you didn't, uh . . ."

"Naw. You an' me go back too long for me to do that. I ain't saying I couldn't be tempted, but this has been a pretty good year. I'm not hurting for money, not so bad that I'd turn in a friend for a lousy reward." Charlie Alligator grinned. "Of course, if the reward gets big enough, watch your ass."

Harlan did not know if Alligator was serious about that or not. He knew that he did not want to stay here long enough to push the issue. "Do me a favor?" he asked.

"Put the word out, Charlie. See if you can come up with any information about any fresh murders. The stinking law is all looking for me, so I figure to see can I do anything about finding the fellow who's been doing those rapes an' murders."

"Do you know who you're looking for?"

"I know that one place he said his name was Harlan. That's what got me in trouble."

Alligator pursed his lips and whistled. "That's not a common name, Harlan."

"Tell me about it."

"I'll ask around. Do you figure to stay here until I know something?"

"Not no way. There's too many people down here could recognize me an' a fair number of them might want that reward money more than they want my handshake."

"But you'll come back?"

"Yeah. I'll come back."

"All right then, Harlan. I'll put the word out, like you said."

"Thanks, Charlie."

"What can I do for you in the meantime?"

"I'll have that steak for starters. Then I'd like to buy a few things. A good serape if you got one. A packsaddle. I been making do with a broken-down old McClellan, but I need a packsaddle. An' of course some eatables, since I don't know yet where I'm going or how long it will take me to get there."

"You got money?"

"A little bit. Not much."

"You need ammunition?"

"No sir, there's only one man I figure to kill an' I got enough to bring him down, I think."

"All right then. Tell me what-all you want and I'll get it ready while you go in the back and have that steak Conception is cooking for you."

Harlan headed behind the curtain that served to separate the store from the Alligator family's living quarters. The dog got up and followed close at his heels.

Chapter Fifty-two

"Mr. Walking Bear?"

Walking Bear nodded. He was of middle years, with deep furrows lining his face and hair that shined with grease. His long hair was tied back with a beaded thong. His skin was dark mahogany. He looked every inch a warrior despite wearing ordinary shirt and trousers.

"Who are you?"

"My name is Earl Woods. Charlie Alligator suggested you might be able to help me."

"What you need, Earl Woods?"

"A bill of sale. I, uh, I lost the original bill of sale for my old pack horse and I need another to replace it."

The Indian grunted. "Two dollar. Advance."

"Charlie said it would only be one dollar."

"Two. Advance."

"Charlie said . . ."

"You want that paper you pay me five dollar."

"But you said . . ."

"I see you before. Down to Anadarko one time. You want name Earl Woods on paper I will write it, but you are Harlan Breen and you are wanted man. Five dollar. Advance."

"All right, dammit. Five dollars."

"You have horse already?"

"Yes, I have the horse. I'm not looking to get the paper and then go steal one to match it."

"Show me." Walking Bear got up from his rocking

chair and reached for a cane. Only then did Harlan notice that the man's left leg was twisted and nearly useless. He hobbled to the door and out onto the porch.

"Good horse. Handsome," Walking Bear said, eyeing the gray.

"Aye, but it's this one I need paper on. I already got a proper bill of sale for that one."

Walking Bear grunted. He slowly made his way around behind the brown. On his way back inside he said, "I got notary stamps from Chautauqua County, Kansas; Grayson County, Texas or Butler County, Ohio. Where you say you buy that horse?"

"Texas, I think."

"You buy it from?"

"Oh, uh, I bought the horse from a man name of, um, Jonathon Quill. And don't forget. My name is Earl Woods."

"How long ago?"

Harlan shrugged. "Couple months, I suppose. That should do."

"Pay now. Come back tomorrow past noon. I will have your paper ready for you."

"All right. Tomorrow." Harlan dug into his pocket and came out with a fistful of coins. He selected a five-dollar gold half eagle and handed it to Walking Bear, who examined the coin closely before he dropped it into his shirt pocket. "Tomorrow," the Indian said.

Harlan was pleased enough to get out of there. There was something about Walking Bear that he did not like. But he needed that bill of sale, dammit.

Chapter Fifty-three

Harlan waited until well past noon before he returned to Walking Bear's shanty.

He dismounted and tied the gray's reins to the wheel of a decrepit farm wagon. The brown was already tied with a wrap around Harlan's saddle horn.

"Sit, Junior. Stay." Harlan was not sure just how much those commands could be trusted, but the dog did sit down. It sat and looked up at him with its tongue hanging out of one side of its muzzle. The *stay* command was not quite so satisfactory. When Harlan headed for Walking Bear's front door, Junior came with him, walking tight against the back of Harlan's calf.

"I've come for my bill of sale," Harlan announced when he stepped inside. Not that there was any other reason for him to be there.

Walking Bear reached into a drawer and for a moment Harlan had the irrational thought that the man intended to pull a gun on him. Harlan damn near went for his own Colt, but all Walking Bear brought out was a rumpled and sweat-stained piece of paper.

Harlan accepted the bill of sale and looked it over. It was a fine forgery. The beaten and battered paper it was written on made it look like the bill of sale had been dragged around in pockets and saddlebags for months on end. The paper, written in what looked to be at least three different hands, certified that the therein described horse was now the property of one Earl Woods of General Delivery, Gilmer, Texas.

A notary seal from Grayson County, Texas, made it an official document.

"All right?" Walking Bear asked.

"Beautiful. You do good work."

"You know where Gilmer is?"

Harlan nodded. "I been through there a couple times."

"All right then. We are done, yes?"

"We're done," Harlan agreed. "Thanks."

The Indian grunted and turned his attention elsewhere.

Harlan left, Junior at his heels. He untied the gray and thought about walking the horses over to Walking Bear's water trough, but suddenly wanted the hell away from there.

He felt a prickling sensation on the back of his neck and across his shoulder blades. He had felt that same thing once before, outside a bank in northern Arkansas. That time Danny Hopwell was supposed to go in with him but Harlan had called off the deal. He'd had to take Danny by the arm and pull him away from the bank to do it, which pissed Danny off no end, as he was already counting on the money they expected to take.

Nothing happened to them that day but two months later a trio of happy-go-lucky cowboys tried to take down that same bank. A guard hidden inside the place cut down two of the cowboys. The third was put away for a term of five to eight years.

Now Harlan wanted away from Walking Bear's place just as far and fast as he could do it. Instead of walking the gray across the open yard he vaulted into the saddle and whipped the horse into a run for the woods that surrounded Walking Bear's shack. The brown balked and tried to fight the halter but had no choice except to run also. That or be dragged off its feet. Both horses bolted into a run and seconds later Harlan heard whooping and hollering behind him.

A flurry of shots pounded the air around him. Two, three, as many as a dozen. Harlan heard the bee-swarm buzz of at least four bullets that passed close by his head, but none touched him.

The shooters, whoever the sons of bitches were, were obviously shooting at him, bless their stupid hearts. If they had aimed at the horses, either one of the horses, they might well have brought Harlan down to where they could get at him. Thankfully they ignored the horses and tried to shoot him.

A dozen jumps and the gray crashed into the under-brush and then quickly into deeper woods.

Walking Bear, that greedy bastard, had to have set him up. *Come back tomorrow to get your bill of sale.*

And it had been delivered just as promised.

So was an ambush staged by a bunch of Walking Bear's friends.

Harlan was about half tempted to wait a day or two until the alarm died down, then sneak back and put paid to that damned Walking Bear.

Except . . . murder was not his game, no matter what anyone said. He was a robber, dammit, not a murderer, not a rapist.

He shielded his face with an elbow and hoped for the best as the gray charged over, under, around and through whatever was before him, ignoring small limbs and avoiding only those that were big enough to crush skulls.

Three or four minutes of that was about all the brush-whipping, arm-pounding, blind jumping Harlan could stand. He waited until they were in a relatively clear patch, then hauled back on the reins. The gray skidded to a sudden, sliding stop and the brown almost ran up the gray's backside to join Harlan in the saddle.

Once the horses were standing still, Harlan listened for pursuit. He heard nothing and assumed that Walking Bear's red brothers were afoot, damn them one and damn them all. And damn that Walking Bear most of all.

Harlan waited for a moment, hoping Junior would catch up with them, but there was no sign of the dog.

Not, at least, until Harlan looked down. Junior was sitting beside the brown horse's front feet, looking up at Harlan like he was eager for another of those fun runs.

"Shee-it!" Harlan said.

Then, his heart returning to something like a normal pace, he gathered up his reins again and clucked the horses forward.

He had his bill of sale and everything he needed to be on the road for a spell. Very likely it would be sensible to go back to someplace where he could once again be Earl Woods instead of here, where too damn many people knew him as Harlan Breen.

"It's back to Kansas for us, boys," he said.

The gray flicked its ears, but that was the only reaction he got from horse or hound.

He turned north, intending to avoid the roads and travel cross country until he had some miles between himself and Walking Bear's Indian pals.

Those rewards were piling up much too high for comfort, Harlan unhappily acknowledged.

Chapter Fifty-four

The town was called Tiberion. In summer it might well have been a green and pretty sort of a place, but now with all the leaves turned brown and fallen it was just dry and dusty and ugly. Harlan rode through the town once to look things over, then turned around and came back through.

There was a small hotel, single story with sun-curled shingles overhead and warped siding down below. Harlan had stayed in more than enough of that sort. A man ended up sharing his bed with a snoring stranger who slept with his boots on and garlic on his breath. Garlic was bad enough on a whore's breath; Harlan could not stand it in a male bedmate.

He rode past and turned down the first cross street he came to, rode the length of that and shifted over to the next street. He smiled when he saw a small, hand-lettered sign that said FULL BOARD. He drew rein there, stepped down, and tied the gray to a sturdy, white painted fence in front of the boardinghouse.

The house looked clean and nicely kept. There were three wicker rocking chairs on the porch. There was no vestibule, the front door opening directly into the house. Harlan tugged the bellpull set beside the door. He heard footsteps inside and remembered at the last moment to snatch off his hat. After all, he was supposed to be a respectable traveler, not some rowdy, go-to-hell bank robber having a blowout.

He wished to hell he was just a robber enjoying a blowout, but those days were gone. Maybe permanently.

The door was opened by a middle-aged woman with a thick waist, gray-streaked hair leaking from her bun and enough tit for two cows.

"How do, ma'am?"

"What are you selling?" she demanded in a sandpaper-rough voice.

"Nothin', ma'am. I'm lookin' for a room. Just for a few nights."

"I have one. Fifty cents a night full board or thirty-five if you only take breakfast here. You don't smoke, do you?"

"No, ma'am. Never do."

"And no women visitors, not even in the parlor."

"Yes, ma'am. I do have a question though. It's about the shed I see out back of your place. I got a saddle horse there an' a pack horse too. Fees at a public stable would likely eat me up. Would it be all right if I turn my animals into your shed? I'd take care o' them, of course. Feed an' water and all. An' I could pay a little bit extra for them, I expect."

"I wouldn't have to tend them?"

"No, ma'am."

"All right. They can stand in the shed. No extra charge if you're providing their feed. Water comes out of the ground free so I couldn't feel right about charging you for that."

"You're mighty kind, ma'am."

"You can put your things here on the porch while you get your animals set. What about him?"

"Who?"

The lady pointed down beside Harlan's feet where Junior was sitting, tongue out.

"Oh. I . . . I guess I'm so used t' him that I forget he's there sometimes. Can he stay too?"

"He can stay but he's not allowed in the bed with you."

Harlan grinned.

"My name is Harris, by the way. The Widow Harris, most call me. Mrs. Harris to my face."

"Yes'm. An' I'm Earl Woods. My friend here I call Junior."

"Well, take your horses around back, or do you want to look at your room before you decide?"

"Miz Harris, I'm sure any room in your house will be just fine by me."

"Don't go trying to charm me. It won't work."

"Yes, ma'am." He said it. That did not necessarily mean that he believed it.

"Breakfast is at seven. Lunch at noon. Dinner at seven again. I don't serve anybody late, so if you don't come on time you don't eat. And I don't wash for my boarders. You'll get a change of bedding every Sunday. There's a couple women who do take in laundry. I can point them out to you if you need. Or if you don't mind doing a woman's work, you're welcome to use my washtub and clothesline. Those are around back. You'll see them when you move your horses around."

"I surely do need my clothes cleaned." He smiled. "It all sounds fine with me, Miz Harris, so if you will excuse me I'll get those horses an' move them off the street."

"I'll meet you at the back door and show you to your room."

"I do thank you, ma'am." Harlan bobbed his head and put his hat back on. As soon as he was settled into his room, he meant to find the local lawman and have a word with the man.

Hell of a thought, that. Him. Actually wanting to talk to a lawman. My, how things did change.

He let himself back out of the gate, untied the gray, and led his pair of animals around to the alley that ran behind this block of houses and along to Mrs. Harris's shed.

Chapter Fifty-five

"How do, Marshal?" Harlan smiled and stuck his hand out to shake. He hoped he sounded nice and easy about it, but inside he was more than a little apprehensive for fear the man might recognize him from a Wanted poster. "My name is Earl Woods, sir, an' I'd like to have a word with you."

"A pleasure to meet you, Mr. Woods. I'm Grant Leiber."

So far, so good. The man did not seem suspicious. Thank goodness.

Leiber was an ordinary enough sort except for the badge pinned to his shirt. He once had been a redhead but now the red was fading, being replaced with gray at the temples and over the ears. He was of middling height with a wiry build and an oversize nose. His Adam's apple bobbed wildly when he spoke, to the point that Harlan found it difficult to refrain from staring. He almost wanted to get into a long conversation with Leiber just to see that knob of gristle jump up and down.

"What can I do for you, Mr. Woods? Have you had some trouble with one of our citizens?"

"No, sir, nothing like that. What it is, y'see, I'm trying to pick up the trail of this Harlan fella that's been murdering and raping and such. But I been out of touch for a few weeks and I was wanting to find out if there's been anything new on the telegraph wires about him. Has he been spotted anywhere that you know of, Marshal?"

"Bounty hunter?"

"Yes, sir, I suppose you can say that."

"Well, Breen hasn't been caught, I can tell you that much. I'm sure that news will be broadcast as soon as it happens. Just to relieve folks' fears if nothing else. Women around here are awful spooky about him being loose again." Leiber shook his head. "To think . . . they had him and they let him get away. That is practically sinful. As for news about him, though, there hasn't been anything in a while. You've probably already seen the flyers on him, haven't you?"

"Actually, no. I haven't."

"Walk with me over to the office, Mr. Woods. I got a delivery of half a dozen or so of those flyers last week or thereabouts. You're welcome to take one if you think it would help."

"Yes, sir, that would be a big help. I've never actually seen the man, you understand. Is, uh, is there a picture on the flyer?"

The town marshal nodded. "There is. Not very detailed but it gives you an idea of what he looks like."

Leiber started off down a side street, Harlan and Junior following. The marshal's office and jail were in a ramshackle building beyond an equipment supply company. Leiber led the way inside and offered Harlan a chair. Harlan sat and Junior curled up beside his feet.

Harlan took one look around and decided he could get away from any jail so shoddily built as this one. The iron bars were stout enough, but the bars over the window in the lone cell were set into a wooden casement. The cell floor was ordinary wood planking and so was the ceiling. Lock a determined man in there for one night and he would be gone by morning, Harlan figured. He felt a little better after he saw that.

He sat back and crossed his legs, waiting patiently while Leiber rummaged through a file cabinet for the Wanted flyer. When he found it, he sat down on the other side of a cluttered desk, belched once and handed Harlan the flyer.

Harlan had to control an impulse to wince when he saw his own name there in large, bold type.

Wanted. Dead or Alive. Harlan Breen. For murder, robbery and indecent assault of females. Rewards totaling $600 or more. If apprehended contact Sheriff Brandon Bates, Dowdville, Corleigh County, Kansas. Reward.

There was a line drawing that was more detailed than a child's stick figure. But not much. For sure no one would recognize him—or anyone else—from that printed image.

Harlan grunted. "It doesn't say anything new, but I'd never seen his picture before." Dead or alive. That phrase kept racing through his thoughts.

"You can keep that if you like. I posted some around town, over at the bank for instance and one in each saloon, but I don't have any use for the rest of these."

"Thanks." Harlan carefully folded the Wanted poster with his name on it. His own name, damn it. Dead or alive. *Dead or alive.* Lord! He folded the flyer and tucked it away in his pocket.

"May I ask you something, Mr. Woods?"

"Of course, Marshal. I got nothing to hide." If you are going to lie, Harlan reminded himself, do it with a straight face and lie like a son of a bitch.

"What makes you think this Breen fellow might be around our fair town?"

"I haven't heard anything to suggest that, Marshal. I

been hunting for him down in the Nations lately. Didn't do no good down there. Not so much as a nibble 'bout where he might be now. So I thought I'd head north for a while. See if I can come up with anything that might point me to him. All that reward money, it's tempting. I stopped here just t' rest up for a day or two, then I'll be on my way again."

"I certainly hope you do find him, Mr. Woods. Breen has to be taken out of circulation. I would like to see the man brought in to be tried and hanged by legal authority, but if that is not convenient, just shoot him down where he stands. The reward will be paid either way, you know."

"Yes, sir." Dead or alive. Shee-it. It was one thing to know that. It was quite another, and much worse, to see it right there in black and white. He could almost feel the words coming off the flyer in his pocket and burning into his flesh.

"If there is anything I can do to help . . ."

"Thank you, Marshal. You been a big help already. An' if you hear anything new while I'm still in town, I'd surely appreciate you passing that along to me."

"If I do, Mr. Woods, you will be among the first to hear it."

Harlan stood and shook hands with the man again. Junior lurched to his feet and followed Harlan out into the street.

Chapter Fifty-six

The seedy little fellow offered his hand to shake. He had dark yellow stains on his smock, unkempt black hair and large, perpetually wet dark eyes. Jarrett had come to know that George Culm was extremely myopic. The man could scarcely see three feet in front of him. Which probably explained why he had chosen to enter the field of photography. He could see close up and that was quite enough to examine a focusing glass or a photographic negative.

"I want to thank you, George," Jarrett said.

"My pleasure, Mr. Jarrett. You're a good pupil. A very quick learner. With just a little practice, I don't doubt you shall be every bit as comfortable with the craft as I am."

"If that is true, George, I suspect it is because of my teacher." Jarrett reached into his coat pocket and extracted an envelope. "The remainder of what I owe you, as promised," he said.

"I hope you won't be offended if I count it before you leave."

"Not at all," Jarrett lied. Indeed he was offended that anyone should think he might try to beat a debt. But then Culm was a common sort of fellow who lacked Harlan Jarrett's breeding.

The photographer opened the envelope, removed a sheaf of currency and began to count, his eyes glistening as he wet his thumb and riffled slowly through the bills. "Three . . . three twenty . . . three forty. And ten makes three hundred fifty dollars." Culm looked up and smiled. "It's precisely correct, Mr. Jarrett. Thank you."

"I shall come by early tomorrow with some lads to load the equipment for me," Jarrett said.

"At your convenience, sir. Everything is already prepared, and I took the liberty of looking over your coach. If you like I can help. Offer suggestions about where things should be placed and so on."

"That would be fine, thank you."

The coach, once a sheepherder's traveling domicile, had been turned into a rolling photographic studio complete with chemical trays, drying racks and light-proof storage bins for both plates and paper, the plates to produce negative images, while the paper would be used for the final photographic print. It was the thought of those that so excited Jarrett. His greatest dreams were about to be realized.

"I'm sorry I didn't have an extra camera to sell you, Mr. Jarrett."

"Don't worry about it, George. I've already ordered one. It's being shipped from Cincinnati. I shall drive up to the railroad and pick it up there."

"That's all the way to Nebraska."

"Oh, I don't mind," Jarrett said, a smile tugging at the corners of his lips. "I always like to see new country anyway."

Chapter Fifty-seven

Harlan reached for a thigh. Mrs. Harris seemed a nice enough woman, but she fried chicken the way Yankees did, first boiled practically to pieces and then battered before frying. Harlan preferred his chicken down-south style, simply coated with flour and popped into the grease.

Not that he was in any position to criticize. This Yankee-fried chicken came free with his board.

He was holding the platter in both hands when a vision floated into the big room where Harlan was dining with two other boarders in the Harris house, one a fellow who worked at Bascomb's Hardware and the other a taciturn man who had not spoken a word of greeting or introduced himself.

The vision who entered the room was, quite simply, the loveliest female creature Harlan had seen since he left Texas. She was small, probably not more than five feet tall, with a peaches-and-cream complexion and gleaming dark auburn hair. She had huge blue eyes, delicate hands and an hourglass figure. A small hourglass perhaps, but a shapely one. She was wearing an apron and carrying a large bowl of mashed potatoes. He was no hand when it came to judging the age of human females but this one was young. Big enough, though. Definitely big enough.

Harlan bounced to his feet, the chicken platter balanced in one hand and that chicken thigh in the other. The other two boarders kept their seats, neither one of them so much as looking up to acknowledge the girl's entry into the room.

The girl gave him a look of amusement and said, "You must be Mr. Woods. Mama told me you arrived today. Don't mind me, Mr. Woods. I'm Brenda." Harlan was too rattled to respond immediately, so she added, "My mother owns this place. I help out here. You'll see lots of me."

Harlan set the platter down and dropped the chicken thigh onto his plate. He grabbed up his napkin and nervously wiped grease off his hands. "I, uh . . . I . . ."

It was one thing to talk to a whore. Hell, you just told them what to do and they did it. That was dead easy. But Brenda Harris was no chippy. And she was, well, she was beautiful. Enough to take a man's breath away.

Harlan stammered a little more. He desperately wanted to say something. Almost anything. But the words would not come. He simply did not know what to say to a girl like Brenda.

"Sit down, Mr. Woods, before your supper gets cold."

"Yes'm."

The girl's blue eyes sparkled, and when she laughed the tip of her nose lifted and the corners of her eyes crinkled.

She had freckles, he saw now. Across the bridge of her nose and a few tiny ones high on her cheeks.

Her teeth were the whitest he ever saw. One of them, right on top in the front, was very slightly chipped.

Her lips were . . . Harlan tried to stop himself from staring at Brenda Harris's mouth. He was making a fool of himself. He was also growing hard and the bulge in his britches was sure to be noticeable. He sat, dropping like a shot and quickly arranging the napkin over his lap.

Those lips. He was still looking at them. Thinking about them. Wanting to taste their flavor.

They were red. And they looked very soft.

"Mr. Woods? Are you all right?"

"I . . . uh . . . yes, ma'am. I'm fine, ma'am."

"It is *miss*, Mr. Woods. I am *Miss* Harris. Now sit down and finish your supper."

"Yes, ma', uh, I mean yes, *miss*." He sat. He might not have learned much of anything new about the killer when he'd talked with Marshal Leiber that afternoon. But he surely was glad he had come here.

Harlan looked down at the chicken thigh in his right hand. At the moment he could not remember how it had gotten there. But he could recall the exact shape and every color shading of Brenda Harris's lips.

Chapter Fifty-eight

"Won't you be going out onto the porch with the other gentlemen for an after-dinner smoke, Mr. Woods?"

"Not me, miss. I don't smoke." Except sometimes, but he saw no reason to mention that. Girls, he was given to understand, preferred men without vices. He looked at Brenda Harris. His mind was blank, filled to overflowing with images of the girl. "How old are you?" he blurted.

"I am eighteen, sir. And you?"

"I, uh . . . thirty-four."

The girl smiled and tossed her head. "Goodness, that isn't too much of a gap, is it?"

Harlan felt his knees go weak. Not too much of a gap. That was exactly what she had said. Not too much. It was . . . he calculated hard to try to do the sums in his head . . . it was eighteen . . . no, dammit, sixteen. It was sixteen years difference. Lordy! He had been sixteen years old and already long living out on his own when Brenda Harris was born.

"Would you care to walk out with me this evening, miss?"

"Oh, I have work to do, Mr. Woods."

"Tomorrow evening then."

She shook her pretty head. "Sorry."

"Do you work every evening?"

"Yes, I do."

"During the day then. I'm new here. You could show me around. I can hire a buggy if you like."

"No. I don't think that would be a good idea. May I ask you something?" She knelt and began fondling Junior's ears. The dog certainly did not mind that. He stood wagging his tail so hard that his entire backside swung from side to side and back again.

"Of course."

"I was admiring your horses this afternoon. Would you mind if I fed them something? Carrots, perhaps. Horses always like carrots. And you needn't tell me to not give them candies or sugar. I already know about that."

"I wouldn't mind. Perhaps I could introduce you to them."

"Perhaps. Sometime. What is his name?"

"Whose?"

"The dog's, silly." Brenda rubbed Junior's head and stood, brushing off her hands on her apron.

Harlan told her. He had gotten to the point where he accepted the name himself, although it had seemed awkward at first. There was no telling what it might have been before the animal had left its owners and took up with Harlan.

"We like dogs here. Can't have one, of course, because the boarders might complain. They might be allergic or something. And we can't afford a horse. Not that we really need one. We never go anywhere. Have you been to lots and lots of places, Mr. Woods?"

"Not so many. Texas, of course. That's where I'm from. And the Indian Territory. I got a lot of friends down there. Here in Kansas, naturally, and over into Missoura an' Arkansas. Couple times out to Colorado."

"You've seen the mountains then," Brenda said. She wrapped her arms close around her as if hugging herself. Hell, Harlan would have gladly done that for her.

He wondered for a moment what she would do if he did indeed hug her. He chopped that train of thought off short, though, when he felt himself begin to grow hard inside his trousers.

"I seen the mountains," he admitted.

"Are they as magnificent as the paintings make them seen?"

"I don't know about paintings, miss, but those mountains, they're *some*. So high it ain't easy to breathe up there. Cold too. Snow on them winter an' summer alike, some places. But there's passes. A body can travel through if he knows where he's going. There's even railroads up real high. You can take a train clear up to Leadville, then switch to a coach t' get across to the Colorado River. I done that once. Not in a train an' coach but I traveled that way." He neglected to mention that at the time he had been part of Billy Everett's gang. Their idea was to raid a shipment of gold from the mines near Leadville. They pulled off the raid all right, only to find out that the mines were shipping ore, not refined gold, and it would have taken a pack train to haul enough ore to make that venture worthwhile. A man's saddlebags couldn't hold enough ore to buy a beer. That was the last time Harlan rode with Billy. He was shot down and killed near Julesburg the next summer, or so Harlan heard tell.

He mentioned none of that to Brenda Harris though. Just smiled and chatted with her about her visions of the high mountains farther west.

"Do you really want to walk somewhere with me, Mr. Woods?" The question came at him out of the blue.

"Why, why . . . yes, miss. I do."

"The day after tomorrow is Sunday. You may escort me to Sunday services if you like."

"Like, um, church, miss?"

She smiled—Lordy, she did have the prettiest smile; it just lit up her whole face and made her eyes seem so bright they scarcely looked real—and said, "That's right, Mr. Woods. Church. We are Methodists, by the way." She smiled that beautiful smile again. "Holy Rollers, some call us. We sing loud and jump around sometimes and shout. We might not be what you are accustomed to in church."

"What I'm used to, y' mean? Why, miss, I never been to a regular church service. Not one inside a real church building. But I did hear a revival man at a camp meeting once. That was down in New Mexico. Which I reckon I forgot t' mention before. Being in New Mexico, that is. Which they tell me is part o' these United States, despite its name."

Brenda's smile became all the bigger. "Wonderful. We shall look forward to you joining us Sunday morning."

Us. Had she said "us"? Harlan did not especially like the sound of that. He had assumed he and Brenda would be walking alone to these Methodist services, whatever that implied.

Still, it would be a chance to spend some time with the girl. She turned to go and Harlan stood there admiring the curve of her butt beneath her dress. He wondered what she would look like without the dress. Without anything at all covering her.

With luck, maybe, just maybe, he would get a chance to find out.

But not Sunday. Not as long as "us" were included. Dammit.

"C'mon, Junior. Let's us go out an' feed those horses."

Chapter Fifty-nine

Harlan was disappointed. The girl had not put in an appearance during breakfast. He had been hoping for an opportunity to chat her up before the church thing the next day. If she were agreeable, they could maybe walk out somewhere after the service ended and get in a little fooling around.

Fortunately there was always suppertime. Surely she would have to be on hand to help her mother then, as that should be the heaviest meal of the day. And in the meantime Harlan had things he needed to do.

He stepped outside, into the chill of the morning, and reminded himself to go buy a coat today. At the moment all he had to keep the cold away was the duster he had taken from that store back east a way, and that would not begin to be enough come hard winter.

He might, he pondered, just might consider staying here for the winter. That was normal enough. A good many paid-off cowhands chose to pocket their earnings and use them to sustain themselves until spring when the ranchers needed hands again.

Not that Harlan was any sort of a cowhand. Nor a goatherder nor farmer nor delivery boy. Although he had done a bit of all those in his time.

No, what he was, dammit, was a robber. And he considered himself to be a good one. He had been mighty successful at it until this sonuvabitch other Harlan stepped in and ruined his reputation.

The book was still open on that problem though. Harlan intended to see to it.

He shivered a little and clucked once to Junior, then walked past the remains of Mrs. Harris's garden, out to the shed and fenced pen where his horses stood. "How're you boys this morning?" he asked aloud, as he forked the last of Mrs. Harris's hay to the animals. The hay was old and brittle but clean enough in this dry air and free of mold. There was no grain for them. That was another chore he needed to tend to.

When he was satisfied that the horses were taken care of, he walked down the alley to the street and found a likely-looking mercantile where he bought a heavy woolen coat—a bright red, double-breasted Hudson's Bay pattern—with a quilted lining and oversized collar. He found some good quality gloves with rabbit fur inside and a long woolen scarf or muffler that he could use to wrap his neck up to his ears when the cold winds blew.

His bill came to almost eight dollars but he considered the amount worthwhile, even though if he did stay here through the winter there would not be any opportunity for him to steal any more.

"Will there be anything else?" the storekeeper asked.

"No, that's all I nee . . . no, wait. Let me change my mind. I'd like five cents worth o' those taffy candies there . . . and are those horehound drops? Another nickel o' them, please."

The storekeeper smiled. "Ten cents' worth. That's a lot of candies, mister."

"I got me a sweet tooth," Harlan lied. He intended to take the poke of candy back to Brenda Harris. Maybe that would help put him in good with her come tomorrow. Might even get him into her bloomers if he were lucky.

He paid for his purchases, put on the coat and draped the muffler around his neck. He stuffed his pockets full of candies and tucked the gloves behind his gun belt.

From the mercantile he headed for the feed store and arranged to have a ton of good quality grass hay and a hundredweight of mixed grain, heavy on the oats, delivered to Mrs. Harris's shed.

"I know the place," the merchant said. "Delivered there before." The man hesitated a moment, then snorted. "You sniffing around after that girl of hers, are you? There's plenty been after that before you, friend, but they didn't do no good. Speculation is that the girl holds on to her cherry so tight she'll likely die with it still the only thing she's ever had between her legs. But good luck to you."

"Oh, no, I . . ."

"Of course you are. Any man with balls has gotta want some of that."

"She ain't bad-looking," Harlan admitted. But that was all he intended to admit.

"She invite you to that church of hers yet?" the feed-store owner asked. "If she hasn't, she will. That's what she does. Invites fellows to services and tries to convert them. Gets them down in front where everybody will be watching and plays up to them. Tells them how happy she'll be if they'll just say some words out loud, like. But believe me, she won't be happy enough to loosen the drawstring on her drawers for you."

"You sound like a man who's been there," Harlan said. The grain seller had to be in his forties, maybe even his fifties. But then Harlan was given to understand that age was not enough to wipe that sort of thought from a man's mind, no matter what it did to his body.

"I been there," the merchant replied. "Made a complete ass of myself. And me with a wife and grandchildren back in Illinois."

"My condolences, friend."

The grain seller shrugged. "Never too old to learn a lesson, right? I'll have your hay and the grain delivered this afternoon."

His errands taken care of, Harlan ambled off down the street with Junior at his heels, in search of a drink. Or maybe two.

Chapter Sixty

Or three or maybe four. Damn but that liquor tasted good. Smooth, it was. Aged in oak, the man said. Harlan put on a snootful.

But he was on time for supper. He was that.

Brenda Harris paid attention to him this time. Whenever she had to serve the table of boarders, she stood at Harlan's side to lean forward with the bowl or platter, the side of her right breast soft and warm against his shoulder when she did so.

Harlan was just drunk enough that several times he contrived to turn his head at the right moment so his cheek pressed against her tit. Brenda smelled of yeast and flour and something . . . vanilla extract? Could be. Whatever it was, he damn sure liked it. He came close to telling her so, close to blurting it out for all to hear. Probably he would have been thrown the hell out of the house if he did that.

For sure he would be thrown out—and likely jailed as well—if he reached up and took hold of one of those beauties inside Brenda's shirtwaist. He thought about it though. Oh, he did think about it. A napkin in his lap covered up the proof of that.

After his own supper he walked out to the shed to check on the horses. Earlier in the afternoon he had gone out to make sure the feed had been delivered as promised and to check on the quality of both. He was still rubber-knee drunk at the time, but he doubted it was possible to get so drunk that he would neglect his horse.

After supper he found the animals quietly nibbling at their hay. Harlan sighed. And thought about Brenda Harris's tits. Thought about the shape of her face and the scent that came off her. Thought about the hundred and one things he would like to do to her. With her. Wondered if that damned old grain seller knew what he was talking about. The man might simply have a severe case of the sour grapes. He might just be so pissed off at the girl for rejecting his advances that he wanted to spoil everybody else's interest in her. After all, why should he bring up Brenda to a complete stranger? Harlan had never seen the man before this morning. Why would he be so anxious to discuss something so personal as his being sent packing by the prettiest girl in town? And him a married man by his own admission.

Harlan brushed the horses a little and cleaned their feet. Then he sat on the pile of freshly delivered hay while he thought about Brenda's tits and the feed man's comments and some asshole rapist named Harlan, and the next thing he knew it was black dark and felt like the middle of the night.

He had a perfectly good bed inside the house. If he could find it in his still rather woozy condition.

And anyway it was mighty comfortable on that pile of hay. Harlan burrowed into it to ward off the cold, closed his eyes and dropped back into a deep, refreshing sleep.

Chapter Sixty-one

"I'm sorry, Mr. Jarrett. There's no package for you."

"Could you please check again. I know there should be . . ."

"Mr. Jarrett. Please!" The railroad clerk sounded exasperated. "I've already looked through the stored baggage. Your shipment simply has not arrived yet."

"But I told them . . ."

"Yes, sir, I understand that, but it is not here. Really. Now, please. I have work to do."

Harlan Jarrett scowled but he had no choice except to turn away from the Dutch door, its top half open at the moment. The baggage clerk, a thin man with pox scars on his face, seemed relieved. This was the third day Jarrett had come to claim the camera he had ordered, and still there was nothing.

He went around to the telegraph office, which was housed in the same depot building, and impatiently tapped the bell to announce himself to the operator, who was nowhere in sight. Jarrett sounded the bell two more times before a young fellow in sleeve garters and eyeshade emerged from a back room.

"Yes, sir?" Harlan Jarrett thought the telegrapher should offer an apology for his tardiness but none was forthcoming.

"I want to send a wire, of course." Damn fellow should know that without having to ask. Why else would anyone come into the telegraph office except

to send a message? Jarrett made no attempt to keep
the irritation out of his voice.

The telegrapher softly grunted something under
his breath, too faint for Jarrett to make out what had
been said. He reached beneath the counter, placed a
yellow message pad on the counter, reached again
and placed a nub of lead pencil beside the pad.

"What did you say?"

The operator looked at him soundlessly for a moment, then said, "Nothing, mister."

"I want to speak with your supervisor," Jarrett demanded.

"Sure. His name is Jake Wilbank. His office is in
Kansas City. You want a ticket?"

"What?"

"A ticket. Do you want a ticket to Kansas City so you
can speak with Jake?"

Jarrett bristled. For a moment he forgot himself. He
came very near to bashing the cheeky fellow over the
head with his walking stick. But that might bring the
law in. And the telegrapher was local. Jarrett was but a
stranger here, without the weight of money and family
influence to support him. It was better to hold on to
his rage. As soon as the camera arrived, he could be on
his way and there would be ways he could vent those
feelings.

"I want to send a message to the B. Adams Camera
and Optical Works, Cincinnati, Ohio."

"Just write it down, mister."

"This pencil is not sharp."

"There's lead showing. It will do."

"I want a better pencil."

"Mister, you can piss your message in the snow for
all I care. But I gave you a pencil. That's the only pencil
I have here."

"I think you are lying, young man."

"And I think you are rude. Reckon that makes us pretty much even." The telegrapher smirked and took half a step backward.

Jarrett did not know what the man intended and he did not particularly want to find out. Grunting his dissatisfaction but otherwise holding his tongue, Jarrett removed the writing wallet from inside his coat, produced his pen and vial of ink, and proceeded to write out his message demanding to know why his camera had not yet arrived.

He handed that sheet to the operator, took a moment to consider his circumstances after laying out cash for the photographic equipment and caravan, then wrote out a second message telling his bank to send more money.

It seemed he would be stuck here for the next few days.

But then . . . oh, my . . . then he would have the perfect reason to visit isolated farms. And Nebraska, he was already learning, was even more sparsely settled than Kansas.

This was, he believed, the perfect hunting ground for a man with his particular tastes.

Chapter Sixty-two

"Mr. Woods! Gracious sakes, you can't go to services like that. Look at you. You're all covered in hay stems. Did you sleep out there with the horses? Whyever would you do such a silly thing? And you promised. You promised you would walk with me this morning. I've been so looking forward to that." Brenda's eyelashes fluttered a little as she decorously, shyly lowered her gaze.

"I, uh . . . I fell asleep," Harlan said. The words sounded lame even to him.

The girl really did have splendid tits. And a taut, round little ass.

She was dressed for church in a dress with frills on the . . . what did they call it? Bodice, that was it. The dress was a shade of pale blue. It went nicely with her eyes and the color of her hair. She was wearing white cotton gloves that barely extended to her wrists. Those would be no good at all for work, but then that was not their intended purpose. She had on a hat. Bonnet? Harlan was not sure exactly what that should be called. It was a little bit of a thing that was pinned to the left hind side of her head. He caught himself. Make that the left rear. Brenda was not a horse, after all.

"Step back out onto the porch. Hurry," she commanded.

Harlan did what she asked. He backed up onto the utility porch at the back of the house. Brenda reached up and began hurriedly brushing the bits of hay off him. The light touching felt rather nice. Nice enough to give him the beginnings of an erection. He really was going to have to get Brenda's bloomers down or else go find a friendly little whore to spend time with. And damn soon, before he got so horny he became excited over the look of a sleek mare.

"Why are you wearing that gun?" Brenda yelped. "Take it off. You can't wear that to services, Mr. Woods. You should know better. Come on now. Take your belt off and put the gun down. Take it inside. Put it . . . I don't know. Put it in the pie safe or something. We don't want to be late. Hurry."

Harlan opened his mouth to protest but he was too late. Brenda already had the door open and was tugging him inside the house.

At least she let him unbuckle the gun belt by himself. Although, come to think of it, it might be interesting if she did help him undress. Beyond a gun belt, that was. He wrapped the belt around the revolver and holster and stuffed the ungainly lump of steel and leather onto the top shelf of the cabinet thing that Brenda opened for him.

"Here. Put it here. Oh, there's some more hay. Come outside. Quick."

She pulled him back the other way, turned him around and frantically brushed at his back and shoulders. After a few moments she said, "That will just have to do. Come along now, Mr. Woods. We don't want to be late."

As it happened they were at least ten minutes early. Early enough that Harlan's butt was already becoming sore from sitting on the hard bench by the time the singing and the shouting started. By the time the preacher tore into his sermon, Harlan was bored and half asleep. He contented himself with imagining how Brenda would look naked. Finally—it seemed forever—the agony came to an end. There was a final prayer. It lasted no more than twelve times as long as Harlan thought it should. And they were, mercifully, free to leave.

"I was wonderin' would you care t' walk out a ways with me?" he suggested, thinking about how Brenda Harris would feel in his arms and what her lips would taste like. He had spent half the dang service glancing at those lips and thinking how soft and moist and pleasant they looked. At her ear. That ear just begged for a tongue to be swirled around inside it. Brenda might not know that. Yet. But it was true.

The girl smiled ever so sweetly. "Why, we haven't time for that, Mr. Woods. Now we will be having our picnic dinner with all the others of the congregation."

"You didn't say nothing about a picnic dinner."

"I didn't?" She smiled. And shrugged. "I thought you knew. We always have our Sunday dinner here on the grounds. Unless it is raining, of course, or snowing. Then we move indoors and eat there." Brenda slipped her hand through his right arm and gazed up at him with seeming adoration.

Damn, Harlan thought. He wasn't sure if he should be extra happy that she wanted to spend the time with him. Or pissed off that she was taking advantage.

"Come along. We want to see everything the ladies brought before Pastor says grace and we start loading our plates. Do you like pork fritters, Mr. Woods? I already know you like fried chicken. Oh, there will be ever so much to choose from. And the ladies of the church are wonderful cooks, bless them. Not as good as Mama, you understand, but really quite wonderful. Come along now, please. I want to introduce you to everyone."

Harlan suffered through more praying and a meal that lasted much longer than it should have. When it had ended Brenda gathered up a basket of leftover food that her mother had prepared, even though Mrs. Harris was needed back at the boardinghouse to provide for her boarders.

Brenda handed the basket to Harlan without bothering to ask him if he would be willing to carry it. But that smile. Those eyes. Gracious.

She had dimples. Lovely.

"Come along now, Mr. Woods. We can go home now."

As soon as they were inside the back door Harlan looked around. There was no sign of Mrs. Harris or any of the other boarders. He set the basket down, turned Brenda around and pulled her to him.

She tasted lightly of cloves and there was a faint floral scent on her. The kiss lasted only a moment before Brenda pulled away, pretending to be shocked. Which he did not believe for a second.

She also pretended the kiss never happened. Instead she turned and opened the cabinet that sat close to the stove. "Please get this . . . this terrible thing out of Mama's pie safe, Mr. Woods."

"Y'know, you could call me Earl now. We know each other good enough for that, don't we?"

Brenda ignored the suggestion and stood beside the open cabinet door, waiting for him to retrieve his gun belt and Colt. He did so and quickly strapped the belt and holster back where they belonged.

"I, uh, thanks," he said.

The girl hesitated for only a moment. Then she smiled again.

Harlan smiled too, thinking about how very soft Brenda's lips were, thinking about the taste of her breath, thinking about what they might progress to the next time. His smile grew wider. Maybe, just maybe this would be a good place to hole up for the winter and never mind that jealous, lying SOB at the feed and grain.

He touched the brim of his hat, then sauntered out through the house to the front porch where the other gentlemen were smoking and visiting.

All in all, he thought, this was not a bad Sunday.

Chapter Sixty-three

"Oh, Mr. Woods."

Harlan paused in the doorway. "Yes, Miss Harris?"

"Are you going out?"

He smiled. "You see that I am. I'm on my way t' feed the horses."

"May I go with you? I saved some pieces of carrot for them."

"Sure. Come along."

"Go ahead then. I'll run to the kitchen to get those carrots and join you out back."

"All right, fine." Harlan put on his hat, nodded to one of the boarders who was sitting in a wicker rocking chair on the front porch, and reached down to give Junior a pat. He was coming to really like the dog. Together Harlan and Junior went lightly down the porch steps and around the side of the house. True to her word, Brenda was waiting for them by the back steps. She had removed her apron and carried a bit of cloth wrapped around something. Carrot pieces, no doubt.

Harlan led the way back to the shed where the horses stood. Instead of slipping through the planks that barred what passed as an alleyway in the small shed as he usually did, he pulled the two top planks back and let them down so Brenda could enter without having to crouch in an unladylike pose.

"Sit. Stay there."

"Are you talking to me, sir?"

Harlan laughed. Junior sat. And stayed.

He took the little bundle of carrot bits from her and set them aside. "We'll let them eat their supper first, shall we? You can do the carrots later." Not that it made any difference to the horses, but this way Brenda would have to stay with him longer.

Harlan clipped a short lead onto the gray's halter and tied it in a corner, then secured the big brown in an opposite corner.

"Why are you doing that?" Brenda asked. "Don't they get along?"

"Oh, they get along fine. It's just that the gray is dominant. If I leave them loose the gray will hurry up and finish its grain, then come over and push the big fella off his. He's older and eats sort of slow. If I let them alone the gray would get most of the feed an' the brown would be left out."

"You know horses, don't you?"

Harlan shrugged. "I depend on them."

"Do you like them?"

"I haven't thought about that very much but . . . yeah. Yeah, I guess I do like them. Come in here and set with me. We'll wait for the horses to finish their grain before you give them the carrots."

"All right."

Harlan opened the gate and led Brenda into the stall where he had put the hay and the wooden bin of grain.

"Where can . . ."

"Set here," he suggested, dropping onto the soft hay by way of demonstration.

"I don't know. We're all alone here. And . . . everything."

He smiled. "I won't bite. Honest Injun."

"I suppose . . . all right then." She very gingerly lowered herself into a sitting position beside him, then carefully arranged her skirt around her legs.

Harlan smiled at her again. And leaned nearer. Then nearer still. His arm slipped around her waist and he gave a little tug. Brenda's lips parted as she raised her face to his.

Half an hour later Brenda's complexion was red and mottled. Her face was flushed and her breath was quick and short.

He could feel that she wanted him as badly as he wanted her. He reached for the buttons that held her blouse closed.

"No!" Brenda twisted away from him and sat panting and crying now, tears running down her cheeks and snot leaking from her nose. "No. Please no."

He reached toward her, hoping to gentle her. And then to ease her back into what they had started. Almost started.

"No." The girl scrambled to her feet, mumbled something that he could not make out and fled, slipping through the bars of the alley gate quite as easily as he could have.

He saw a last flash of skirts and she was gone.

Harlan felt something cold and moist in his palm. He looked down to see Junior offering what comfort he could. Harlan rubbed the dog's ears, then stood.

"Come along, boy. I need t' go find me someplace warm t' take care of this yearning betwixt my legs. It's powerful, I'm telling you." He smiled. "There's got t' be a fifty-cent whore in this here town. Hell, I could even go a dollar's worth this evenin'."

Harlan and the dog checked on the horses and let them off their tethers before leaving the shed, then walked out to the street and along toward town.

He was sure he knew just who to ask about where to find that whore he was looking for.

It occurred to him that Brenda never had fed those carrot bits to the horses. Next time, maybe. With luck.

Chapter Sixty-four

Harlan slid his tongue inside Brenda's mouth and wiggled it around some. At the same time he was feeling of her boobies with his left hand while his right arm was around her, holding and comforting her.

This was . . . he thought back. Only about the fifth time he'd had her alone out here in the shed. That was fine. Just fine. He was moving along toward getting where he wanted to be.

A whore was one thing. A whore would let a man release some of the pressure in him. But a whore was not the same as a real girl. Brenda was definitely the real thing. It would be a pleasure to take her, and Harlan expected to have that pleasure just any old time now.

He judged her breathing, which was getting heavier and heavier. He murmured sweet words into her ear, letting his lips flutter and move against her ear and his breath flow warm into it.

Brenda groaned. Harlan took that as his cue. His left hand slipped down away from her breast and found the hem of her skirt. Slid beneath the skirt and ever so lightly up the inside of her leg. Found what he wanted and began very gently to stroke with the tip of one finger.

Brenda squealed. Her hips began to move. Then she became rigid and cried out, a short sound that was almost a bark.

Harlan smiled, his lips thinning even while they nibbled on Brenda's earlobe. She was ripe. Oh Lordy, the girl was surely ripe. Next time. Real soon, anyway. Next time she would fall. He would have her for sure.

After that it would just be a matter of teaching her how to do the things he liked best.

That could wait, though, until after her first time.

Harlan could scarcely stop himself from trying to take her the rest of the way now. But she was not ready. Not quite. First she had to learn to accept this. And then to want it. After that . . . after that it would be easy, just a matter of tipping her over the final edge.

Harlan kissed her and mumbled the silly things she wanted to hear. He loved her. She was the best. He *respected* her. Yeah. Sure he did. Or so he said. But what did the girl know? Girls were such excitable creatures. Gullible too. Harlan surreptitiously wiped his finger on Brenda's petticoat, then brought his hand out and went back to stroking her breast.

None of this gave him what he needed, but it was a process. It took time. And this evening, hell, there was always Fat Betty over at the whorehouse. She would do. For tonight.

"I love you, Earl."

For just a moment there, Harlan forgot who it was the girl was talking about. Then he smiled and kissed her and told her how he loved her back.

Things here were going just fine. For sure this would be a good place to spend the winter.

Chapter Sixty-five

"Good morning, Earl."

"Good morning your own self, Cyrus." Harlan smiled and nodded, then greeted the others who were waiting for their turn under the barber's shears.

"In a hurry this morning, Earl?" Cyrus Roche asked with a faint smile. It was nice of the man to ask, even though he and Harlan both knew it would make not a lick of difference whether he was in a rush or not. Cyrus would not hurry his cutting, probably not for the president of the United States. Roche was slow and deliberate. But friendly, and he gave a good haircut, always smooth with no flyaway spikes sticking up.

"You know me, Cyrus. I got nothing better t' do anyhow." Harlan unbuttoned his coat and hung it and his hat on one of the coat trees Cyrus provided for his customers.

"Help yourself to a seat then, Earl. I'll let you know soon as I'm ready for you."

There were three other fellows, mostly older gentlemen, already waiting in the chairs that sat against the side wall. Harlan did not know any of them to talk to, but he had seen them around town and of course they would be familiar with him too.

"You're Woods, aren't you?" one of the old fellows asked. He did not look like he really needed a haircut. Or a shave, for that matter. Harlan guessed he was just there to gossip and pass the time.

"Yes, sir."

"Jason Stewart," the old boy said. He struggled to his feet and offered his hand. Harlan shook with him.

"It's a pleasure, Mr. Stewart."

Stewart introduced the other men as well. They nodded and seemed pleasant enough, but did not stand up or offer to shake hands.

"Would you care to read the Kansas City newspaper, Mr. Woods? It's the latest edition. Got here on the stagecoach just last night."

"Why, thank you, Mr. Stewart. Yes, sir, I would." He smiled. "I always like t' keep up with what's going on in the world."

Stewart produced a folded newspaper that was already limp from folding and refolding. Obviously these men and likely a number of others had already had the chance to read it.

Harlan sat down, crossed his legs and spread the newspaper open in his lap.

He could read. A little. Enough to make out the biggest headline, that was for sure.

"The Murderer Breen Strikes Again." And then in smaller type, "Family of Five Slaughtered in Goodson, Neb."

"Shit," Harlan muttered aloud. He bent to the rest of the story.

The killer, this other Harlan, had left Kansas. Fled the state, most likely. Obviously he was finding the pickings to his liking up north in Nebraska, despite the onset of winter.

"How far is it up to the Nebraska line?" Harlan asked of no one in particular.

"A hundred fifty, maybe a hundred seventy-five miles," Cyrus said.

"More like a hundred sixty," Jason Stewart put in.

"I'd say the hundred seventy-five," another of the old codgers opined.

"And Goodson? Anybody know where it is?" Harlan asked.

He got a few blank looks and two shakes of heads. No one knew. That was all right. He could figure that out when he got there.

"Thanks." Harlan stood and reached for his coat and his hat.

"What about your haircut, Earl?"

"Later, Cyrus. It'll have t' wait until later."

Harlan went to the mercantile and bought ready-ground coffee, four slabs of smoked hog jowl and a peck of rice. At the farm supply he purchased two nose bags for the horses. In good weather he did not mind just pouring their grain onto the ground, but if there were snow, especially deep stuff, he thought it better to feed in a bag.

He bought a good belt knife and a whetstone. Bought a box of cartridges for his .45, thought about adding another box of shells for the shotgun but decided against that. Shotgun shells were heavy and if one box was not enough, it would mean he was dead and a dozen boxes would not have done it.

He bought a light ax and a short-handled spade.

"I don't generally see this sort of sale come this time o' year, Earl. You traveling soon?"

"I'm thinking about it, Stan."

"Be careful then. Storms can come up or who the hell knows what else. You be careful, Earl. We want you t' come home safe, you hear?"

Harlan was halfway back to Mrs. Harris's boardinghouse before he realized what it was that Stan had said. "Come home," the man had said.

Home. Was this home now?

Lordy! That was something that had never crossed Harlan's mind. Not until this moment.

He had not had a home, not the real thing, in a helluva long time.

And the truth was that no one knew him here. Not the real him. They knew a man they called Earl Woods. Not a soul among them had ever met Harlan Breen.

Still, it was not so awfully far to some of the places where he and the boys had pulled their robberies. It would not be impossible for someone from one of those places to see him and to remember him.

On the other hand . . . if this were home and if he were Earl Woods . . .

"Son of a *bitch*!" Harlan spat into the teeth of a cold winter wind.

He stopped in at the boardinghouse long enough to haul his gear out to the shed, then loaded the big brown and saddled the gray.

There was no need for him to go back inside the house. Brenda would just bawl and make a fuss. And it wasn't like he owed anything. He was paid up through the end of this week.

Harlan took down the bars at the entrance to the shed and led his horses out into the pale winter sunlight.

He stepped into the saddle, took a wrap of the brown's lead rope on the horn and pointed the gray north.

A hundred seventy-five miles to Nebraska. More or less. How long that took would depend on the weather for the next few days.

Wind was one thing. It was miserably uncomfortable but wind by itself would not slow him down.

Snow, that was another thing entirely.

"Let's hope the snow holds off," Harlan said aloud. The gray flicked its ears in response and Junior, who was trotting along beneath Harlan's near stirrup, wagged his tail and looked up at his master.

Chapter Sixty-six

Harlan scowled as he looked upward toward the steely gray clouds that were scudding overhead. The temperature had to be freezing or close to it, and the air smelled of ozone.

All right, dammit," Harlan said aloud. "There's no hotel nor anyplace where we can get inside, so we'll hole up for the night in that thicket yonder." He gigged the gray into a lope, the brown and Junior following, and made it to the timber in twenty minutes or thereabouts.

Long practice made short work of preparing a camp, and he had a fire going and a bed laid out in no time. Preparing supper was as easy as tossing a couple chunks of jerked beef—or possibly mule, as the meat was stringy and tough—for Junior and selecting one for himself.

There was no creek to dip fresh water from, so he settled for a sip or two from his canteen. He poured a little into a cup for Junior but gave none to the horses. They had had a fill-up at the last water they'd crossed, not more than a few hours earlier. That would have to do until they chanced across some more.

Once that was out of the way Harlan lay down and pulled his blankets close around his ears.

His thoughts were not necessarily pleasant ones. The hat, for instance. Handsome as it was, he was wishing now he had kept the woolen cap. Or, better yet, bought a knitted stocking cap that would come down over his

ears. His ears were so cold they ached. Three days on
the trail north and already he felt like he had never
been warm a single day of his life.

He inwardly grumbled as well at having to leave
Brenda Harris just when she was ripe and ready. Another evening, two at the most he figured, and he would
have had her cherry. The girl tried to act cool and above
it all with the boarders, but Harlan had reason to know
that inside she was hot and ready for the picking.

All his good work and now it would be some other
son of a bitch who would reap the reward.

He was still thinking about Brenda when he fell
asleep that evening.

Harlan woke before dawn to a light dusting of hard,
granulated snow. It was colder than ever, he thought.
Cold enough to freeze a man's ass off if he dropped his
drawers to take a squat. That, he decided, could wait
until he found a proper place, so he could be out of the
wind while he dumped.

He had no choice, though, about taking a leak. His
bladder was so full he was sure it would burst if he
didn't relieve it. He pulled his coat tightly around him
and stood, letting his blankets fall in a heap.

Harlan stepped over to the nearest tree and unbuttoned, then anointed the tree trunk. Junior immediately snuggled into the warm blankets Harlan had just
vacated.

He thought about taking time to boil some coffee but
abandoned the idea. He did not have much water left
in his canteen and anyway was hoping to find someplace where he could get inside and warm up. Maybe
get a hot meal and some coffee made with better water
than what he had been getting out of the creeks and
rills along the road thus far.

He did give Junior a little more water and poured

a cup or two into his hat for each of the horses before breaking camp and repacking the brown.

It was still dark when they started north again but not quite as black as it had been. Dawn shouldn't be long coming.

Chapter Sixty-seven

Harlan buried his nose inside the rim of the mug and for a moment just inhaled the steam rising off hot coffee. Lordy, was there anything that smelled better than fresh brewed coffee?

The coffee was too hot to swallow, so he set the mug aside and asked, "D'you have a saucer or something like it?"

"No. Sorry."

Harlan picked up his cup and wandered through the cluttered little store until he found something that would serve. He removed a flowerpot from its pottery base, set the red clay pot aside and poured a small amount of coffee into the base, then set that on the floor for Junior.

"I'll be damned. The dog drinks coffee?"

"You see him, don't you? Him and me, we're each the only company the other has when we're travelin'. I've kinda got used to sharing with him." Harlan blew into his mug, then took a tentative sip. He smiled. "You make good coffee."

"So good even dogs like it," the storekeeper said with a chuckle.

"Mind if I have a refill?"

"Help yourself. He can have some too," the man said, inclining his head toward Junior.

Harlan poured the mug full, set it down and got around to unbuttoning his coat. A wave of heat from the potbelly stove reached him. It was more than welcome.

It was still frigid outside but so far the snow was holding off, save for a very small dusting of granules that were as much ice as they were snow. They swept down on the wind and gathered as white streaks in the ruts from wagon wheels or in small half moons where hoofprints had formed during more moderate weather. Now the ground was frozen as solid as the creek surfaces.

"Good," Harlan muttered. "Mighty good." He looked around, picked out a few canned goods and carried them to the counter.

"Those things will freeze and bust wide open if you don't have anyplace to protect them from the cold," the storekeeper warned.

Harlan cussed and snapped his fingers. "You're right. Thanks for reminding me." He was not accustomed to this manner of cold. And he really did not want to become used to it.

"I got jerky, of course. Everybody carries jerky, especially this time of year. Got hardtack too. And ready-ground coffee. Bacon, that's always good for a trail food. The fats stay with a man and help keep you warm. You could get some flour and lard and make it up into a dough. Won't matter if that freezes and it shouldn't get so hard that you can't work it in your fingers."

"All right. I'll take some of each of those things."

"You going to be going far?"

"Damned if I know," Harlan said. "I'm looking for a place, name of Goodson. Any idea where that would be?"

"Oh, sure. That's easy enough. Right now you're about a dozen miles due east from Goodson. The road that runs across just north of town takes you right to it. Go up past a sod house with a chicken coop set beside the crossroads of this here road with another running east and west. When you find that, turn left. Goodson will be right smack in front of you."

"How big a place is this Goodson?"

"Pretty good size. I'd say six, seven hundred folks."

"They got a lawman there?"

The storekeeper nodded. "Aye, I know him well. Nice fella. Ned Edwards is his name. There's no jailhouse or anything like that. You can generally find Edwards in the post office or sometimes Garrison's saloon. Goodson isn't much but Edwards works the law full-time. The town pays him a little and the sheriff pays him something to act as a deputy for this end of the county. And of course he gets to collect fees from time to time. I don't know what it all adds up to, but I guess Ned don't need much, for he seems to get along on that."

"Works out of a saloon, you say. Drinking man, is he?"

"Not much. It's just that Garrison's is where the fellows like to hang out. You know how that is, I expect."

"I do," Harlan admitted. He glanced toward the front window but he already knew what he would see out there. Gray sky, gray buildings and gray-black tree trunks. If he ever got this mess straightened out, he was going to have to think about finding someplace that stayed warm and green all the year long. Damn, but he hated the very thought of having to bundle up and head out into the cold and the wind again.

"'Bout twelve miles, you say?"

"Around that, yes."

"Is there a hotel in Goodson?"

"No, but Garrison has his rooms in back for the whores. He'll rent them out to travelers if need be."

"You've been a big help, friend. How much do I owe you?"

"That would be . . . let me see . . . a dollar ten should do it." The storekeeper smiled. "No charge for the dog's coffee."

Harlan paid the man, buttoned his coat and pulled on his gloves. He ducked his chin deep into the muffler around his neck and headed back outside, Junior at his heels.

Chapter Sixty-eight

Goodson, Nebraska, was gray and ugly. But then at the moment the whole damn world was gray and ugly. Gray and ugly or not, Harlan was glad to get there anyway.

He found the livery barn and took his horses inside. There did not appear to be anyone there to tend the place, so Harlan stripped the gear off them, the sweat on their backs steaming in the cold when the air reached them, and dumped his gear against a wall.

Leaving wet places on their hides in this weather, even indoors out of the bite of the wind, would be asking for sickness to strike them, so he rummaged in the various bins and boxes until he came up with some discarded grain sacks. He used those to rub down each animal and gave Junior a few swipes of the rough cloth too, lest the dog feel left out.

He carefully inspected the grain that was available and added cracked corn to the mixed grains before separating the gray and the brown and feeding them. Corn promoted heat in an animal and Harlan figured that was just exactly what his horses needed in this miserable weather.

Once he had the horses settled, he spoke to Junior and stepped back into the frigid cut of the wind. His eyes watered and the tip of his nose began to hurt, almost feeling like it was burning, but all he could do about it was to bury his face deeper into his muffler and tug the brim of his hat lower.

The sky still looked snow laden and menacing but there was no snow falling, not even the hard, sandlike spicules he'd encountered farther south.

If there was a sign announcing Garrison's saloon Harlan failed to see it, but the bright lamplight and sounds of laughter were obvious from the sidewalk. He stepped inside and found twenty or more men crowding a small room that had a crude bar at one end and a number of tables scattered across the sawdust.

Conversation slowed when the door opened and a gust of icy wind swept in with Harlan and Junior behind it.

Conversation stopped entirely when Harlan removed his hat and began to disentangle himself from his muffler and coat like a turtle coming out of its shell.

Strangers, he gathered, were not common in Goodson, Nebraska.

There were two other dogs already in the place. They left their masters long enough to come sniff Junior. There were no tails wagging but they did not offer to fight either, and soon enough they finished their inspection and went back to their places.

Harlan figured it would take a little longer for the human population to do what passed for asshole sniffing when folks encountered unfamiliar people.

He stood there taking his time about smelling the sharp, bright scents of beer and corn whiskey, sawdust and spit and unwashed men. He could not see any whores at the moment but there was a hint of lavender in the air. That suggested the presence of some painted ladies. Well, it did unless somebody around here had found a way to make lavender bloom in the dead of winter.

Harlan pulled his hat back on and shucked out of the coat. There was an already heavily encumbered coat rack beside the door and it would have been acceptable to simply pile his coat on top of all the others, but he preferred to drape both it and the muffler over his shoulder and keep them with him.

The men in the room were mostly wearing bib overalls and clod-buster shoes, suggesting that this was farm country and not ranch land around Goodson. That suited Harlan fine. His experience suggested that farmers were no less intelligent than ranchers or cowhands, but they were a damn sight slower to act. They could be bulldog stubborn once they did move, but they tended to ponder and to deliberate longer. And townspeople, well, them a man could not make any assumptions about, as they ran the gamut from Slow Willie to Slick Sam and back again.

Harlan gave the good gentlemen of Goodson time to look him over, and then he found a place at the bar.

"You got coffee? Anything hot?"

"I got wot you need." The bartender had an accent. German, maybe, or Polish, something on that order. Likely then he was not Garrison but a hired man.

Whoever the man was and wherever he was from, he did indeed have a magic elixir to chase the cold. He poured a mug of something—Harlan had no idea what it was—and set it aside. He took an iron poker, opened the door of a glowing hot stove and shoved the tip of the poker deep into the coals inside. A minute or so later he removed the poker from the fire and jammed it into the mug of liquid. Steam rose and Harlan thought he could hear a sizzle as heat transferred from metal into the liquid. The result was a warm drink that the barkeep set in front of Harlan.

"One bit, eh."

Harlan laid down a quarter before he picked up the

mug. He sank his nose into it and breathed deeply. He was smiling when he looked up again.

The drink was not exactly a cider. But not a wine either. A mixture perhaps. Whatever it was, it smelled good enough to eat.

Harlan settled for drinking it.

Once it hit his belly, a delicious warmth surrounded it and quickly spread through him.

"You, sir, are a boon to all of humanity," Harlan told the barkeep, saluting the bewhiskered man with the mug before taking another long swallow.

"You want the udder bit?" The bartender pointed toward Harlan's quarter still lying on the bar. Two bits. Two drinks' worth.

"Hell, yes," Harlan said with enthusiasm. One more of these and he should go past warm and be feeling practically hot.

The bartender busied himself with refilling a few beer mugs, then started building that second drink for the newcomer.

In the meantime Harlan noticed that a man who had been sitting at a table in a far corner was now standing close on Harlan's right side. And he was not paying any attention at all to the barkeep.

"Something I can do for you, mister?" Harlan asked.

The gentleman, who looked like all the other patrons in the place, turned his lapel back. There was a very small polished metal star pinned there. Harlan had to squint and lean closer to make out the single word lightly engraved into the metal: Marshal.

"Ned Edwards," Harlan said. "Just the man I'm looking for."

Chapter Sixty-nine

"If you got a minute," Harlan said, over the loud buzz of many conversations, "I need t' talk with you. Is there someplace quieter than this?"

"There's a cafe. Should be fairly empty at this time of day," Edwards said. "Is it important though? I'm in the middle of a hot cribbage game at the table over there."

"Important enough for me t' walk away from the rest o' this toddy," Harlan told him, indicating his mug.

The marshal smiled and shook his head. "No need to prove yourself. I'll step back over there and tell my friends that duty calls. You gag that drink down and put your own coat on. Then we'll go have us that palaver."

Edwards went back to the table and leaned down, speaking with the other men there. Harlan downed his second drink almost as quickly as he had the first and as quickly began to regret the fact. The drinks were stronger than he had given them credit for, and it seemed he was somewhat out of practice when it came to imbibing spirits, for his head felt just a wee bit light after that one hit his belly. He would have to be careful when he spoke with the marshal.

He pulled his coat back on and wrapped the muffler around his neck, then presented himself beside the town marshal, Junior sticking practically underneath his feet as well.

Edwards smiled. "You can tell you aren't from

around here. A Nebraska man won't hardly notice a cool, refreshing zephyr like we've been having lately."

"You can turn yourself into an icicle if you like, Marshal. Me, I intend to live a while longer if you don't mind. Your zephyrs will knock a Texas boy plumb off his feet. And that's coming from someone who's lived through a hurricane, rode drift in blue northers and once found a covey of quail that froze in midair. Didn't need to shoot those birds, Marshal. We just picked 'em outa the sky like fruit off a tree."

"Convenient," Edwards agreed.

"Yes, sir, but it caused a problem for us. Once we got the birds back to the bunkhouse an' they thawed out, they jumped up and started flapping an' flying again. We had a terrible time rounding them all up."

"I can see how that would be a problem. In this door here, if you would. I know, there's no sign, but trust me. It's a cafe. Everybody around here knows that, so there's no point in paying for a sign, I guess."

Edwards opened the door and motioned Harlan ahead of him, then stepped inside behind him. The place was laid out as a cafe, all right, with half a dozen round tables, each with four chairs around it. Only one of the tables was occupied, plus there was a stove with a bald, sweating cook standing over it.

"Coffee, Ned?" the cook ventured.

"Two, please, and something for this gentleman to eat. Something that will warm him up."

"I got some chili here hot enough to warm him and three people standing near him."

The cook looked at Edwards. Edwards looked at Harlan. Harlan nodded. Chili sounded just fine and the hotter the better.

"We'll sit over here where we can't be overheard too easy," Edwards suggested, walking to a table in the front corner and pulling off his coat and knitted cap.

Harlan sat in the corner and shrugged off his coat. He laid his hat on an empty chair between Edwards and himself. Junior took a seat on the floor at Harlan's side and a moment later he lay down.

The cook brought their coffee on a tray and a steaming bowl of chili too.

"The chili will be too hot for my dog. D'you have something he could handle?" Harlan asked. "I don't mind paying for his grub if you got anything like that."

"I could crumble some biscuits into a pie plate and cover them with raw eggs, maybe add a little tinned milk and mix it all up. How would that be?"

"Sounds fine."

"It will cost you the price of a full meal though. I want you to understand that."

"I'll pay. That's not a problem."

"It will only take a minute."

Harlan tried the coffee. Either he was still exceptionally cold or the coffee was exceptionally good. Either way he was pleased.

"That gets the formalities out of the way," Edwards said. "Most of them anyway. Would you mind telling me who you are and why you need to see me?"

"My name is Earl Woods, Marshal, and I'm looking for a fellow who's been murdering folks and raping girls down in Kansas, maybe over in Missouri too. I know his first name is Harlan. That's straight from a witness. Some say his last name could be Breen." It hurt Harlan's gut to have to add that and further sully his own name, but he did not think he had much choice about it.

"I read in a newspaper," he went on, "that you've

had a killing up here that might've been by the same fella. This man likes to pick isolated homes to hit. He seems t' have a knack for putting folks at ease. They get to trust him easy. One place I already been he actually sat down an' had dinner with them before he murdered them all. Shot them from up close but kept a young girl alive long enough to do some awful things to her before he did her the kindness of killing her."

"What is your interest in this, Mr. Woods?" the marshal asked.

"There's rewards offered for him down in Kansas, Mr. Edwards. Marshal, I mean."

"Ned. You can call me Ned, Earl."

Harlan nodded. "Anyway, I'd like to see the place where he did his murders up here. I rode all the way up from the south o' Kansas just for that, just t' get on his trail, so to speak. To see where he was so's maybe I can get a better idea of where t' look for him next."

"I assume you are asking about the Hefley murders," Edwards said.

"That's the name the newspaper had, yes, sir."

The cook appeared with a plate of supper for Junior. It reminded Harlan that he had not taken time to tuck into his own meal yet. He tried a tentative spoonful of the chili and nodded, satisfied. The stuff was hot enough that its temperature did not matter. It would stay hot on the basis of the peppers alone.

"Jim and Laura and their children lived about five miles north from here. That is outside my jurisdiction, but once I heard they were dead I had to go out and do what I could, of course. God knows that wasn't much. Just like you say with this family down in Kansas, there were indications the Hefleys invited the stranger to eat with them. There was an extra place set at the table anyway and signs that he did indeed eat there. Not dinner though. Breakfast. There were fried eggs left on a platter and some ham slices. Biscuits. A little redeye gravy remaining in a bowl." The marshal sighed. "Laura was a good cook. I've eaten at that same table myself so I know."

"You knew the family then," Harlan said.

The marshal nodded. "I know everyone around here, of course, but Jim and Laura were friends. We came out here on the same train, traveled together all the way from Chicago. Homesteaded at the same time on land not far apart. Our children went to school together. Yes, Mr. Woods, I knew that family."

"Would you mind if I was t' ride out there an' take a look at their place?"

"There isn't much to see. The neighbors have gone in and pretty much cleaned the place out or so I understand. I haven't been back myself since . . . well, since it happened. But if you like I can ride out there with you tomorrow, Mr. Woods. If you don't mind, that is."

"No, sir, I'd be glad for both the guide and the company."

"Then we can go about . . . excuse me a second." Edwards looked across the room, an expression of mild annoyance crossing his face. "What do you want, Gerald, or has a swarm of ants crawled up your pant legs to make you so fidgety?"

A lanky, weathered man wearing the local uniform of overalls and red flannel long johns squirmed in his seat at the other table. "Can you . . . can I, uh . . ."

"Dammit, Gerald, if you got something to say, come over here and say it. Can't you see that I'm busy talking with this gentleman?"

"I just . . . Marshal, I need to have a word with you. In private, please."

Edwards looked at Harlan and shrugged. "Excuse me for a minute, please."

"Take your time, Marshal. I'm wanting to get around some more o' this chili anyway."

Junior had already finished his meal and was noisily shoving the tin plate around on the floor, trying to lick up any last vestiges of what must have been a good supper from a dog's point of view.

Edwards walked over to Gerald, leaned down and listened for a bit. Harlan went back to eating.

Moments later the marshal was back beside Harlan's chair. "Done with your meal, Mr. Woods?"

"Yes, sir."

"That's fine." Edwards pulled out a pistol and placed the muzzle behind Harlan's right ear. "It would be best if you would hold still now. Real still." To the men at the other table he said, "Come get that shooter off his belt, boys, and look him over for other weapons while you are at it."

"You have a real interesting way of getting a man's attention, Marshal. Could I ask what this is about?" Lordy, surely there was no way anyone here could have figured out that he was Harlan Breen. Not even if they had seen those Wanted flyers with the piss-poor drawings on them.

"Bank robbery, Mr. Woods. I understand you robbed a bank down in Waldo Springs, Missouri. Now kindly put your coat back on and come with me. Quietly, if you please."

Harlan put on his coat and accompanied the marshal. Quietly.

Chapter Seventy

Harlan remembered that Waldo Springs bank. It had been pretty fat for a small-town country outfit. He and Little Jim Toomey took it down one fine afternoon. They took, if he remembered correctly, a little over four thousand that day, mostly in paper money. The newspapers the following week said it was over twelve thousand in gold that was stolen, but that was just so they could claim that much from the insurance company. Harlan sometimes wondered just who in hell they were robbing from, the banks or the insurance companies.

But he surely did not remember any such person as this fellow standing here beside Marshal Edwards.

"I remember his face clear as daylight, Ned. Him and a real big man came into the bank. I was down there visiting my brother and his family, and he had to go to the bank that day for some reason, I disremember what. Anyway, Lars and me was in there when the two of them walked in. This fella was wearing a nice suit and a duster. The big man was dressed like a farmhand or like that. Didn't even figure them to be together until I saw they both was carrying pistols. They shooed us customers over to one side where the big man watched over us, while this fella went behind the counter and got the money out of the vault. Oh, he was one cocky son of a bitch, I tell you. Cocky."

Cocky? Harlan wasn't trying to be cocky, dammit. Menacing maybe. He could accept that. But not cocky. Cocky was silly.

"He says his name is Earl Woods and he's wanting to collect the bounty on the man that murdered Jim and Laura Hefley," Edwards said, still keeping a gun pointed at Harlan's head. That was not a sight that Harlan found encouraging.

"Could be his name really is Earl Woods, just like he says," the witness said. "I never heard a name for either of them robbers. I just know this is the man. He's growed a beard since but I recognize him. I sure as hell do, Ned."

The marshal nodded. "You did good, Gerald. Mr. Woods, or whatever your name is, we don't have a proper jail in town here so what I'm going to do is handcuff you to a post. An indoor one. You don't have to worry about that. I won't let you freeze to death before I send you back to Missouri for trial."

"Damn, that's good of you, Marshal. I don't suppose you'll listen to me if I tell you I never done that robbery down in Missoura."

"You're right. I won't listen. Someday," the marshal mused, "someday I'm going to run into a man that *doesn't* claim he's innocent. I'll be so startled I'll probably let the son of a bitch go. What I'm going to do now, Mr. Woods, is to take a step back. I don't want you to turn around. That might lead me to thinking you're up to something, and I'll shoot you. No, what I want you to do, without turning or moving your feet much, I want you to put your coat and scarf and hat back on. We'll be going outside again in a minute here. Then I want you to hold your hands behind you so I can put the handcuffs on you. Then we'll head over to the mercantile. There's a fine timber smack in the middle of the room there. I've used it before to chain prisoners and all of them survived, so I expect you can too. Now do as I said, Mr. Woods. Nice and careful, put your things on and button up. We'll be outside again in just a moment here."

"Shit!" Harlan grumbled.

"Do you need to? I can take you by the outhouse on our way over to the store if you like. Otherwise it will be morning before you get another chance to go."

"Then I'd at least like t' take a piss," Harlan told him. He was thinking—blindly hoping, really—that the rest break might allow him somehow to get loose. But then not all jailers were as stupid as Gordon Dobbs down in Missouri had been. He grinned. "If I'm gonna be your prisoner though, dammit, I expect the town can pay for my supper. An' I got two horses stabled over at the livery. You can pay for them too, thank you very much. Now kindly lead the way as I got no idea where we're going."

"You won't get my back quite that easy, Mr. Woods. Gerald. Would you please lead the way to Sam's store and Mr. Woods can follow you? Then me and this pistol will bring up the rear. How does that sound, Mr. Woods?"

"I got no problem with it, Marshal. Once you get me locked up nice and tight we'll have us a talk an' get this thing straightened out." He tried to make his voice sound light and easy, but the truth was that those steel bracelets felt cold and nasty when they locked around his wrists. "Lead on, Gerald. I'll be right behind you."

Chapter Seventy-one

They treated him decently enough. Harlan had to admit that. They gave him a wooden armchair to sit on and put a puffy pillow on the seat so it wouldn't be too uncomfortable. The marshal set the chair only a few inches away from and facing a stout upright timber in the middle of the floor, presumably put there to hold the roof up.

"Sit down, please, Mr. Woods."

"Yes, sir." Harlan would turn rabbit and run if he had even a ghost of a chance to get away, but there was no sense in making Edwards and his friends angry in the meantime. It did occur to him, though, and not for the first time, that maybe his much-abused "good" name was no longer quite as good as it used to be. It just might be time to become someone else. And some*where* else while he was at it.

Harlan took the indicated seat and waited to see what they intended next. Moving his handcuffs to the other side of the post was what he expected. It was not what Marshal Ned Edwards did.

"Cover him, Gerald," the marshal said.

"What, Ned?"

"Take your pistol out," Edwards said patiently, "and point it at him. If he tries to run away, shoot him."

"I'm not sure . . ."

"It's all right, Gerald. If he tries to run away I'm sure I will have time to shoot him myself. Never mind the gun. Just stand behind him and keep an eye on things, will you?"

"Yes, sir. I can do that."

Edwards brought some shackles and chain out from behind the store counter—this was a task he obviously had done before—and carried them to the other side of the post. "Extend your legs, Mr. Woods. A little further, please. Gerald, give the chair a shove. Push it right up against the timber, eh?"

Harlan felt Gerald shove the chair, passenger included, across the wooden flooring until the timber was practically sitting in Harlan's lap.

"That's fine, Gerald. Mr. Woods, I'm going to pull your boots off you. I won't take them anywhere. They'll be right over there. But I need to get at your ankles."

The marshal knelt and quite expertly tugged Harlan's fine and fancy boots off his feet. True to his word, he set the boots side by side where they would be out of the way but where Harlan could keep an eye on them if he liked.

"Now hold still. I need to get these tight." Edwards slipped the heavy steel shackles around Harlan's ankles, right leg first and then the left, and locked them into place. They were too tight for him to wriggle out of, and if he tried to walk with them still on he would tear his skin up pretty quickly, but they were fine as long as Harlan did not fight them.

The chain that connected the shackles appeared to be strong. Not that Harlan could really tell. With the thick timber practically in his face he could not reach his feet anyway.

Edwards stood and came around to Harlan's side of the post.

Now comes the abuse, Harlan thought. With both

hands and feet secured this marshal can do anything
he damn pleases.

What Edwards pleased to do was to say, "Now
hold your wrists up to where I can get at them, Mr.
Woods."

Harlan was more than half expecting a cuff upside
his head at the very least, but he did what he was told.

"Thank you." Edwards produced a small key and
proceeded to unlock the handcuffs. "There. You don't
need those on too. They don't serve any purpose now
except to make you uncomfortable."

Edwards found another chair somewhere in the store
and dragged it over to Harlan's prison post. "Now, Mr.
Woods. You were saying you wanted to talk with me
about your innocence." He looked up. "Don't you be
going anywhere, Gerald. Whatever this man has to
say, I want you to sit here as a witness to it. You can
fetch that crate over an' upend it to sit on." Edwards
smiled. "Mr. Woods, you have my full attention. Go
right ahead and have your say."

Chapter Seventy-two

Harlan Jarrett was not happy. Still, a man sometimes had to make the difficult decisions even if they meant forgoing immediate pleasure in exchange for future reward. His mother had taught him that, and she was right. But then she was always right.

It was simply too cold to continue this trek through the wilderness. Relatively speaking, that is.

The countryside here certainly looked like a wilderness. It was barren and drab and frozen.

The fact was that it was simply too miserably cold to be enjoyable, even given the delights a man of Jarrett's tastes might encounter hereabouts.

He had concluded, therefore, that his best course for the immediate future would be to turn back east. He had been trending westward ever since leaving Kansas, finding Nebraska much to his liking. But now, with this bitter cold slicing deep to the bone, Jarrett was rolling eastward, the hooves of his team clattering sharply on the iron-hard ground and the iron wheels grinding.

His intention was to return to the river—Missouri? he wondered, or would it be the Mississippi that lay due east?—no matter. Whichever of the great rivers he encountered he would sell the photographic wagon there—it had certainly served its purpose and he could always buy and stock a new one if he wanted to—or even abandon it. He did not need the money. He could afford to walk away from this wagon and a dozen more just like it.

A riverboat, one of the better ones if he had anything to say about it, would provide warmth and comfort as well as transportation.

He could take the boat south. To New Orleans. A man with money in his pockets could find anything he wished for in New Orleans. Or almost anything. As for those other things, well, he could wait. Springtime would come again in due course and he would venture out again. Westward. Perhaps to north Texas or on to New Mexico.

Anywhere there were farms without close neighbors, Harlan Jarrett could find his pleasures.

He looked over his shoulder and tried to judge the height of the sun. Not that there was much daylight at this gray time of year even at high noon. Miserable damned country, he silently grumbled.

He saw a lane and hauled on the lines until his team turned into it. The horses picked up their plodding pace into a spanking trot, perhaps sensing feed and shelter ahead.

Jarrett pulled them to a halt in front of a handsome, commodious barn and nodded to the man who came shivering out of a low-roofed sod house nearby.

"How do you do, sir?"

"Mister, if you're selling something you are shit outa luck here. I got everything I need except for the wherewithal to buy more of it."

"Actually, sir, I am seeking a place where I might stop overnight. I am cold and I am tired and I would give anything right now for a hot supper and a warm place where I could eat it."

"Anything?" the lean farmer asked. The man seemed as gray as the landscape around him.

Jarrett smiled. "Almost anything." The farmer had

not introduced himself, Jarrett noticed, and did not seem inclined to do so.

"My old woman has some porridge on the stove. Oat porridge. She cuts up some dried apricots in it and it ain't bad. You could have some of that if you'd pay for it."

"I would pay."

"How much?"

"How much would you want?"

"A dollar?" The farmer sounded uncertain, obviously wondering if his asking price was so steep that it would keep the visitor from staying to pay for his meal.

"A dollar would be fine," Jarrett assured him. "And a dollar each for my horses if you would take care of them as well. And of course I would pay more for a warm place to sleep tonight and a bite to eat before I get back on the road tomorrow."

The farmer looked at the sky, then at Jarrett. "You won't want t' be traveling tomorrow. You see them clouds? Feel the way the wind is dying down? It'll start snowing tonight, sure as I'm standing here."

Jarrett assumed the man was just trying to leach a little more money from him at those exorbitant rates. A dollar for a bowl of porridge? Scandalous!

"Light down," the farmer said. "I'll have my boy take care o' your stock when he tends to mine."

"Thank you very much." Jarrett set the brake and wrapped the driving lines around the whip socket, then climbed stiffly down from the wagon. Boy, the man had said. Jarrett hoped there were girls too. At least one. This would likely be his last opportunity to play until next spring and he wanted to take full advantage of it.

"Come along then. You don't want to stand out here any longer than you got to."

Jarrett followed the man into the soddy. He had to duck his head and bend down to keep from hitting his head on the chunk of log that served as a lintel. Inside, the sod house smelled of dirt and dampness even at this frigid time of year.

There was only the one room with a small table in the center, with stools rather than chairs placed around it, a cheap sheepherder-style stove on one side and a single bed pegged into the wall on two sides. There were no photographs anywhere in sight, no decorations at all. A boy of fourteen or so who had been sitting at the table jumped to obey when his father ordered him to take care of the livestock.

And there was a woman. She was not much of a woman but in the absence of any daughters she would have to do.

At least she had large bosoms. A man could always get some pleasure out of those, particularly if they were sensitive.

And there was the sheet iron stove. It was glowing red. There was a poker lying nearby atop a wood box. Hot pokers were . . . useful. In oh so many ways.

Jarrett looked at the woman again. He visualized her. Naked. Shrieking in pain. The red-hot poker . . .

He smiled. The farmer smiled back.

As soon as the boy returned from taking care of the animals, Jarrett thought. There was no need to wait. Not even for food. Anticipation of his real joy, so soon to come, swept his appetite away.

Harlan Jarrett at that moment was a very happy man. Even if these people had no daughters.

Chapter Seventy-three

Harlan Breen was well and truly pissed off. He had wasted two whole days back there in Goodson, chained to that sonuvabitch timber, while the telegraph wires grew hot—at Harlan's own expense—sending wires back and forth between Ned Edwards and Sheriff Brandon Bates in Corleigh County, Kansas, trying to establish Harlan's bona fides as bounty hunter Earl Woods.

Edwards had gotten in touch with Bates at some length and tried to reach Nels Jesperson but could not. He did, however, exchange wires with Marshal Julius Brandt in Waltrop, Kansas, where Harlan had established himself as Earl Woods.

Among those three they satisfied themselves that Earl Woods was who he said he was.

Oddly enough, Harlan thought the most telling thing in his favor was the set of initials inside his hat brim, for why would a man named Breen be wearing a hat with the initials of the bounty hunter Earl Woods?

Now that he was past and done with it, Harlan thought the whole thing funny as all billy hell, what with those lawmen certifying that he was not who in fact he was. As if they knew.

But it had still cost him two full days when he could have been chasing after this son of a bitch Harlan-whoever, who was so near to ruining his life.

And now to top everything else off, it was snowing thick and heavy. The wind had nearly died, but the snowflakes were getting heavier and bigger. A man could scarcely see a hundred yards ahead.

As if to prove that point, Harlan saw a mud wagon pulled by a pair of cobs materialize out of the whiteness. Harlan reined his horses over to the side of the road so the wheeled vehicle could keep to the ruts that had formed during milder weather and now were frozen solid where they lay.

Junior barked but the wagon horses ignored him.

"Sorry about that, mister," Harlan told the driver, a large, well set-up gentleman perched on the wagon box.

"No harm done," the driver muttered.

"Where're you bound?" Harlan asked, mildly curious about what would bring a man out on a day like this.

"Omaha," the fellow said. "Then south to someplace warmer." The man had an accent. Almost but not exactly like the British remittance men talked. Something back-east snooty, Harlan thought.

Harlan grinned. "I can sure understand that. See any strangers hereabouts?"

"I wouldn't know. I happen to be a stranger in this country myself. I've been traveling, creating a photographic record for the Museum of Natural History back east."

"That sounds interesting," Harlan lied. "Well, good luck to you."

"And to you." The driver gave his team their head and they walked off at a good clip. As they passed Harlan noticed some gold lettering on the side of the wagon: H. JARRETT, PHOTOGRAPHIC ARTISTRY.

Photography. Now that was something Harlan sure did not understand. It was all pure magic to him.

He touched the brim of his hat and dipped his chin

and got a nod back from the driver, then Harlan reined his horses back onto the road and headed west once more.

A mile or so on he came to a lane and with a sigh turned into it. It was not that he really expected to learn anything, but he was stopping and talking to everyone he could find. Had they seen any strangers? Heard any odd noises? Did they know anything about the recent murders?

The snow was falling harder now, blanketing the frozen earth. Harlan noticed that the photographer had come up this lane too. Harlan could see the tracks of his wheels coming out and joining the public road. In another hour it would not be possible to see anything, he was sure, not if the snow continued to fall at this rate.

There was a large barn at the head of the farm lane and a small sod house. Beside the pump Harlan found a bucket with water that had not yet frozen over. Which probably explained what had brought the photographer here. He'd stopped to water his horses.

"Hello? Is anyone here?" Harlan called. "Would you mind if I draw some water for my animals? Hello?"

There was no answer so he took the opportunity to refill the bucket, offering it first to the gray and then to the brown. He gave Junior a drink too, then took a few swallows himself. He would rather have whiskey on a day this raw, but water would just have to do.

"Hello?" he tried again. "Is there anybody here? Can I buy a meal off you folks or some hot coffee? I can pay."

A whiff of smoke on the chill air suggested that someone was or recently had been up and around. It was, what, late morning or close on to noon. If there was anyone home they should be cooking their midday meal about now. Perhaps they just could not hear.

Harlan tied his horses to rings bolted to the side of the barn—convenient, that—and headed for the house with Junior close on his heels.

Once they reached the entrance to the soddy, though, Junior whined and drew back.

"What's the matter with you, boy?" Over the past several months Harlan had come to like the shaggy black and white dog. He had not seen Junior act like this though.

"Hello?" he called.

The door to the soddy was ajar. Harlan tapped politely on the wood, and the door swung partially open.

He looked inside, hoping to find whoever lived here.

Instead . . .

"Oh, shit!"

Harlan did not go in. One look told him all he needed to know and then some.

"Shit," he repeated again.

Then, realizing, he whirled and headed for the horses at a dead run.

Those tracks in the snow. A gentleman traveler. A scientific gentleman at that. H. Jarrett. H.!

Harlan yanked the gray around, the brown dutifully following, and put them into a canter even before they passed the pump.

Chapter Seventy-four

"Hold up there a minute, mister. Whoa."

"What is it you want, sir?"

"Your name's Harlan, is it?"

"That's right. Harlan Jarrett."

"My name is Harlan too. Harlan Breen. Mr. Jarrett, you have caused me a world o' trouble. Killing, raping, God only knows what-all else you done."

"I have done no such . . ."

"O' course you have. I seen your tracks comin' out o' that farm lane back there. An' I seen what of a mess you left inside. How many dead did you leave in there, Jarrett? How many before them?"

"You can prove nothing, sir."

"Those tracks . . ."

"Will be completely obliterated long before you could find any sort of constable or policeman and get one back here. There is nothing, not one iota of evidence, that could possibly tie me to those murders."

"You know about them then," Harlan said. "You as good as admit . . ."

"I admit to nothing. And let me tell you something, Mr. . . . . Brin, was it?"

"Breen."

"Yes. Mr. Breen. Let me tell you something, sir. I am from an entirely respectable family. A family with both money and influence. Do you really think a wild accusation made by . . . what is it that you do for a living, Mr. Breen?"

"I rob people."

"Really?" Jarrett seemed genuinely interested now. "That is wonderful, Mr. Breen. We have something in common, you and I."

"Mister, we ain't nothing alike."

"Oh, I make no claims about that. But both of us have to be wary of the law, Mr. Breen." Jarrett smiled. "So I seriously doubt that you will be able to make trouble for me. If you try, I can promise I will get off scot-free. I will have the finest lawyers available." He laughed. "And it would distress you to learn how venal and greedy judges are. After all, they were all lawyers before they became exalted above mere mortals. Many of them, so many, can be bought for a relative pittance. As for you, you would be the one to end up in prison. I would see to it. I would hire witnesses who would testify under oath that they personally witnessed . . . well . . . things much like you saw back at that farm just now. You would be the one labeled a murderer, Mr. Breen. You would hang by the neck until you were dead. I promise you that you would. So why don't you be a good chap and go on about your business, Mr. Breen? Go away, please, and do not bother me any further."

The son of a bitch was probably right, Harlan thought. This Jarrett had money and position. He could buy his way out of trouble with the law. There was probably no point at all in taking him in and turning him over to Ned Edwards or to anyone else. There would be no rewards paid. Not to Harlan Breen anyway.

And there would be no reclaiming his good name. That was finished for good and all.

Still, it just graveled Harlan's gut to think that this snooty bastard would be free to prey on still more girls and young women. He could slaughter and rape with impunity. The law that was such a threat to Harlan Breen would not touch Harlan Jarrett.

Harlan felt dizzy. He closed his eyes. Felt himself swaying in the saddle. "Dammit t' hell," he grumbled aloud.

He heard Jarrett's laughter. A wave of utter disgust swept through Harlan Breen.

He opened his eyes to find a smirk on Jarrett's handsome features.

"You bastard!" Harlan cried.

"Yes, what of it?" The man laughed again.

Harlan calmed himself. Tried to think this through. His name was destroyed now. His career, if one wanted to call it that, was in tatters, his gang gone off to other pursuits without him. He had a couple hundred dollars, two horses and a dog. Not much more.

He could not go back to Brenda. If he had been recognized as a bank robber by somebody in an out-of-the-way piece of shit like Goodson, Nebraska, how much more likely was it that eventually he would run into someone in the south of Kansas who recognized him as the despised Breen?

Dammit, that girl had been just about to give it up too. He could feel how close she was to ready. Now some other asshole would eventually be getting the benefit of all of Harlan's preparations.

And there Jarrett sat, smug and satisfied. "You understand," Jarrett said. "I can see it in your face that you do."

"Yeah. I reckon I do," Harlan said. "There's no way I can take you in an' pretend that you're Harlan Breen. No way I can collect all those rewards."

"I didn't know there was reward money being offered. How much?"

"The last I heard," Harlan said, "they toted up to something over a thousand dollars."

"Is that a great deal of money to you?"

"It's seeming like more an' more, the longer this goes on," Harlan admitted.

"All right. A thousand dollars. And ten percent more to sweeten the deal." Jarrett took out a wallet, dug deep into it and extracted a sheaf of hundred-dollar bills. He counted out eleven and held them out toward Harlan.

Men had started off with a hell of a lot less, Harlan reflected. He kneed the gray over closer to the photographer's wagon and took the bills out of his hand.

"You are fortunate that I'm in such a good mood today," Jarrett said. "I could have killed you instead." He returned the wallet to his coat pocket, displaying the butt of a small revolver when he did so.

It was Harlan's turn to laugh. "Of a sudden I'm feeling pretty good, Mr. Jarrett."

"It's the money," Jarrett said. "It has a way of making a man feel good. And by the way, I think I will kill you."

Jarrett reached for the pistol he had already exposed.

Harlan had not exactly been expecting that but he was prepared for it. His Colt came out of the leather smooth and easy. The barrel lined up with no hesitation.

"Say now . . . !" Jarrett objected, startled.

Harlan triggered the .45 and a lead slug buried itself in Harlan Jarrett's forehead, snapping his head back and sending his hat flying.

The man's body, probably already lifeless, toppled sideways off the driving box of the mud wagon and fell into the snow beside the front wheel.

Harlan rode around to stop the gray over Jarrett's

body. He stepped down long enough to retrieve the man's wallet from his coat, then took more time to unbutton his britches and take a piss on the corpse.

He tucked himself in and buttoned up again, climbed back onto the gray, thought for a moment, then unslung the shotgun from his saddle horn and carefully, deliberately fired both loads of buckshot into Harlan Jarrett's crotch.

"For those folks you left in the soddy up the road there," he said.

Harlan felt better after he did that. He carefully reloaded both his revolver and the shotgun, trying to think this through while his hands were occupied.

Harlan Breen might as well be dead. To all intents and purposes he already was dead.

But Earl Woods still lived, by damn. Earl Woods was just fine.

Earl Woods sighed. Then smiled and sat up straighter in the saddle.

It was warm in California, he'd heard. And no one there would know a thing about a robber called Harlan Breen.

Earl Woods could . . . hell, he could do anything he damn pleased. Make a completely fresh start on life.

Why not?

Earl Woods reined the gray horse away from the stationary mud wagon. Junior was still busy sniffing at Harlan Jarrett's body. The dog tentatively lapped at the blood flowing out of the red wreckage where Jarrett's privates used to be.

"That's disgusting, Junior. Leave be." Earl started down the road. He whistled for the dog to catch up.

They could go down to the railroad, he figured. Take the train all the way to San Francisco and head south from there. When he reached a place where they said he could throw his coat away, that was where he would settle down and stay.

Maybe even live a virtuous and upright life, and wouldn't that be a kick in the head?

"Come along, dog. We got us a ways t' go."

Five-time Winner of the Spur Award

Will Henry

There is perhaps no outlaw of the Old West more notorious or legendary than Billy the Kid. And no author is better suited than Will Henry to tell the tale of the young gunman . . . and the mysterious stranger who changed his life.

Also included in this volume are two exciting novellas: "Santa Fe Passage" is the basis for the classic 1955 film of the same name. And "The Fourth Horseman" sets a rancher on the trail of a kidnapped young woman . . . while trying to survive a bloody range war.

A BULLET FOR BILLY THE KID

ISBN 13: 978-0-8439-6340-3

"Conley is among the most productive
and inventive of modern Western novelists."
—Dale L. Walker, *Rocky Mountain News*

BARJACK AND THE
UNWELCOME GHOST

Marshal Barjack likes to keep peace and quiet in the tiny
town of Asininity. It's better for business at the Hooch
House, the saloon that Barjack owns. But peace and quiet got mighty hard to come by once Harm Cody came
to town. Cody's made a lot of enemies over the years and
some of them are hot on his trail, aiming to kill him—
including a Cherokee named Miller and a pretty little
sharpshooter named Polly Pistol. And when the Asininity bank gets robbed, well, now Cody has a whole new
bunch of enemies . . . including Barjack.

Robert J. Conley

"One of the most underrated and overlooked writers
of our time, as well as the most skilled."
—Don Coldsmith, Author of the Spanish Bit Saga

ISBN 13: 978-0-8439-6225-3

☐ **YES!**

Sign me up for the Leisure Western Book Club and send my FREE BOOKS! If I choose to stay in the club, I will pay only $14.00* each month, a savings of $9.96!

NAME: _____

ADDRESS: _____

TELEPHONE: _____

EMAIL: _____

☐ I want to pay by credit card.

☐ **VISA**   ☐ **MasterCard.**   ☐ **DISCOVER**

ACCOUNT #: _____

EXPIRATION DATE: _____

SIGNATURE: _____

Mail this page along with $2.00 shipping and handling to:
**Leisure Western Book Club
PO Box 6640
Wayne, PA 19087**
Or fax (must include credit card information) to:
610-995-9274
You can also sign up online at **www.dorchesterpub.com.**
*Plus $2.00 for shipping. Offer open to residents of the U.S. and Canada only.
Canadian residents please call 1-800-481-9191 for pricing information.
If under 18, a parent or guardian must sign. Terms, prices and conditions subject to
change. Subscription subject to acceptance. Dorchester Publishing reserves the right
to reject any order or cancel any subscription.

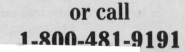